I0669284

By SHELTER SOMERSET

NOVELS
Alaska Hunt
On the Trail to Moonlight Gulch
The Rule of Sebastian

Between Two Worlds
Between Two Promises

Published by DREAMSPINNER PRESS
http://www.dreamspinnerpress.com

The RULE of SEBASTIAN

SHELTER SOMERSET

Dreamspinner Press

Published by
Dreamspinner Press
5032 Capital Circle SW
Ste 2, PMB# 279
Tallahassee, FL 32305-7886
USA
http://www.dreamspinnerpress.com/

The Rule of Sebastian
Copyright © 2012 by Shelter Somerset

Cover Art by Paul Richmond
http://www.paulrichmondstudio.com

ISBN: 978-1-62380-128-1

Printed in the United States of America
First Edition
November 2012

eBook edition available
eBook ISBN: 978-1-62380-129-8

To Joseph

WEEKDAY TRAPPIST SCHEDULE

(Winter)

3:00 a.m.	Rise
3:30 a.m.	Vigils, first of seven prayer "offices"
4:15 a.m.	*Lectio divina*, "divine reading" of Scripture
5:15 a.m.	Breakfast; personal needs
6:00 a.m.	Lauds, sunrise prayer
6:30 a.m.	*Lectio divina*
7:30 a.m.	Eucharist
8:30 a.m.	Terce, "third hour" prayer (Grand Silence ends)
8:45 a.m.	Morning work assignments
Noon	Sext, "sixth hour" prayer
12:15 p.m.	Lunch
12:45 p.m.	None, "ninth hour" prayer
1:00 p.m.	Optional siesta and prayer
2:00 p.m.	Afternoon work assignments
4:30 p.m.	Dinner
5:30 p.m.	Vespers, sunset prayer
6:00 p.m.	Community activities; personal needs
7:00 p.m.	Compline, night prayer (Grand Silence begins)
7:45 p.m.	Retire

TRAPPIST GARMENTS

Tunic: White ankle-length habit worn during the day and at
              sleep, confined at waist with leather belt.

Scapular: Black calf-length hooded garment worn over the tunic
              during daytime.

Cowl: Full white, woolen cloak with wide sleeves and hood
              worn in chapel.

Footwear: Inexpensive leather sandals; work boots.

– I –

"Hurry! Come help! Come help!"

Sebastian sprinted from his cell, where he had been engaged in *lectio divina*, to see what the commotion was about. He found Brother Casey sitting on the wood floor in the entrance foyer, replacing his sandals with a pair of the common work boots stowed under the bench. Beneath his tunic, he wore snow pants. Casey stopped tying the bootlaces long enough to look up at him. His brown eyes grew wide, frozen ponds caught in a sudden spray of the overhead lights.

"What is it, Casey?" Sebastian asked. "Are you all right? Did you hurt yourself?"

"I'm fine," Casey said, refocused on tying the boots, "but there's someone—I think a man—lying outside in this blizzard. He appears unconscious. I don't think it's one of our brothers. My eyes didn't deceive me. Can you pull on some snow gear and follow me outside?"

Skeptical but alarmed, Sebastian wasted no time minding the latest of the monastery's postulants. He sat on the bench next to him and pulled on socks, snow pants, and sturdy boots. Minutes later, clad in their parkas with their scapular hoods pulled over their heads to ward off the blowing snow, they dashed outside into the storm. Sebastian drew his hood back enough for a clearer view, jerking his head from one angle to the next to avoid the hard-driven snow stinging his cheeks, but he had no idea what he searched for.

Casey pointed to one of the library's arched windows, where light cast a dull yellow over a snowbank. "I was seated in the library for *lectio divina* when I noticed something in the snow," he shouted above the wind. "At first I thought it was a mound of sheets that might have blown from an open window in Brother Giles's cell. You know how forgetful he can be. But then I was certain it had a man's shape."

Up to their knees in snow, they circled around where Casey claimed he had spotted the man. Rushing wind swept a patch of the fast-accumulating snow, and in a flash Sebastian discerned the same mound of color. He motioned with his head for Casey to follow. "I see him, come on!"

They dropped to their haunches by the lifeless figure and cleared the snow around him with their bare hands, exhaling thick, vaporous breath. The more they dug, the more Sebastian was certain they would uncover a dead man. Two more brothers wrapped in parkas and secured in boots scurried outside.

"May God have mercy on his soul. Is he dead?" Brother George hollered from the buried footpath, where the blowing snow iced his thick eyeglasses.

Sebastian removed his fingertips from the man's carotid artery. "He's alive," he shouted above his own pounding heart, "but barely."

"Who is he?" Brother Eusebius asked, standing beside them and looking on with deep lines marring his forehead.

"I've never seen him before," Sebastian said. "We'll have to find out later. Let's get him inside before he freezes to death."

"I'll go fetch the abbot." Brother Eusebius dashed along their boot tracks, already smoothed into a subtle groove from the relentless wind and snowfall.

Sebastian gathered the unconscious man in his arms and carried him inside the warmth of the abbey while Casey and Brother George shielded him from the elements. Six of the abbey's twelve brothers were already waiting by the front door, pelting them with questions. But Sebastian had no answers, and his main objective was to hurry the man to the infirmary and get him beneath several layers of bedcovers.

He shouted for someone to get Brother Jerome and shouldered his way through the brothers.

Once inside the infirmary, Sebastian and the others rushed to undress the stranger and dry him with soft cotton towels. The brothers' palpable interest in the man did not surprise Sebastian. He caught the flush that blemished their faces when he slid off the stranger's wet jeans and underwear. And he detected a puckering of their lips when the first trace of body odor reached their nostrils before they tucked him into bed and cocooned him in woolen blankets.

Firm muscles now lay underneath those three sturdy blankets, which were tucked around him snugger than a baby in swaddling. His breath came in short gasps, lifting the blankets every fifteen to twenty seconds. Sebastian worried that the young man, perhaps twenty-one or twenty-two—about the same age as Casey and Brother Rodel—might not make it.

Lying in bed, he appeared almost surreal, a dark Adonis poised for death after his mysterious ascent along southwest Colorado's San Juan Mountains. Color had returned to his cheeks. Ruddiness accentuated the subtle brown of his skin. But he was still out cold.

The brothers pushed against the bed to the point that Sebastian had little room to turn. He couldn't help but notice a high energy emanating from them. Excitement had replaced their humdrum abbey lives.

"What was he doing in the middle of the snowstorm?" Brother Lucien asked in his typical quirky English lilt, stealing the thoughts straight from Sebastian's head.

"It's a perfectly good question," Sebastian said. "I'm unsure how or why he's come to us. Had anyone witnessed him hiking up?"

"I was in my cell studying Scripture, and the few times I glanced outside I saw nothing," Brother Hubert said, adjusting his black-framed glasses over his rosacea-coated nose. "But with all this blowing snow, how could I?"

"Yes, I know. I was in my cell as well," Sebastian said, almost disgusted with himself for having failed to see the man. "But I hadn't noticed a thing."

The others said they'd spent their rest periods in other parts of the abbey and hadn't noticed anything either.

"Do you think he'll survive?" Casey directed the question to Sebastian, flexing his fingers from the cold that probably still stung them.

"I'm sure he'll be fine," Sebastian said, providing the handsome young brother one of his stealthy signature winks to reassure him.

"I hope he lives. I really hope he does," Brother George said, rolling his chubby hands in front of his scapular. "I want to see him with opened eyes. They must be brown, I'm sure."

"Could he have gotten lost while skiing?" Brother Rodel asked in his typical whispery voice. He was as reserved as a turtle, yet with the stealth of a cat. So many times the five-foot-two brother had sidled close to Sebastian without his realizing until he'd spoken.

"He wasn't dressed for skiing," Sebastian said. "He had no skis, no poles or ski boots, unless he'd left them elsewhere."

"This is a pickle," said Brother Giles, who, at seventy-two, showed signs of reverting to a childlike emotional detachment from the abbey, a trait Sebastian had grown to envy. Even the gout that had confined him to a wheelchair failed to dispirit Brother Giles. He wheeled closer to the bed, the squeak of the chair punctuating the awed silence, and nudged aside Brothers Lucien and George. "Certainly is a pickle, I'll say." He rubbed his grizzled beard. "Maybe he's one of those nature hikers."

"What person goes hiking in the mountains in the dead of winter without proper attire?" Brother Micah said, scratching at his expanding forehead and curling his thin upper lip. "Don't you think so, Brother Sebastian?" He softened his sour tone and gazed at Sebastian with ardent blue eyes. "Don't you think he couldn't possibly be a nature hiker?"

"Yes, I agree." Brother Sebastian patronized Brother Micah, as he often did. "I don't think he's your typical rugged outdoorsman. He was wearing only those worthless hiking sneakers, and I didn't see any snowshoes. Even if he was dressed properly, it's unlikely he'd be joy hiking in this snowstorm. I think he's come to the abbey on purpose."

"But what for?" Brother Lucien asked.

"Maybe he's come to us out of desperation, to find solace from a tragedy," Brother Hubert said.

"He reminds me of the Lord our Savior, napping in the stern of the boat as he and the disciples crossed the Sea of Galilee," Brother Giles said with a grin. "Look how he lies so helpless and peaceful."

The brothers gazed at the sleeping figure in silence until Brother Eusebius rushed into the room with Father Paolo following close on the hem of his tunic. The abbot parted the band of brothers with a sweep of his flowing sleeve. Sebastian noted the hint of smoldering juniper wafting off his garments from the incense he liked to burn in his private office. Father Paolo leaned into the unconscious figure, his breath inches from the young man's nose.

A smile twisted one side of the venerable sixty-year-old's pale face. According to Brother Hubert, who seemed to have the abbey secrets whispered to him by the finches that clustered in the cloister garden even in winter (did he know Sebastian's dark secrets too, and the reason why he'd come to Mt. Ouray?), the abbot had retreated to the abbey more than twenty years ago to escape the pressures of parish life. Ten years later, resident brothers had elected him abbot.

Accepting Father Paolo's complete authority at Mt. Ouray was perhaps the most difficult transition for Sebastian. A stoic man used to leading (or as his father used to say, "Stubborn as an old dog, like a good Irishman should be, a Harkin through and through"), Sebastian had found himself biting his tongue more often than not whenever facing the abbot's leadership.

Leaving his worldly goods back in Philadelphia had come easy— he'd had few worldly goods to sacrifice (two hundred seventy thousand in savings had gone straight into the abbey's purse)—but renouncing his inclination to command had proved more painful.

Once he'd committed to the idea of professing his vows after he'd arrived at Mt. Ouray four years ago, he'd learned to take the abbot's orders silently and with deference. Although the abbot often relied on him as his second in command, for Sebastian stood tall and strong and the others naturally looked to him for guidance, a fresh, pestering resentment had begun to nag Sebastian.

He gulped down his rising angst and waited for the abbot to comment, anticipating his characteristic Portuguese accent that always sounded as if he held a mouthful of marbles.

The father stood erect and adjusted his wire-framed glasses, eyes still focused on the stranger. "Any idea how he came to us?"

"No one saw him hiking up," Brother Micah said.

"It's as if he fell out of the sky," Brother Hubert said.

"Like an angel," Brother George breathed.

"There's no identification on him," Sebastian added, his voice resonating in his ears, more forceful than he'd intended. "He was carrying only one small knapsack, that yellow pack over there on the table," he said in a softer tone. "Inside we found two protein bars, a frozen bottle of water, nothing else. No wallet or anything. Not even a cell phone."

He explained how they'd discovered him wearing only hiking sneakers, a thin parka, and day clothes, absent of any other outdoor gear, and how they'd undressed him and packed his clothes in a bag for Brother Hubert to launder. "I turned the pockets of his jeans inside out," he said. "Shook the knapsack upside down. No clues, not even a stub from an airline ticket or motel receipts."

"You can tell by his battered feet that he hiked a long ways," Casey said. "We cleaned him as best we could."

"We've refrained from administering any first aid until Brother Jerome gets here," Sebastian said.

"Has he been notified?"

"He was in *lectio divina* when I went to call for him." Brother George twisted his head toward the door. "Praise be to God, here he comes now."

Old, weathered Brother Jerome, suffering from osteoarthritis, lumbered toward the brothers. He had once been a physician in lay life and, according to Brother Hubert, was widowed, with three sons. His medical skills had proved invaluable to the secluded abbey, nestled nine thousand feet in the Rockies, fifteen miles from the closest village, and cut off from civilization in winter. Unable to keep up with the seasonal snowfall, the forest service closed the road that passed Mt. Ouray from November to April. No one could come or go until snowmelt. Or so Sebastian thought.

Brother Jerome fumbled in a drawer and removed a pocket flashlight, stethoscope, and blood pressure meter. He stepped up to the bed, pulled open each of the stranger's eyelids, and peered at the pupils with the flashlight.

Brother George stood on his toes. "See, I told you he had brown eyes. I told you."

Next, Brother Jerome exposed the stranger's midsection to the subdued gasps of many of the brothers, and listened through the stethoscope while everyone held a collective breath. He moved slowly, careful not to raise his arms above his shoulders, since this caused him great pain.

While he took the stranger's blood pressure, Brother Jerome uncorked the instrument from his cartilage-shattered ears and began to feel around the man's ribcage and stomach. Then he removed the sphygmomanometer and secured the covers around him. He next examined his hands and feet. Some of the monks flinched when Brother Jerome uncovered the blisters and blue swelling at the toes and fingertips.

Sighing, Brother Jerome tucked in the man's hands and feet and stood straight with a pained expression. "Feet and hands have some frostbite. Nothing too horrible. Mild hypothermia, from the looks of his pupils. We'll have to keep him good and warm."

"Will he survive?" Father Paolo asked.

"I'm unsure. Breathing is labored, but his heart sounds strong. Blood pressure isn't bad. Doesn't seem to have any visible signs of internal injuries, which is a blessing."

"How long do you think he was out there?" Sebastian asked.

"From the looks of him, maybe no more than a handful of hours. He must be a strong boy to have gotten this far without more serious injuries."

"That's what I was thinking," Sebastian said.

"Ideally, he should be taken to a hospital for tests," Brother Jerome stated with a wince. "But there's little hope for a helicopter or even a snowmobile to make it through this storm. We'll have to wait for it to clear. There's not much to do but keep watch over him and pray he awakens. And even then, I'm afraid, it might get worse."

"Get worse?" Brother George's dark eyes widened behind his thick glasses.

"He could suffer cardiac arrest."

"We'll pray for him," Brother Hubert said. "He'll need divine help."

"I think he's already had much of that just by reaching us," Brother Eusebius said. At more than six foot, the middle-aged monk towered over the others, save for Sebastian. The light fixtures hanging above reflected off his golden sphere of a shaved head.

Many of the brothers followed the abbot's lead and made the sign of the cross over their black scapulars. Sebastian peered at the dark figure. His chest rose and fell slowly and methodically. The interim between breaths seemed to have shortened. A good sign.

"God must have had a hand in bringing him to us," Brother George said. "Why else would he have come here? I do hope he makes it."

"He's young and strong looking," Brother Jerome said. "That's his best chance for a full recovery."

"That and prayer," Brother Hubert said.

"There's still the question of where he came from," Brother Eusebius said.

"Maybe he's from Monfrere," Brother Lucien said. "A villager seeking our divine help."

Sebastian shook his head. "Monfrere has only one hundred residents. We'd recognize him if he came from there. He's a stranger. A young man in search of something."

"You already said that," Brother Lucien said with his usual sneering tone. "Searching for what?"

"I have no idea," Sebastian murmured.

"Desperate men resort to desperate actions," Brother Eusebius said.

"You think he's a criminal?" Brother Rodel's dark eyes grew wide. "He's come here to escape prosecution. That's why he risked his life to reach us. He seeks asylum."

"A criminal?" Brother George's jaw dropped.

When they'd undressed him, Sebastian had noted that no tattoos marked his flesh, unusual for a young man of his generation. If he were a criminal, the way Brother Rodel worried—the way Sebastian had also considered—he'd most likely have been branded as a member of the Trinitarios or a dozen other street gangs Sebastian knew to exist. His hair was not too long, not too short, and he had a heart-cut diamond earring piercing his left earlobe. Sebastian doubted he was AWOL from the military. The closest military post was in Colorado Springs, three hundred miles away. And he was circumcised, which meant he'd most likely been born in the United States.

"Shouldn't we inform the police?" Brother Micah said.

"No need to notify the authorities," Father Paolo said with a deepening of his voice. "If he has come for asylum, St. Benedict instructs that we provide him with comfort and protection, regardless of what he's done. All guests who present themselves to the abbey are to be welcomed as Christ."

"Never in the near twenty years that I've lived at Mt. Ouray has anyone visited the abbey in the dead of winter," Brother Hubert said. "It's impossible."

"Whatever brought him here, he not only wanted to find us, but he *needed* to find us," Brother Eusebius said. "Determination and God's helping hand allowed him to travel this far and survive."

"Do you think someone dropped him off in a snowmobile?" Brother George darted his eyes from one brother to the next. "Maybe someone else is out there lost?"

"It's unlikely he has any companions," Sebastian said. "Nonetheless, even a snowmobile or ATV would've proved near impossible in this weather."

Brother Micah shook his head. "Unless… Unless…."

"Unless what, Brother Micah?" Brother Eusebius said.

Brother Micah flushed. "Oh, never mind any of that. I'm thinking of silly legends."

"He might die. We have to accept that," Brother Lucien added from alongside the abbot, spewing his English drawl with a glorified emphasis, which Sebastian noticed he did whenever he wished the brothers to judge his intelligence above anyone else's. Twenty-five years in the United States had probably taught him that Americans stereotyped the British by their accents as brighter than average.

"Praise God, he survives." Brother George made the sign of the cross with marked fastidiousness. "How horrible it would be if he'd traveled this far only to die in our very own infirmary."

"He will not die," Brother Giles said, yanking on his beard. "I have a feeling in my old bones he'll make it. God has not brought him to us without a reason. He will survive and live here among us. He will become a brother."

Brother Giles's optimism silenced the brothers. Many trembled in anticipation, and some, Sebastian suspected, with uncertainty. Brother Eusebius's shoulders rose to his ears. Brother George rubbed his hands, mirroring Bother Giles's childlike expectation. Casey gazed toward the stranger, dreamlike, lost.

"Do you think he might really want to become a brother?" Brother Micah asked.

A soft, peculiar grin formed on the side of Father Paolo's face. "We're jumping to conclusions," he said. "Before we have him profess, if and when he awakens, we must learn what his intentions are for coming here."

"I hope he's not a criminal," Brother George said. "That would be horrible."

"He's a mystery, indeed." Sebastian surprised himself that his words had come out as a whisper rather than remain inside his mind as the mere reflection he'd intended.

Casey jerked his head to Sebastian. He caught the apprehension in the young postulant's chestnut eyes. For some reason, Sebastian believed Casey needed assurance—the way Brother Micah often did. He shook himself from his reverie, smiled, and gave him one of his stealthy winks. Casey flushed with a smile and spun back to the stranger.

Imitating a mother goose gathering her goslings with her wings, Father Paolo ushered the brothers toward the doorway. "Let's give the patient some peace and quiet," he said. "We'll have Brother Jerome watch after him, with Brother Rodel assisting. Come along. We can ask God to have mercy on the stranger while we fulfill our responsibilities to the abbey. Make sure you stay clear of the infirmary. No wandering over to sneak a peek. Curiosity will hinder your duties and the stranger's recovery. Remember our mission, *Opus Dei*."

The brothers shuffled for the corridor, glimpsing over their shoulders at the unconscious figure with wonder and dejection pinned in their eyes. Father Paolo held Sebastian back and waited for the others to fade away. "Are you certain you have no idea where this man might have come from, Brother Sebastian?"

"I'm afraid I am," he said. "The snow had covered his tracks, and I couldn't tell which direction he might have traveled from."

The recessed lighting glinted off Father Paolo's wire-framed glasses. "Very odd. Very odd."

Sebastian was glad to take leave of the abbot. While walking to his winter workstation, he pondered more about the young man lying unconscious in the infirmary. Brother George had been right.

The stranger seemed to have fallen from Heaven.

– II –

TUCKED in a corner of the sacristy, Sebastian and Brother Eusebius crafted rosaries from coffee beans, which they sold in the abbey gift shop to summertime tourists and retreatants. He no longer grumbled about the absence of windows. The abbot believed they'd focus more on their task without the outside world stealing their concentration. Four blank walls surrounded them. Two of the sacristy's walls faced the corridors, one the kitchen pantry, and another one abutted the abbot's private office.

Although the brothers were permitted to discuss pertinent work-related issues during their working hours, the abbot frowned upon unnecessary speech. Biting his bottom lip, Sebastian crafted the rosary he'd started during the morning work period. He reached into a bucket full of shellacked and drilled coffee beans, and with a pair of needle-nose pliers, he placed a bean on the pin and curled the clasp ninety degrees, securing it to the previous s-clasp. Next he rolled the pin to meet the head of the adjoining bean. He repeated these steps several more times for the Hail Marys until he reached the centerpiece, Hail Holy Queen.

Using light pressure, he leveraged a bean onto the Hail Holy Queen, making sure not to snap the bean (a bucket nearby was half-full of fractured coffee beans), and fastened it to the silver s-clasp. Bead by bead, he worked his way toward the cross attaching the First Mystery, the Glory Be, and two Hail Marys. At that point, his fingers ached. He rested his hands in his lap. Despite the abbot's wishes, the urge to speak overcame him. He cleared his throat.

"Do you think he's doing well?" He did not need to elucidate who he'd meant by "he," for he suspected the stranger resided in the forefront of each one of the monks' minds, Brother Eusebius included. Certainly Brother Eusebius would have thoughts on the matter. An educated man with a doctorate in theology from the Catholic University in Washington, DC, he'd always expressed a keen understanding of human nature.

Sebastian returned to the rosary, twisting an s-clasp with the pliers onto the last of the Hail Marys, and waited for Brother Eusebius's thoughtful reply. He appreciated the gentle clink of the beans and silver wire in his hands in the ensuing silence.

"I think he'll survive," Brother Eusebius finally said, his downturned eyes focused on his lap, where he clasped a Hail Mary onto the rosary he'd been working on since yesterday.

"Does his presence bother you, Brother Eusebius?" The way it did himself, Sebastian wanted to add.

"Yes," he said without pretense. "A little."

"It is odd how he came here to us."

Brother Eusebius repositioned the rosary he was working on across his lap, pliers in left hand. "I suppose we all ended up at the abbey under unusual circumstances."

Sebastian toyed with the notion of asking Brother Eusebius what "unusual circumstances" had brought him to the abbey. They'd worked shoulder to shoulder for two years, but he knew little about the middle-aged monk other than what Brother Hubert had told him. He had come from a small town in Georgia, had converted to Catholicism when he was a teenager, and had moved to Washington to pursue his degree. What unknown tales might a learned convert hold? Enough that he'd sought penance by joining the Trappists?

Sebastian could not deny that he'd left his own unmentionables behind. Turning his back on his hometown of Philadelphia, he'd come to the abbey searching for escape too. Oh, of course, Center City sparkled with a gem's brilliance, as do most of America's downtowns.

Skyscrapers shimmered, the downtown streets, impressively clean, glittered. But beyond the soaring steel and white sidewalks, decaying neighborhoods radiated outward in far-flung indifference. The ribs of a hand fan run over by a truck.

Even city activists with heartfelt intentions had discarded hope. "I realize that it's a lost cause," one community leader had told him after a youth gathering he'd organized at Penn Park had left two teens dead and four wounded in a shoot-out. "I brought them together to show them peace and unity, but didn't realize they're incapable of even playing together without the slightest disagreement evolving into bloodshed." The man had shaken his head, his eyes pinned toward the Delaware River and his back to the city and all its nonsensical, adolescent violence.

For Sebastian, it was the west that had beckoned him. Coming to Colorado meant no more wishing or trying. No more facing the horrible reality of a life fouled by urban decay and chaos, a bureaucratic slow burn that had left his life and so many others shattered. Much like the coffee beans in the reject bucket.

He prayed for Philadelphia, for its future. What did it matter? Many great cities throughout history had fallen to ruin. Let Phoenix, San Diego, Dallas, and Las Vegas rise as the new urban centers. He was glad to rid himself of the east coast.

Sebastian took refuge among the men at Mt. Ouray, where, despite their quirks, they got along well. Good Samaritans, most of them, the way Luke's parable described honest, decent men. No fear of being shot or killed here, he chuckled to himself, attaching another coffee bean with a delicate jingle of the silver wire. If only life could be fastened as smartly as a handmade rosary, he mused.

He still figured a crushing past had brought the stranger to them. A desperate man, like Sebastian, like the others, like perhaps even the august Brother Eusebius, seeking refuge from the world's ambiguity and violence. With nowhere else to go, the stranger had faced the blizzard to reach their grounds, only to collapse a mere fifty yards from their snow-covered doorstep.

So young, Sebastian realized. He'd seen it before. Defeated by life before a chance to experience any of it, in turn to become a wrecking machine. So young and misguided. This one, however, who had struggled to reach their sanctuary, might harbor some fraction of hope.

Clinking of silver wires and rustling of coffee beans blanketed the resulting silence. Sebastian pinched a bean he'd wanted to toss into the dud bucket due to its odd shape. Then, deciding to use the oblong coffee bean as the Our Father bead after all, he said, "Maybe we're making too much of our guest."

"I pray that he lives and that we may learn why he's come." Brother Eusebius fixed his eyes on his work. "Prayer can often be the only solace in a world of riddles."

The tone of Brother Eusebius's voice lacked its usual rich clarity that afternoon. Sebastian wondered if he had more qualms about their guest than he had led Sebastian to believe. He took the cue from Brother Eusebius, attached a cross to the rosary, and remained quiet for the remainder of the work period.

Later, at dinnertime, the brothers gathering in the dining hall appeared likewise pensive. The only missing brothers were Brother Jerome, who ate his meal in the infirmary while watching over the stranger, and the eldest brother, Brother Augustine, who could no longer leave his cell without assistance. Brother George had already washed and fed him. Each brother stood by his wooden chair (except for Brother Giles, who remained in his wheelchair), chanting the responses to Father Paolo's Latin prayer.

They sat after the abbot closed the Bible and crossed himself, and ate in silence, as the Trappist order demanded. Sebastian had grown used to the fleshless meal of tomato soup, bread, cheese, and lentil casserole that had been a part of the Trappist diet for centuries. He had lost twenty-two pounds since entering the abbey, last time he checked. A good thing, he figured. Before leaving Pennsylvania, he'd resented his expanding paunch.

With still no information coming from the infirmary, the brothers ate slower and more ponderously than usual. The clink of dinnerware, the clearing of a throat accompanied the snap and hiss from the fireplace at the end of the dining hall.

Sebastian glanced at the brothers. Their darting eyes expressed a thousand thoughts and worries. "I wonder if he's doing well," Brother George's dark, round eyes asked. And Brother Rodel's expression held onto the fear that the stranger lying in their infirmary might be a criminal.

Even after the passing of dinner and Vespers, the infirmary remained closed and silent. The monks grew restless. By Compline, Sebastian noticed their chanting had become less audible. Finally, just before everyone took to their separate cells for Retire, Brother Jerome emerged from the infirmary to give word that no change had come over the stranger.

Father Paolo instructed Brother Jerome to remain in the infirmary through the night to guard the stranger's well-being. The other monks closed their cell doors with envy in their eyes. They wanted the young man to recover, but they also craved to stand over his bed and gaze at him, as if he were a blessed icon.

Sebastian slept little, spending most the night on his back, piecing together the puzzle of the stranger. Why did the stranger's mystifying arrival bother him? Sebastian yearned for his awakening so that he might release his secrets. Yet deep inside he also wanted to keep them forever sealed.

The following morning, the Grand Silence irked him more than usual. The other brothers had tossed and turned most of the night too, by the looks of their frazzled and drawn faces. All through Vigils and *lectio divina*, he figured they harbored the same unsaid question as he: Had their stranger survived the night?

Lumbering even more slowly, they lined up in the kitchen to plate their breakfasts of corn mash, fried potatoes, and scrambled Egg Beaters, suppressing yawns and scratching at their eyes. Brother George had taken Brother Jerome his breakfast tray, but once he'd returned to the kitchen, he shrugged with a light smile. The stranger still breathed, but there had been no change.

Brother Micah, the abbey's cellarer, made sure to keep the breakfast bins full. No bacon or ham to go with Sebastian's scrambled eggs. Delores, the abbey's St. Bernard and the only female within fifteen miles, nudged her cold, wet snout at Sebastian's hand while he served himself. He gave her a bit of scrambled egg and patted her head. She trotted over to Brother Giles, one of the few brothers who indulged the old girl, and he fed her corn mash from the tray balanced on his lap.

In the deadened silence and under the stark fluorescent lights, each one of the brothers' peculiarities stood out. Sebastian tolerated his fellow monks as best he could, following Christ's instruction to love all mankind like brothers, to embrace them with open hearts, regardless of their flaws. Brother George, suffering from pyrophobia, flinched from the warming flames under the serving bins when he served himself potatoes and, once again, knocked Sebastian's tray, spilling his corn mash onto the tiled floor. Delores was happy to clean up. Brother Micah, dish towel forever clenched in his left hand, glowered at shaky Brother George.

As always, Casey brushed against him while serving himself. Little Sebastian minded that. Many times Casey served Sebastian first, like now. Casey spread cream cheese on Sebastian's blueberry muffin and grabbed his bread from the toaster, as if worried Sebastian might burn his fingers. Casey never poured himself a cup of steaming black coffee without topping off Sebastian's. Sebastian cared little for Brother Micah's disapproving glares.

Sebastian carried his loaded tray to the cloister, where he reclined on the floor by the warm, buzzing radiators and gazed outside at the garden. He couldn't see much in winter at five thirty in the morning, but he enjoyed the silent mornings, imagining May, when the tulips Brother Hubert had planted would bloom in radiant colors of yellow, red, and orange, and the lilac shrubs would blossom with purple buds.

Casey strolled past him with his tray, the echoing click of his sandals against the terracotta tiles filling the stillness. He claimed a spot catty-corner to Sebastian, where two juniper shrubs hidden behind snow drifts pushed against the window, the same spot he always took whenever Sebastian ate breakfast by the garden.

Sebastian found Casey trailing him around the abbey, like Delores following Brother Micah in the kitchen, sweet. Of course, there was nothing he could do about it. Temptations meant nothing to Sebastian. He had lived with unfulfilled yearnings his entire life. Why should he give in to them at a monastery, of all places?

The eldest of six, Sebastian had kept his homosexuality secret since he'd first realized his attraction to boys in the sixth grade, while playing shortstop at the Berks County Catholic Summer Sports League. Although he'd proved himself a capable athlete, keeping his eyes off the other boys in their tight baseball uniforms had proved difficult. Especially considering he'd gone to Catholic school until the twelfth grade and then on to a Catholic university in Philadelphia, and he'd interacted with few girls other than his two sisters and mother and a handful of sourpuss nuns.

He had played "games" with a few of his friends, but no one had ever mentioned homosexuality except in a negative way. "Homo" was the preferred word choice whenever any of them did something the others discouraged, like missing a ball between the legs that should've been easily scooped up in the infield dust.

He was certain his family suspected, yet he never came out to any of them. A few times his father and a few of his siblings had expressed through innuendo that if they knew anyone gay, they wouldn't mind. No matter. He rarely dated and could recall only once bringing home a "beard" for the family to meet. Sebastian, a captain of the guards, sheltered his private life. Gregarious and friendly to a fault, colleagues had told him, though he preferred people never get too personal.

During college he'd had three boyfriends, but they'd dropped him after a few months. Sebastian had assumed they'd lost interest, misunderstanding his introspective side. With a shrug, he'd given up on the notion of dating and relationships, graduated with honors, and taken to the real world. Until his life shattered and his only refuge was inside Mt. Ouray.

He finished breakfast with Casey's furtive glimpses lingering after him, washed his dishes in the kitchen sink, and went to take a quick shower before Lauds. Casey trailed him into the shower room.

Seemed he always showered whenever Sebastian did. Or was it the other way around?

Casey never made eye contact with him while they slipped off their bathrobes and stepped into the separate stalls before yanking the curtains closed. Never indicated any awareness that Sebastian spent extra time under the steaming jet, waiting to fall flaccid before stepping back onto the clammy floor mat.

Sebastian tried to avoid glancing at Casey. Once or twice he couldn't help but look. Supple and smooth. His hair, shiny like onyx, falling over his forehead. Perfect. His type. Casey, as usual, maintained a casual posture, his eyes averted, as if Sebastian weren't there. Sebastian suspected Casey deliberately posed for him.

Dried and dressed in a fresh tunic and white cowl, Sebastian stepped into line outside the chapel for Lauds with only a few minutes to spare. They waited for the abbot's lead forward. With his hood covering most of his peripheral vision, he spied Casey, smelling of Ivory soap, edging behind him. Father Paolo entered the corridor and motioned for them to follow.

Their hands left the folds of their cowls long enough to reach for the holy water and cross themselves. Heads bowed in silent prayer, they took their positions in the pews. Scents of burning candles and dry wood met Sebastian's downturned nose. The rising sun would normally ooze through the arched stained glass windows, aligned precisely so that the morning sun's rays would bathe the crucifix hanging on the high altar. That morning, the snowstorm shrouded the chapel in murky shadows.

While they recited Psalms 148 to 150, Sebastian noted the wandering eyes of the brothers, which peeked from above their psalmodies toward the side door closest to the infirmary. Even the most devout would have difficulty concentrating on prayer without speculating about the stranger. The brothers' expressions altered little while Casey read from the Gospel and they followed with the responsory.

Hallowed and haunting, their melodic voices reached to the high wooden beams. The singing of the Canticle of Mary was perhaps the most chilling for Sebastian. *Magnificat anima mea Dominum....* Briefly, Sebastian lost himself in the poignant hymn, and even forgot about the stranger. But only for a moment.

As the brothers' voices eased to a stop, he opened his eyes and imagined the young man lying unconscious in the infirmary, near death's doorstep. Sebastian prayed for his speedy recovery. He also prayed that his presence might signify positive change for the abbey, apart from the odd and ominous sensations indented on Sebastian's soul.

They recited the Lord's Prayer and the closing, led by Father Paolo, after which Sebastian retreated to his cell to engage in *lectio divina*. Glad to have parted from the others, he hoped that immersing himself in divine reading might steal away his incessant concerns about the stranger and the other irritating thoughts that never seemed to leave him.

By Mass, the abbey rumor mill suggested the young man's condition had yet to change. For the first time in many months, Sebastian wished for a quick passage of the Eucharist so that he might learn something. He mumbled the words of the Gospel with a painful knowledge that what lurked inside his mind was not marvel for the Paschal Mystery of Christ's suffering and resurrection, but fear and worry.

With the communion wafer still stuck to the roof of his mouth, the Grand Silence ended, and Sebastian shuffled to the sacristy to fashion rosaries alongside Brother Eusebius, as he had each winter for the past two years.

– III –

CASEY worked at his station in the abbey office, doing whatever administrative tasks Brother Lucien or Father Paolo requested. At present, he answered phone calls and e-mails for prayer requests and inquiries into monastic life from prospective postulants. Because he'd graduated with a bachelor's degree in English, the abbot fancied utilizing Casey's writing skills.

Reading a short inquiry from a curious high school senior in Minnesota, Casey recalled his own letters to Mt. Ouray when he first recognized the nudging call to join the monastic vocation. His mother had clutched the curtains to keep from collapsing after he'd informed his parents about his decision to join the Trappists. His stepfather had stared at him as if he'd flown into the living room on wings. "Why did I waste all that money on your college education?" he'd said once he'd shaken off the initial shock.

He never expected his parents to understand his choosing life inside a monastery. They knew he was gay (he'd come out to his family when he was twenty), and that had made it all the more confusing for them to grasp, he supposed. He imagined their roller-coaster ride of emotions—first learning that their son was gay, followed by the jarring news that he wanted to join an austere religious order.

Casey never bought into the Church's condemnation of homosexuality. From his personal experience, the Church was loaded with gay men. At college he'd experienced numerous come-ons from the Jesuit students and faculty. And there was that time he'd overheard a friend of his mother's divulge her embarrassment at finding Internet porn on one of the priest's computers at the local Catholic parish office, where she worked as a secretary. "Priests are men," was his mother's thin reply while they'd sipped coffee at the dining table. Casey never did learn what type of porn his mother's friend had found, but he couldn't help but assume the pictures were of men.

The Church drew an odd alliance of men, attracted by the desire for a family they feared they'd never find in a society that viewed them as outsiders. Focused on ancient rituals in a world of cascading velvet and satin, flowing robes and brilliant stained glass, swirling incense and glittering gold, monks and priests came together for a new kind of brotherhood. In the Church's open censure of homosexuality lay a tacit endorsement.

Father Paolo and Brother Lucien's close relationship was silently accepted inside the monastery. At the moment, they convened in the abbot's private office, discussing whatever issues they deemed important, the stranger most likely, or doing whatever else they did in private. They spent many hours inside his office, sharing a bond tighter than that of husband and wife. Lately, Casey sensed their relationship hovered near the skids, like any long-term relationship might.

Casey had little doubt Brother Sebastian was gay. He'd concluded soon after his arrival in October as a postulant that Sebastian had sought monasticism for much the same reasons as he and the others had. Of course, a handful of the monks, homosexual or not, led devout lives, fixed to their vows. Sebastian hadn't intimated his sexual orientation to Casey, or expressed any interest in him beyond a naïve and needy postulant. He hadn't crossed an improper line, as the father had done once. Still, Casey knew. He always knew.

The tall brother with the shiny russet hair and soft blue eyes that captured the abbey's dim lighting like a gold chalice had attracted Casey his first day as a summer retreatant. So often he'd fantasized seeing those bright eyes gaze down at him while he lay alone on his simple twin bed, in his cell that always smelled of old houses. Loneliness at the abbey could sometimes seize him, especially at night during Retire when lights went out and silence was enforced.

Casey hadn't professed his solemn vows, but if all went well, he foresaw lying prone at the abbot's feet within the coming years, while his family, disbelief marking their faces, watched. A lifetime of consecration wouldn't be so bad, not with Brother Sebastian to share it.

His "real" family had failed to provide Casey with the love he sought. An amalgamation of individuals with nothing more in common than a shared roof over their heads. Less even than what he felt with his fellow Trappist brothers.

A biological father he had never really known, a stepfather too consumed with his aerospace job, a mother so focused on building her social stature in the community that she never held his stare longer than five seconds, a younger brother who never seemed to go anywhere without an iPod attached to his ears, and his younger sister, a junior at Casey's alma mater, always peered at Casey as if he were a complete stranger. He couldn't even remember holding a conversation with her.

His eldest brother, a graduate student at Kansas State, had expressed the most interest in Casey one afternoon in Casey's bedroom, after he'd learned of his discernment. Trenton, as if personally wounded by his decision, had pressed Casey as to what he expected to find at a monastery.

"It's where I should go," Casey had told him with a shrug. The typical uncomfortable lulls had reared between them while Casey pretended to study at his desk. "It's hard to put into words."

Casey wasn't running from himself, as Trenton had alluded to that afternoon, the sharp sunlight piercing his bedroom window. No, Casey had answered a call he was certain God had placed to him. *You will find love and beauty inside a monastery*, the voice had whispered one night while he'd lain in bed.

His baby brother hadn't even hugged him good-bye when he departed for Mt. Ouray. Only his mother had given him a cursory embrace. John, his stepfather, had supplied the obligatory firm handshake. "Try not to get into trouble," was all he'd said before Casey stepped onto the Greyhound in downtown Hutchinson for the sixteen-hour trip to Telluride, flute case sturdy by his side.

He'd had a special relationship with his maternal grandmother, but she had passed away two weeks after Casey's fourteenth birthday. He sensed Grandma had stood behind him with her hand on his shoulder when he'd climbed onto the bus that day. After her death, about the only demonstrative affection Casey experienced came in the form of dreams.

The monks at Mt. Ouray loved and accepted him. Or at least they professed to. They had little choice. St. Benedict, in his fifteen-hundred-year-old *Rule*, ordered that all monks love and embrace one another as their true brothers. More than what he experienced from his immediate family.

Casey never once imagined that someone might come along and compete for Brother Sebastian's attentions. What if Brother Giles's inane ramblings proved true and the stranger in their infirmary chose to remain at Mt. Ouray? Casey couldn't live without anyone loving him, thinking him special.

He wished he'd never spotted that strange man lying in the snow. Horrible to think such things. If not for Casey, the snow would've buried the man alive, keeping him undiscovered until the spring thaw. Even if Brother Sebastian had an interest in Casey, what might come of a mutual attraction? Sebastian, who had entered the abbey three years prior to Casey's coming to Mt. Ouray, stood on the cusp of taking his solemn vows. For all Casey knew, Sebastian had no intention of breaking that promise.

Sighing, he mulled over what to put in a nice letter to the confused high school boy from St. Paul. He glimpsed at the "how to write to postulants" note Father Paolo had tacked to the bulletin board beside the computer. Over time, Casey had learned to disregard most of it. A short response would be best. He typed the e-mail in thirty seconds and pressed "send." The father would follow up with more letters if the boy was serious enough to write back.

He mentally shook his head when Brother Lucien stepped outside Father Paolo's office, with a stronger stench of juniper incense wafting after him. Face flushed, he dashed about the office, shuffling papers, opening and shutting cabinets. His brushing Casey with his tunic sleeves while he hovered about only rubbed Casey's emotional sores all the worse. The abbot's right-hand man, Brother Lucien had exhibited an odd contempt for Casey.

The worst came one week after his arrival in October, when Father Paolo had insisted on instructing Casey with private chanting lessons in his office. The fireplace was lit on each occasion, and chocolates and wine sat ready for him on the round table. God might have blessed Casey with polished writing skills and sensitive flute-playing lips, but singing would never be his strength. Nonetheless, the father had continued to praise him. "You own a wondrous voice. A great gift from the Lord." After five lessons, Casey had begged off.

He wondered if Brother Lucien's animosity toward him derived from the same reason Casey felt scorn for the stranger.

Once Brother Lucien disappeared again inside Father Paolo's private office, Casey breathed a bit lighter. He grew bored. The phones remained silent. He wished he could get onto his favorite websites, but Father Paolo had blocked everything but the abbey's homepage. Not even his favorite weather site was accessible.

Only Brother Hubert, who administered the abbey's public website, had privileged and unlimited access to the "off limits" computer on the other side of the room. Father Paolo had given a strict order, forbidding anyone else from using it. If he found out, he would intern the offender in his cell, without exception save for toilet needs. Casey could not tolerate solitary confinement. Not when he was battling for the attention of Brother Sebastian.

The few times they'd shared the office, Casey had spied Brother Hubert typing in a special password. From his desk, Casey had noticed the brother scanning different websites or making much use of Google. "Research for the website," Brother Hubert had once told him after he'd caught Casey staring.

And much of what Brother Hubert had said was true. Upon Father Paolo's requests, Brother Hubert would supply Casey with notes he'd compiled from his Internet research and ask that Casey write up a new entry to lure young men considering discernment. The father would edit his entries with a pointed eye for detail. "We're seeking *healthy, virile young men*," he'd once said as he added the extra words on the printout copy with his sharpened red pencil. "Not just *men*." And sure enough, the new language went into the page headed, "Interested in Becoming a Monk?"

Flustered, Casey focused on his work again. He read several e-mailed prayer requests, one from a woman in Colorado Springs. Her twenty-six-year-old son suffered from lymphoma. Would the monks please say a special prayer for him? Casey printed the request and placed it in the "prayer tray." He wrote a simple reply that the brothers would pray for the woman's son and for her to find patience and understanding in God's love. The other prayer requests appealed for the same. Either a friend or family member suffered from a disease or drug addiction or depression, and they sought whatever help they could. The brothers took the requests seriously. During Vespers, they would read aloud each ailing person's name and beseech God's mercy.

Casey printed the latest of the prayer requests and considered a few of his own he wouldn't mind adding to their pile that morning.

Worktime passed, and Casey, along with the other monks, entered the chapel for Sext. He'd hoped to hear something about the stranger. But not until late afternoon did abbey hearsay report that the stranger had stirred from unconsciousness. "He hasn't opened his eyes or spoken," Brother Rodel had whispered to them while they filed into the dining hall to take dinner, "but he's alive and kicking. Should be better in a few days."

Heavy sighs had flowed from the grinning brothers. So what? When would they learn the reason for the man's arrival at Mt. Ouray or how he'd ventured so far in such impenetrable weather? In a few days, when he'd regain full consciousness, like Brother Jerome had said? Brother Sebastian seemed the most faraway when he'd heard the news, and Casey feared he was thinking of the young man's flexing muscles.

They had sacrificed much to care for him. Like they did for the aged Brother Augustine, he knew Brothers Rodel and Jerome had cleaned the young stranger whenever he needed it, ensuring he slept on fresh sheets. The annoying envy had glowed in the other brothers' faces, including Brother Sebastian's. The entire abbey buzzed about the "angel come to them on gilded wings."

Later that night after Compline, with news from the abbey grapevine affirming the stranger continued to mumble and squirm and kick at his sheets, Casey prayed by the foot of his twin bed in his lonely seven-by-ten cell, asking God to forgive him. Over his folded hands, he peered at the statuette of the Virgin Mary the abbot had given him his first week as a postulant, and mouthed Psalm 119.

His lips ached with dryness as he whispered God's instructions. He recalled Christ's chapped lips when he entered the place of the skulls, where his crucifixion awaited. He'd rejected the wine soldiers had given him to drink, refusing to even moisten his lips with it. Casey's suffering was a trip to a theme park in comparison. But to his young soul, pain wielded no prejudice.

At the end of his recitation, he slipped off his sandals and scapular and climbed into bed, still cloaked in his tunic. *Let them sleep clothed and girded with cinctures or cords*, St. Benedict proclaimed. Often Casey wanted to strip the garment from his body and sleep nude, the way he had back home in Kansas. He supposed it was for the best. Temptation came less often without fidgety fingers finding his warm flesh.

Did Brother Sebastian, alone in his cell, ever strip off his tunic and falter with temptation?

Was he doing it now, while thinking of Casey?

Or did he picture the beautiful dark stranger in the infirmary?

Casey rolled to his side, wrapped his tunic tight around his body. The usual moldy smell, along with the darkness, engulfed him. Whichever way he turned, the same stale barrenness met his wide gaze. At only eight thirty at night, he still had difficulty falling off to sleep right away.

Outside, the snowstorm raged on. The windowpane rattled above his small desk, where he stowed his theological texts and chanting guides. The shadowy shape of his flute case rested on top. He squeezed his slender pillow, biting into the cotton. Had he lost Sebastian before ever embracing him?

He tossed and turned the night, until giving up on sleep about two hours before Brother George's signature rap on each of the cell doors to rouse them at three in the morning for Vigils. Restless, he sat at his desk and read Alban Butler's *Lives of the Saints* under the faint glow of his desk lamp.

He took refuge in the saints. They sought a life grander than the status quo that Casey had lived. They found caves and deserts, away from civilization, far more accommodating than the world of man. Casey often wondered if any of them had been gay. Outcasts longing for acceptance from a greater power.

Wind continued to wail outside while he drew inspiration from his choice saints. At least the snow had stopped for a time. He rested his eyes a moment, and was about to switch off the lamp and try to salvage what remained of sleep when he heard the alarm ringing in the corridor. Only once since his stay had the emergency bells heralded them, when an electrical fire had broken out in the kitchen the day before Thanksgiving.

What now? he thought, snapping his book shut. Without bothering to pull on his scapular or slip on his sandals, he peeked into the corridor.

The other monks were gathering outside their cells in various states of sleepiness. Brother Hubert's tunic draped over his hunched body, uncinched, and for a moment Casey stood staring in shock and amusement. He noticed Brother Sebastian's strong calves while he struggled into his sandals.

Panic etched their faces. They gazed about, expressing concern that a fire might force them into the snowstorm. Sebastian calmed them above the din of the bell.

"No need for worry until we find out what's happening," he said.

Right then the bell stopped, and Brother Rodel scurried up to them from the bowels of the abbey.

"He's gone," he shouted, hands clenched by his sides in anguish. "He's gone! He's gone from his bed! The stranger is gone from the infirmary!"

"Are you certain?" Sebastian asked.

"Brother Jerome and I searched everywhere. He's gone!"

– IV –

BROTHER RODEL hurried them to the infirmary in a flood of white tunics. The hard slap of many sandals and the squeal of Brother Giles's wheelchair sounded odd to Sebastian in the darkest morning hour. Their shadows chased them—and then seemed to surround them in mockery. Once inside the infirmary, they stared in disbelief. Brother Rodel had not mistaken a bad dream for reality. The stranger's bed sat empty, the bodiless IV pushed against the far wall, the tube dangling like a dead snake. Brother Jerome's wide, moist eyes exposed his fears and shame.

"I was asleep in the bed next to him," he said, his eyes tearing behind his crooked glasses. "I didn't hear him get up at all. Didn't hear a thing. It was Brother Rodel who woke me."

Father Paolo and Brother Lucien, the last to reach them, breathed heavily by the door. Both appeared frazzled. Brother Lucien, in the process of cinching his tunic, glanced about, dazed-looking and flushed. Brother Rodel laid pleading eyes on the abbot.

"It's my fault," he said. "I'd been awake, sitting in a chair by his side watching over him, since he'd been stirring so much. I worried he might pull out his IV. I went to use the bathroom for no more than ten minutes. When I returned, he'd vanished. Just like that."

"We looked everywhere," Brother Jerome added. "When we realized there was no finding him, we pulled the alarm."

"What could've happened to him?" Brother George said, wringing his hands. What remained of his brown hair sat mussed atop his round head. "He couldn't possibly have gone back outside, you think. Not out there again, in all this snow?"

"What should we do?" Brother Micah asked while looking in Sebastian's direction.

"Let's break up and look in every nook and cranny," Sebastian said.

"What if he's dangerous?" Brother Rodel's eyes expanded. "What if he's an escaped convict like I feared, and he's hiding, waiting to jump us?"

The brothers flinched. Brother Hubert shook his head, and tears fell from under his dark-framed glasses. "I don't want to believe it," he said.

"We have nothing to fear in God's house," Father Paolo said. "Now let's begin our search before we may never find him."

The brothers' long shadows fanned around them as they spread throughout the abbey. Heavy sighs and grunts traveled along the cavernous corridors. Brother Giles wheeled about on the wings of a phoenix on a desperate mission, hesitating only when he turned sharp corners. The squeal of his chair ricocheted off the walls. Some of the brothers even looked inside baskets and drawers too small for a lapdog. Delores kept close by Sebastian's side. Urgency for the hunt shone in the St. Bernard's big brown eyes.

"Find him, girl, find him," Sebastian whispered, hoping the eight-year-old hadn't lost her instinct to track and retrieve. She'd proven to be a master at catching the abbey's numerous mice, especially in winter when they took refuge indoors from the cold and snow. Certainly she'd uncover a grown man.

He searched in the six vacant cells, as well as in Brother Augustine's at the far end of the corridor, where he appeared undisturbed and asleep on his bed, peered into the two toilet stalls in the bathroom, looked around the dining hall alongside Brothers Rodel and Micah. Not even the mousetraps went undisturbed. In the sacristy, he pushed aside the storage boxes until Brother Hubert rushed in, glancing about, lost and aimless.

"Anything?" Sebastian asked him.

He shrugged, his eyes still moist with fretful tears and the blood vessels on his nose ready to explode. "Nothing at all."

"Come on, girl."

Moving stealthier than a cougar, Sebastian hugged the perimeter of the cloister while he peered into the darkness of the snow-riddled garden. When nothing turned up, he ordered Delores to follow him into the library. He ran from arched window to arched window, halfheartedly straining to look for the stranger lying in the snow the way Casey had first discovered him, realizing he'd have no such luck.

Then an idea struck him.

"Let's go, old girl. Follow me."

With Delores close by Sebastian's hip, her tail wagging like the rotors of a windmill, Sebastian sprinted off, swinging right then left through the long stretches of corridor. He was about to switch on the kitchen light by impulse, but curtailed the movement. Mulling over an idea, he restrained Delores by the fur on her neck and whispered for her to stay quiet. Lingering aromas of Brother Micah's tomato soup made the hunt seem like a game.

Sebastian glanced into the dark. Residual light from the corridor highlighted the pots and pans hanging from hooks and the kitchen knives stuck to the magnetic wall strip. He wanted to chastise himself for ensuring none of the knives went missing and worried that Brother Rodel—and he—might have been right about the stranger's criminal intentions.

Inhaling a heavy breath, he squatted by the St. Bernard's melon-sized head and whispered into her floppy ear, "Find him, Delores. Go ahead. Find him, girl."

Delores, comprehending her best friend's order, scuttled about the kitchen, stopping only to nibble on crumbs on the terracotta tiles missed by Brother Micah's broom. She left smear marks from her nose on the stainless steel cabinet doors, and seemed little interested in what was behind them. But near the pantry she scratched at the door and let loose a high-pitched whimper. Sebastian scurried over. He opened the door carefully. Darkness prevented seeing even the cans and boxes stored on the high shelves. Without any further deliberation, he switched on the pantry light. He jerked back, gaped.

In the corner, curled in a tight ball and clutching a box of saltines to his chest, the stranger shook like the branches of an aspen in a stiff breeze. And he was naked.

Sebastian did not wish to frighten the stranger any further. He pacified his shock with a smile, kept his left hand still by his side while he grabbed Delores's neck with his right.

"Did the alarm frighten you?" he said, using his softest tone. "Don't be afraid. You're safe here. Don't worry. No one will hurt you. We were only worried where you ran off to."

Thin streams of dried blood streaked his naked body, from when he must have ripped the IV tube from his arm. Sebastian could imagine the horror the man must've experienced upon gaining full consciousness and finding himself lying in a strange bed inside what to many outsiders appeared to be a prison.

Sebastian spotted a chef's smock someone had tossed on top of a sack of brown rice. Mindful to avoid upsetting the stranger, he gingerly reached for it, squatted to the man's eye level, and handed it to him. "You can use this to cover yourself. Go ahead."

The man stared at Sebastian with large black eyes. Slowly, he took the smock from Sebastian with a trembling hand and draped it over his body.

"There. That's better, isn't it?"

Brother Micah stopped short behind Sebastian. In a flash, he gasped and dashed off, calling for the others to come to the kitchen. Seconds later, the brothers herded by the pantry door, gaping at the shaking stranger.

By then Sebastian had already shuffled closer to ease the young man, and was whispering for him to remain calm, doing the best he could to ignore the brothers pushing behind him.

"You're in a Trappist monastery," he said. "Mt. Ouray at Monfrere in Colorado. You're safe here. We wish to help you."

The stranger held up the smock to his neck and pivoted his shoulders away from Sebastian's hand. Sebastian pulled back.

"We found you outside, lying unconscious in the snow. You've been recovering in our infirmary. Would you prefer to go back there and rest? We'll take you. You have nothing to fear."

"He must want more than crackers," Brother Eusebius said, his baritone voice a sudden blast in Sebastian's ears.

"I'll get him some vegetable broth." Brother Rodel scampered off, followed by cabinets opening and shutting and pots and pans banging.

"What made you think to look for him in here?" Brother Micah asked Sebastian.

"I guessed he'd be hungry after his long sleep and follow his nose to the kitchen."

"That's ingenious," Brother Micah whispered.

"It was Delores who found him." Sebastian patted the hound's head as she squirmed to get closer to the stranger. Casey, using a cracker that had fallen to the floor, lured her out of the pantry. Behind Sebastian, Father Paolo cleared his throat.

"Let's get him to his feet and return him to the infirmary," he said. "It's not proper to allow him to eat on the kitchen floor like a dog."

THE stranger spooned the steaming vegetable broth into his mouth while the brothers hovered around his bed, layering him in shadows. They gazed upon him as if he were Lazarus raised from the dead. In many ways, he was. Brother Jerome had instructed Brother Rodel to reconnect the IV to his arm, and the tube rustled while he ate. Once he had acclimated to the broth's temperature, he laid aside the spoon, which captured the lone ray of light between the brothers' fused shoulders, and gulped from the bowl.

"Steady now," Brother Jerome said. "You don't want to overstuff yourself. It's best if you eat slowly."

"How are you feeling?" Brother George asked.

The stranger nodded while he tried to slow his gulps. "I'm good, I guess. Am I…. Am I really in a… monastery?"

"You are indeed," Brother Giles said. "You've been with us for two whole days now."

Brother Rodel took the emptied bowl from him. "Would you like some more?"

The young man looked at him, almost pleadingly, and his ebony eyes emanated shame and desperation. "If you don't mind."

"I'm afraid that's not a good idea." Brother Jerome held Brother Rodel by his sleeve. "He can have some more later, perhaps at lunch, when he's stronger. Too much right now will make him sick."

Sebastian worried about the state of his health, but he couldn't help but wonder more who lay in their infirmary. *The Lord knows the thoughts of men*, proclaims Psalm 94.11. The Lord, but not Sebastian Harkin. "What brought you to us in the dead of winter?" he asked. "We've been anxious to learn."

"Yes, please tell us," Brother Hubert echoed. "Why did you come?"

The stranger swallowed and seemed to fall into a daydream. His black eyes stared beyond the brothers' merged shoulders, through the wall into the corridor. "I… I don't know why I came here."

"You can't recall," Sebastian said, his forehead pained with wrinkles, "or you traveled here with no clear reason?"

"I can't recall," he said.

Brother Eusebius mellowed his deep voice. "You can trust us now, son. Isn't that why you came to us? To seek help with something? Don't fear confiding in us. Tell us why you came."

The stranger shook his head. "I told you. I can't remember."

The brothers shot each other puzzled glances.

"Are you sure?" Sebastian said.

"All I seem to remember are the initials JC. Maybe that's my name or a nickname. Or maybe it's where I'm from. I can't remember anything."

Father Paolo drew his hands to his chest. "You can't remember anything else?"

"I swear, that's it."

"What about your age?" Sebastian asked. "Your hometown? Your family? Can you picture any of it in your mind?"

"Not really. I know I'm not from here, though. But then maybe...." He dropped his eyes to his knees beneath the heavy blankets and sighed. "How would I know if I can't remember?"

The brothers observed him, allowing him time to gather his thoughts.

Brother Micah broke the contemplative silence, a leer seared into his insipid voice. "Why can't he remember anything?"

"He's got amnesia." Brother Jerome folded his arms across his white tunic, which was still askew from when he'd awakened in a hurry. "It's not uncommon when one regains consciousness after a lengthy period. The high altitude might have made it worse. It's been known to happen."

"Amnesia?" Brother George frowned. "Now we'll never learn anything about him."

"Most likely it'll be short term," Brother Jerome assured. "He'll remember things, I'm certain. I've seen it before in my day. He'll snap out of it."

"What do we do in the meantime?" Brother Giles asked.

"I suggest we give him some added rest and breathing room," Brother Jerome said, urging his fellow brothers back with a flounce of his arms. "Sleep is the best thing for him now. I'll keep watch over him."

"We're in time for Vigils," Father Paolo added, ushering everyone to the door. "Let's do what Brother Jerome requests and fetch our cowls before withdrawing for the chapel. Come along. You too, Brother Rodel. Our guest is in fine hands. Give him room."

Sebastian lingered behind. The young man who could only remember the initials "JC" peered at the ceiling, frozen in a daze. Reluctant obedience stole Sebastian's breath when he obeyed the abbot's command and turned to leave, although he longed to stay and ask the stranger a million more questions.

"GLORY be to the Father," the brothers sang out, following each of Father Paolo's readings from the cantorum. Next they stood and intoned the canticles. Their droning voices rubbed against the chapel's acoustical walls, wispy, like smoke from an extinguished candle. Wafting aimlessly and with finite expectation. Their voices flowed over the awareness that the stranger who now resided in their abbey home was fully conscious. And in the midst of winter, without any means for him or any of them to get off the mountain, in an odd way, he was their prisoner.

Or was it the other way around?

Vigils ended, and each monk returned to his private *lectio divina*. Sebastian hoped to find clues to the stranger in his thoughtful reading of Scripture. They had waited on a bed of nails to learn something about him. The mysterious man had awakened. The answers to his identity and for his arrival at the abbey still slept deep inside him. Sebastian had never imagined he'd suffer from amnesia. Little to do now but wait until the young man's memory improved.

As the morning progressed, Father Paolo permitted the monks to cater to the stranger's needs whenever Brother Jerome or Brother Rodel requested help. Sebastian noted the excitement in their eyes, shimmering in the abbey's recessed lighting, whenever Brother Jerome or Brother Rodel gave the signal they needed someone to fetch food, drink, or toiletries for their patient.

They made excuses to shuffle by the bathroom when the young man the brothers now referred to as "JC" took a good twenty minutes to wash and freshen himself. Brother Lucien sat on the bench inside, waiting in case he took a sudden relapse. The coveting that cut into his fellow monks' faces irked Sebastian rather than tickled him. JC's awakening was akin to the resurrection of Christ, by the way the brothers carried on.

Supplied with a fresh tunic, JC remained in the infirmary under Brother Jerome's care. He appeared anxious and confused whenever the monks neared him, baffled perhaps as much as Sebastian, as much as any of them. The brothers tried desperately to bring a smile to his face.

During their morning work period, Brother Eusebius kept his judgments to himself. He narrowed his dark eyes and fastened the coffee beans to the s-clasps, speaking only to ask where they'd stored the Hail Holy Queen centerpieces. Neither he nor Sebastian could explain the mysterious man.

Sebastian waited until after None, when he knew that Father Paolo had summoned Brother Jerome to his private office, before defying the abbot's request that they refrain from bombarding JC with questions.

With the other brothers occupied in *lectio divina*, he slinked inside the infirmary, where JC slept soundly. He persuaded Brother Rodel, instructed to remain by JC's bedside, to give them privacy. Little Brother Rodel hesitated only a moment before leaving to pray at the transept in the chapel, at Sebastian's pushy suggestion.

Seated next to him, Sebastian observed JC's rising and falling chest. He fantasized entering his head and peeking into his dreams. Maybe then he might learn something about him. Sebastian's presence must have stirred him. Shimmering dark eyes flashed open. He sat up, still looking as if they'd caged him against his will. Sebastian resisted laying a reassuring hand on his shoulder.

JC grabbed for his knapsack, which was lying beside him, the only possession they'd found on him. Earlier, Brother Rodel had shown it to him, and he'd refused to let it go.

"Do you remember the knapsack?" Brother Sebastian asked him, eyeing how he clutched it.

"Yes, I mean… no. They said it was mine. I want to keep it."

"Of course, you may keep it."

Sebastian smiled at JC and leaned closer to him. "Are you feeling more relaxed among us?" he asked, although clearly JC was not. "We've been fussing over you a bit, haven't we?"

"I'm... I'm still confused about everything."

"None of your memories have come back?"

JC shook his head. "I keep trying to think hard, but nothing comes to mind."

"Has anything come to you in your dreams? Maybe that might help piece together the puzzle."

"I don't remember ever having dreamed," he said with darkness to his tone.

Sebastian grinned to encourage a connection between him and the stranger. Perhaps then JC's mind might open up. Something lay trapped inside him. There had to be a way to pry it out. "Puede entender mi?"

JC's eyes popped. "I can understand your Spanish."

"I guessed you might be Latino. It might help us learn who you are."

"It's weird how you can forget everything else, but still understand languages," JC said.

"That's perfectly normal. Does Philadelphia or Baltimore ring a bell in your mind?"

"No, they don't."

"What about Ohio or Cincinnati?"

"I can't remember. It's like my mind is frozen." He peered at Sebastian. "Why do you ask about those places?"

"You and I share a similar twang," Sebastian said. "I'm from Philadelphia. It's possible you might be from there, or somewhere else in the mid-Atlantic. Perhaps along the Ohio River. Sometimes you can trace the migration of Americans by their accents. Did you know that people in Philadelphia sound similar to people from Cincinnati?" He chuckled. "And yet they're over five hundred miles apart. Isn't that something?"

"It still doesn't mean anything to me," JC murmured.

Sebastian repositioned himself closer to JC, but stopped when the man flinched. Was there a reason for his distrust? Had he been running from something? Sebastian wanted to believe he'd lost his memory. He didn't sense that he was a criminal on the lam. Yet he might harbor a past he wished to forget.

Hadn't they all?

Swallowing his own transgressions, Sebastian sat stiffer, his hands firm on his thighs. He smiled wider to relax him. "Are you an expert backpacker of some kind? Maybe an outdoor enthusiast? An extreme sports athlete? We get lots of those types in the Rockies."

"Don't feel like I am."

Sebastian pursed his lips. "Did anyone bring you here, do you remember? One of your friends, maybe? Can you picture anyone's face in your mind?"

JC shook his head.

"Well, we didn't find any other sets of tracks, or even yours, for that matter. There was so much blowing snow. Amazing how you survived. We think of you as sort of a miracle."

JC flushed and faced the far wall, where the IV, disconnected from him since lunch, stood in the corner. "Isn't that place, Philadelphia, where you said I might be from, isn't that far from here? Where is it you said I am? Colorado? Why would I come from so far to a place like this?"

"Whatever reason brought you here, you must truly have wanted to see us badly enough. So for that, you should take comfort that you've arrived."

JC turned back to him and showed fine white teeth. His first smile since Sebastian had laid eyes on him. No denying his beauty.

"You wouldn't happen to have a cigarette, would you?" he asked. "I'm craving one. I guess I'm a smoker."

Sebastian chuckled. "I'm sorry, we're forbidden to smoke here. I used to smoke when I was your age. When I wanted to quit, I ate carrot sticks to help with the cravings. I can bring you some if you like. We keep them fresh in the cellar."

"That's not necessary, Father, but thanks."

"Please, call me Brother Sebastian. I never underwent ordination for the priesthood. I'm a brother of the O.C.S.O., Order of Cistercians of the Stricter Observance."

JC crinkled his brow. "I thought you said you guys were Trappers."

Sebastian's grin hurt his face. He'd once made the same mistake when he was JC's age. "Trappist. It's the same as Cistercian. A more reformed order, you might say. A group of Cistercians concluded that they'd become too worldly and sought more seclusion. The name Trappist is kind of a nickname. It comes from the small village of La Trappe in France, where the brothers had moved hundreds of years ago."

A lull lingered between them for what seemed minutes. JC roved his eyes around the room, as if gauging an escape. Sebastian continued to smile to lessen the unease. He made sure to respect JC's personal space by keeping his hands to himself, but he leaned toward him slightly to suggest a hint of authority.

"Can you think of any names other than 'JC'?" he said in a soft tone. "A family member perhaps? A surname? Anyone's face come to mind?"

"There is a name that keeps popping into my head lately, other than JC, but I don't get why. I can't put a clear face with it."

"What name is that?"

"Manny."

Prickly shockwaves traveled up Sebastian's stiff arms. "Don't worry over things too much," he said, swallowing the sour taste left on his tongue. "Your memories will come back to you sooner than you think. Brother Jerome said so. And then we'll be able to help you sort out why you've come to us."

Brother Lucien broke their intimate chat. "I gathered I might find you here, Brother Sebastian. Father Paolo wishes to see you right away. He's in conference with Brother Jerome and wishes for you to join them. Don't worry. I'll watch over our special guest."

FATHER PAOLO sat at his large mahogany desk, drumming his broad fingertips on the polished top. The burgundy velour drapes were pulled shut, and the office was dim. Pope Benedict XVI's portrait hung above the abbot, while the fireplace, lit with small, lapping flames, snapped and hissed. Shadows danced over the ruby carpet. Brother Jerome sat across from the abbot in a Bergère chair, clutching the padded armrests. Sebastian stood by the threshold, waiting to be noticed—and yet hoping not to be. Neither man was speaking. They seemed trapped in a gully, unsure of which direction to carry their discussion. Father Paolo lifted his eyes to the doorway.

"Ah, Brother Sebastian. Please, come in. We've been waiting for you." He gestured toward the chair beside Brother Jerome. "Shut the door and take a seat, will you."

Once Sebastian situated himself in a chair identical to Brother Jerome's, the abbot peered at him and said, "We've been discussing our unusual visitor, as you might have guessed. Brother Jerome agrees that in a day or two he might be well enough to move into one of the vacant cells. But he has misgivings. I wanted you to clear our standoff."

"What's that?" Sebastian asked, though not without hesitation.

"Brother Jerome still believes he should be transported to a hospital once the weather clears. He wishes to call for the forest service, or even a costly helicopter from the hospital in Telluride."

Sebastian found himself white-knuckling the armrests. "Perhaps we should ask JC what he wishes."

"Wise words, Brother Sebastian," the abbot said.

Brother Jerome adjusted his glasses over his nose, careful as always not to raise his arms too high above his shoulders. "I suppose that makes the most sense. If he chooses to stay here and falls ill again, I can treat him the best I can."

"Is there a chance he might?" Sebastian said. "I mean, fall ill?"

"Not really. I've given him a full physical. His youth and fitness will persevere, I'm certain. His feet and hands have almost fully healed."

"What if he chooses to stay?" Sebastian asked. "We don't know anything about him. He still can't remember anything."

Father Paolo glanced toward the fireplace, where smoking embers leaped and arched toward the hearth. Small flames reflected in his eyeglasses. "Do you think his memory loss is genuine?" he asked.

Sebastian mulled over his thoughts before responding. Innocent until proven guilty. That notion had been branded into his brain. "I… I suppose he's being sincere."

"I must admit, he seems to be on the up and up to me," Brother Jerome said. "Memory loss really isn't so unusual after one suffers from unconsciousness, especially at this altitude. He might've taken a hit on the head before we found him, although he has no visible signs of contusion. That's one of the reasons I wanted to send him to the hospital, for tests to—"

"We've already settled that, Brother Jerome. We'll ask if he wishes to remain. We can't cast him out. It would go against the *Rule*. Besides, there's no way off the mountain until the storms pass. You know how February is in the Rockies. It might be days, weeks. Has he mentioned anything about his religious convictions?"

"I'm around him most of the time, and I haven't heard him utter one word about Our Lord. In fact," Brother Jerome said with a scrunch of his nose, "he's made a few downright disrespectful comments, if you ask me."

"I'm sure he's unaware of what he's saying," Father Paolo said. "He's been ill. He's clearly of Spanish heritage, is he not? He must've been raised Catholic. The Latinos are very devout, the last pious Catholics left in America, in my opinion. When I first came here in 1975, my parish was a quarter Latino even then. Today, across the United States, priests recite entire masses in Spanish."

"He wasn't wearing a crucifix when we found him," Sebastian said. "He wasn't wearing any jewelry at all, other than the heart-shaped diamond in his left ear. I suppose a crucifix might have fallen off in the snow."

"And even if he wasn't wearing one, that doesn't disprove his devotion," the abbot said. "My grandfather was devout to his bones, and he never wore a crucifix around his neck."

"Even with a hampered memory, how could anyone forget his belief in God?" Brother Jerome mumbled.

Sebastian noticed the sweat beads appearing on the brother's bald scalp. Holding his breath, Sebastian fixed his eyes on the ruby carpet. He could feel the burn of the abbot's dark eyes studying him, and he squeezed the armrests harder. The ceaseless smell of juniper incense in the private office had never seemed more pungent.

"Why else would he have traveled here?" the abbot uttered finally. "His coming here through impassable weather and terrain, his devotion must be gigantic. Reminds me of the old women of Vila de Seda, where I grew up as a boy in Portugal. They would walk to church on their knees for miles uphill to prove their subservience to the Lord. Much like our JC has."

"What if he's an escaped convict, like Brother Rodel worried?"

Under his brow, Sebastian peered at Brother Jerome. He sighed, relieved on hearing the older brother murmur those words. Mounds of unanswered questions piled up around JC. His devotion—if he had any—could not have been the sole reason that had conducted him to the abbey's grounds in the dead of winter. He had come to see them for a profound need. A need that might have stemmed from a strong, personal pledge. Sebastian sensed religious convictions had not been behind it.

"I've checked with the local prisons and police bulletins," Father Paolo said. "There's no news of escaped convicts or anything of that nature in the area."

Sebastian stared straight into Father Paolo's pale face. "No APBs?" he asked.

Firelight glinted in Father Paolo's eyeglasses. He positioned his chin parallel with his desk and seemed to sneer at Sebastian. "All-points bulletins? No, Brother Sebastian, no authorities are looking for this man."

His mouth dry, Sebastian said, "Maybe we can encourage him to remember more."

"I know you've been sitting with him," the father said. "I don't mind you flooding him with questions, if he cares to speak. You don't need to trick me. I'll overlook your insubordination, considering the circumstances."

Shame warmed Sebastian's cheeks. He lowered his eyes to his lap. "Thank you, Father."

"Well, has he opened up about anything?"

Sebastian shook his head. "He doesn't remember a thing." He almost mentioned JC's recalling of the name "Manny," but for some reason refrained from sharing the information with Brother Jerome and the abbot. What importance did it have for them at the moment, anyway?

Father Paolo took several deep breaths before going on. "We must care for him, then. If he chooses to remain once the blizzards pass, we'll embrace him as our brother. The way Christ and St. Benedict prescribed." He gazed toward the fire and grinned. "Perhaps Brother Giles was correct. Perhaps our guest will join our brotherhood and lay prostrate at my feet in the distant future and become a professed member of our community."

The sizzling fireplace shrouded Sebastian with a veneer of hollowness. Through the drifting shadows of ambiguity, he sensed the standoff had ended. The father had won. His word always triumphed, despite Sebastian's and Brother Jerome's wishes to notify the proper authorities.

"If you learn who he is," the abbot said, pressing his palms on the polished desktop and standing, "please keep me posted before you tell the others. Not that his past matters, but for the sake of his family, anyone who might be missing him, if his memory recovers we should notify the proper people, and we certainly do not wish to alarm anyone."

"Yes, Father," the men said in unison, standing to take their leave. "Whatever you wish."

– V –

AS SOON as Brothers Sebastian and Jerome left his private office, Father Paolo stretched across his Victorian desk chair, allowing the skirt of his tunic to spread over the burgundy leather. The wool fabric chafed his skin, but he enjoyed the flow of the skirt around his shins, especially when he sat. A few minutes later Lucien entered, locked the door, and took his place by the father's feet. How nice that Lucien knelt before him, as he often did after the passing of another stressful morning.

The fireplace reflected off Lucien's white skin. Even in the scant light, Father Paolo detected the age lines and sagging skin of his beloved Lucien. He no longer found him physically attractive—and he certainly no longer regarded him as a challenge—but he relished the worshipping, the adoration. The obedience.

Father Paolo had no doubts about his minion's loyalty to him. Lucien would die for him—perhaps even more. Like the Belém soldiers who guarded Portugal's Presidential Palace, Lucien, his obedient servant, catered to his every need, his every wish.

And that he had an Englishman, one plucked from upscale roots, at his beck and call made his worship all the more pleasing. Lucien's obedience would impress his long deceased grandfather, a man who'd clung to the fantasy of Portugal's long-lost colonial power while Britain's continued without end. The Iberian explorers had even beaten Britain to the New World, clutching onto Brazil when Captain John Smith was nothing but a daydream for a small Lincolnshire farm girl yearning for marriage and children. Portugal was the first to establish the spice trade to India, before the British had seized its spoils for the Crown.

His grandfather had sympathized with the Nazis, and Father Paolo shouldn't care about what he might think. But then almost every one of his grandfather's cronies had supported the Nazis in spirit, if not in deed. And there was something grandiose about it all—the idea of the European continent expanding. The glory of colonization. Powerful and seductive. Spreading civilization and glittering empires.

Yes, those days of colonial rule had long dissipated. But no harm came from luxuriating in the splendor of the far-off past, all while spreading one's arms wide for the unforeseen spectacular future and the wondrous present.

Here he was, abbot of a monastery in the New World itself— America.

It was all his, bequeathed to the Church by Mrs. Kalil Dalakis, a laywoman wanting to atone for her late husband, the maligned publisher of three newspapers who'd lost his mind during the long, isolated winters, and was alleged to have practiced Satanism. She had donated the land to the Catholic Church upon her death in 1957. Her reparation was to gift the land and all the buildings on it, including the two-thousand-square-foot cottage situated behind the abbey, which they used as a lodge for paying guests in summer. She had but one stipulation—that the Church use the land to build a Trappist monastery. Apparently, one of Mrs. Dalakis's ancestors had been a Trappist in Champagne, beheaded along with his fellow monks during the apex of the French Revolution.

No fear of beheadings now. Not in the twenty-first century. Not in his secure abbey, nestled in the San Juan Mountains, surrounded by mile after mile of unrefined beauty. Serenity swept over him. Luxurious comfort in the old-fashioned environs, saturated with gifts, large and small, bestowed on him—and on the abbey—by the Mrs. Dalakises of the world. Medical supplies, food, wine, tools, furniture. A ceaseless parade of largess by patrons, far and wide.

Father Paolo found opulence in all of it. In the simplest piece of wood carved by local Monfrere craftsmen, or the slow flow of melted wax down a long-stemmed candle handmade by bored retirees, or the tiniest glint in a glass full of ruby wine presented to him by the ladies' auxiliary. All of God's goodies reeked of perfume and shined like jewels.

If his grandfather could see him now. His pobrezinho. Abbot of an entire monastery, all three hundred fifty-three acres of it.

Avô would be proud, indeed.

Thank God for guilt-ridden, middle-aged women.

The monumental blizzard from the past few days continued to hurl snow at the window. He favored winters the most. The harsh weather kept the eyes of the Church away. Mt. Ouray was his domain in winter, and he need not share it with anyone. His to rule as he deemed fit. The snow, like the great walls that once barricaded Jerusalem and Jericho, prevented unwanted visits. No interfering cardinals or bishops or nearby parish priests.

No one could advance past the snowy fortress.

But somehow their mysterious visitor, JC, had.

Father Paolo hadn't stopped thinking about the stranger since he'd first heard of his discovery. Once he had seen him lying in the infirmary, he knew. The Lord had sent him. How his heart had skipped a beat when he'd seen JC curled on the floor of the pantry. A frightened animal, naked save for a scanty chef's smock covering him. And his eyes. Simulating the most elegant, rich coffee or the gracefully carved ebony mantelpiece of his chapter house, gifted to him by the Colorado Carpenters Union. The young man had nearly pulled the floor out from under Father Paolo. He had stared, wordless and without breath.

He could persuade the stranger to stay. He was sure of it. He hadn't earned his doctorate of divinity from Loyola University in Chicago for nothing. He had the mind, the intelligence, to convince people to genuflect to his will. Brothers Sebastian and Jerome had no power against him.

Only twelve monks! He needed more, or else the Church would relegate Mt. Ouray to priory status, with less standing among the hierarchy than abbeys enjoyed. Church officials would quit courting him for favors. Money from benefactors would dwindle to a pittance.

Three more young men would guarantee the official "abbey" designation.

If he were to join their order, the young stranger would help Father Paolo with his goal to lower the average age of the brothers from forty-five to at least thirty-eight. The abbey website proclaimed the need for the accession of younger men. "Come, young men. Come and stand with the Lord!"

He'd instructed Brother Casey to write young retreatants and those considering discernment to find a home at Mt. Ouray. E-mail after e-mail. Press them—that was the goal. Utilize the twelve-step sales pitch to the hilt. He'd learned the technique from a Mormon missionary in Chicago. They sometimes even employed a private service that specialized in hunting down discerning Catholics.

Too many of the younger postulants and novices failed to preserve. Those who professed lasted, on average, seven years. He believed young Brother Casey might linger much longer than the others had. He'd come to Mt. Ouray seeking love and acceptance. No doubt he'd found that. Brother Sebastian should keep his interest. And short-statured Brother Rodel? A mere year with them and he'd already declared an interest in lying prostrate at the abbot's feet. How nice if JC joined their tight brotherhood, the way the inane Brother Giles had foreshadowed.

Of course, the older novices always brought larger purses to the abbey. Lucien himself, when he'd professed at thirty-two, had dropped nearly one million dollars into the abbey's treasury. But money wasn't everything.

Sweet Lucien squirmed by his feet. Guttural sighs issued from his mouth. For the moment, Lucien's veneration took Father Paolo's mind away from JC. Lucien hugged the father's lower legs. Father Paolo glanced at his thinning hair and the shadows that filled the deepening lines along his neck. He was aging, yes, but he was all his.

Father Paolo spread his legs apart, relishing the quiet and solitude with his English underling by his feet. The smell of pheromones emanating from under his tunic aroused him. Lucien took notice. He reached up the father's skirt. Pleasure pushed back Father Paolo's head. He moaned.

Lucien moved to his knees and positioned himself fully before the abbot. His bottom protruded toward the fireplace, so that Father Paolo could only imagine the delight of times past. They hadn't engaged in such intimacy in many months. Lucien's submissions had come in other ways.

With a languishing, dreamy posture, Lucien placed his head under the father's tunic and took his arousal into his warm mouth. Father Paolo closed his eyes, let his head rove against the headrest. He gripped the armrests, massaged the firm leather. Lucien's looks might have faded over time, but his oral skills had improved with age.

In place of Lucien, the father imagined the darker and younger JC. He had dreamed of it since that first afternoon when he'd gazed upon his unconscious form. The hot desire had ignited sensations more intense than that ludicrous spark that had shimmered in the eyes of the other monks. Brother Rodel, Brother George, Brother Hubert. They each desired the stranger. But in his abbey, JC belonged to Father Paolo.

One brother, he knew, might suspect his feelings. He always looked apprehensive around Father Paolo, as if he held a moral divining rod before him. Brother Sebastian. Astute. Too astute. Useful in keeping the brothers in line, but he often fretted about his possible sedition. Oh, he had no doubts Brother Sebastian's entering the abbey derived from sincere intentions. At times, however, his presence was worse than pouring salt into wine.

An uncomfortable alliance had to be forged between them. Father Paolo had understood that reality the first few days of the tall postulant's stay at Mt. Ouray. He needed him not so much as a henchman, but to keep him close to his hip to gauge his movements.

They often exchanged disagreements, but of the kind that came from Brother Sebastian's insinuation: "Are you sure, Father?" Or his reluctant yielding: "Whatever you wish." Of course whatever he wished. He was the abbot. Brother Sebastian's implications bordered on insults.

Yet he harbored no dislike for Brother Sebastian. Hatred never came to Father Paolo's soul. He overflowed with love. Adoring everything and everyone. Even as a boy, he knew only happiness and joy, and sought to spread it. He'd spent countless hours dancing and singing in Vila de Seda's lively square, existing for everyone's smiling faces, not the coins the onlookers tossed at him (even if he and his grandfather had needed the extra escudo).

His desire for power had no price tag. He wanted only to give love, to bring to his bosom those who demanded affection and understanding, like so many of those who sought solace behind the abbey's walls.

Selfishness did not guide his motives.

If only more of the world understood his tender intentions, and willingly submitted to him and his wants.

He allowed the sensation of warmth and love to flow through his middle-aged muscles as Lucien worked on him deeper. The spasms came slower and slower with age. But when they escalated to the point of finality, the sensation had no more diminished than when he'd been a fledgling adolescent, hiding behind the arbustos, which smelled of citrus, to spy on the older boys swimming nude in the Catholic youth center's outdoor pool while he'd pleasured himself.

Tightening his throat, a heated sense of pure euphoria, accented by a rush of triumph, shot through him. He released into Lucien's mouth for what must've been the hundredth time since Lucien's arrival at the abbey nine years ago. They had been lovers almost from the first day.

Father Paolo shuddered, grunted. Lucien removed his head from under Father Paolo's tunic and grinned at him. Exhaling, Father Paolo patted Lucien's balding head.

"Thank you, my love," he uttered. "As always, you pleased me greatly."

Keep the underlings contented with compliments, he urged himself. *Always make them feel wanted.*

Father Paolo flicked the skirt of his tunic over his legs and stood.

His forever-churning mind bypassed his English minion as he straightened his garments. After twenty-four hours of minimal sleep, waiting, pacing, wondering, hoping, he knew.

Once their guest gained more strength and they'd moved him to his own cell, he'd summon him to his private office.

– VI –

THREE days had passed since the stranger the monks now called "Brother JC" had regained full consciousness. In that time, his strength improved. Underneath his white tunic and black scapular (worn as awkwardly as a hippopotamus in lingerie, Casey noted), he carried a firmer physique. His appetite increased to the point Brother Micah bellyached that they'd run out of food before the spring thaw.

Healthy enough to take dinner with them, he'd peer through the steam from his meal and, like an eight-year-old boy, absorb every grain of wood, every fluttering strand of hair poking from the older brothers' balding scalps. Casey and the others had no idea how long he'd stay on, but the abbot seemed eager to keep him. The continuing snowstorms rolling over the San Juan Range gave neither any choice.

When they'd moved him into his own cell, he'd acted as if they'd shown him a room at the Hyatt Regency in downtown Wichita. The fresh sheets, laundered by Brother Hubert with the custom-crafted detergents gifted to the abbey and typically reserved for paying guests, had filled the tiny room with the scent of sandalwood. With his knapsack clenched in both hands, he gazed around, delight watermarked on his face. Wide-eyed alertness had replaced his furrowed brow.

Only when the brothers engaged in Mass and the seven prayer stations did JC show dissatisfaction. His eyes remained sleepy, and his cheeks a tincture of ochre. When entering or leaving the chapel, he never bothered to cross himself with the holy water. He might as well have been placed in the middle of a cattle roundup, Casey quipped to himself whenever watching him.

Now that he could move about unaided, Father Paolo assigned him to work with Brother Micah in the kitchen. He barely had time, the way the brothers spoiled him. Each seemed determined to make an impression on the newcomer by teaching him Latin or escorting him around the abbey during siesta to show him the grounds.

Casey's resentment had intensified after spying Sebastian slink into JC's newly appointed cell during siesta, twice thus far in as many days, at least. What took place behind the door, ajar so that Casey must twist his neck like a contortionist if he attempted to peer inside? So often Casey had fantasized being the one alone in a cell with Sebastian, the door closed to keep out prying eyes. The only eavesdropper the statuette of the Virgin Mary the abbot had gifted to each monk and the new postulants, including JC—which had set the brothers talking.

Casey stayed clear of Brother Sebastian and wore his hood up more often. Right when he'd begun to believe the older brother was enjoying his closeness, Brother Sebastian had transformed his fondness for Casey into infatuation with the dark stranger, Casey was sure.

He evaded eye contact with him, and when Sebastian took his breakfast to his usual nest by the cloister garden, Casey no longer followed him. Instead of lingering inside the showers, he waited in his cell until he saw Sebastian—russet hair wet and shiny and smelling of Ivory soap—pass his room in his bathrobe before he grabbed his toiletry bag and headed for the showers.

Surly as a rabid squirrel, Casey took scant pains to conceal his displeasure with the new arrival. He wanted to be kinder. He'd look heavenward, mumble a few psalms, reach for God's assistance. *I trust in your unfailing mercy; my heart rejoices in your salvation. I will sing to the Lord, for he has been good to me.*

Lucky theirs was a silent order. Something told Casey he and JC wouldn't speak to one another even if they stood face to face at a party. The times JC worked in the kitchen alongside Brother Micah and him, Casey found himself averting his eyes from both.

JC would lurch about the kitchen, following whatever orders Brother Micah pummeled him with. From the corners of his eyes, he'd watch JC haul boxes out of the walk-in freezer, or fumble about with a rag and bucket of soapy water, leaving a wet trail on the terracotta tiles, to the mortification of Brother Micah.

The worst of it came one day when JC and Brother Micah, elbow to elbow, chopped vegetables for soup. JC had cut hard into the uncooked potatoes without first placing them on the chopping block. "Watch what you're doing," Brother Micah finally exclaimed, breaking the silent custom. "You can't use my good knives on the bare countertop. You'll ruin them."

He snatched the chef's knife from him and wielded it in his left hand as if he wanted to plunge it in JC's chest. With a lighter tone, he added, "Be more careful next time, why don't you?"

Brother Micah, the forty-six-year-old who'd resided at the Abbey for seven years and venerated Sebastian more openly than Casey, expressed contempt for JC for perhaps the identical reason Casey did.

Yet Casey never felt likewise toward Brother Micah. Nearing middle age, Brother Micah lacked the looks of the youthful JC.

When Brother Micah left the kitchen to begin his siesta after his uncomfortable outburst, Casey, scrubbing the lunch dishes, nearly fell into the sink full of sudsy water upon hearing JC's sharp voice behind him.

"That one doesn't seem to want me around much," JC said from where he swept the floor.

Casey, unused to casual chitchat during the work period, collected himself before responding. "Brother Micah?"

"Yeah, he never looks at me and always grunts."

Had he noticed Casey's own displeasure? With his billowy sleeves cinched to the elbows, he sunk his arms deeper into the soapy liquid, hoping to cleanse his sins. "He's that way," he said. "He's like that with all of us." But not with Brother Sebastian, he wanted to add. He scrubbed a food bin extra hard with the scouring brush. "Don't worry. He has a grumpy nature."

"You're a lot like me," JC said. "How old are you?"

"Twenty-three."

"I'm twenty-one. You're the only one I can relate to here. Unlike that other guy our age. He's kinda loco."

"You mean Brother Rodel?"

"That's the guy."

Shy and retiring, Brother Rodel did come across aloof, but Casey knew he was a harmless man. He carried around the same lost look Casey figured stained his own countenance now and then. Wonder, intrigue, and embarrassment resided in his eyes, browner than Casey's. The two were peers, yet they had failed to establish a firmer connection. They had a lot in common too. At least physically. Same black hair, same pursing lips. Perhaps Brother Rodel's bashful nature made it difficult to get any closer.

All of the brothers had found a close friend among each other, pairing off the same as in any social group. Brother George had connected with the old and decrepit Brother Augustine, whom he cared for like a baby. Brothers Hubert and Micah had established a bond in which they shared secrets, or so Casey had heard. Brother Lucien and Father Paolo's relationship was known to everyone. And Casey had Brother Sebastian.… He hoped they shared something special, anyhow.

Casey wanted to splash water on his face to temper the heat burning his cheeks. "Brother Rodel is a nice guy," he said.

"I can figure out why a loco like that would come to a place like this, but why you?" JC asked him. "Must be kinda weird to give up so much."

Casey held back a chuckle. "I guess it is kind of different here. But I have strong faith."

"Faith in what?"

"God, of course."

"Oh, sure."

Despite his lapse in memory, JC didn't seem thickheaded or intentionally crass. Casey tried to gauge if he might slip up. He still worried he might be tricking them, hoping for a means to stay at the abbey without giving away his sordid past.

"What brought *you* here?" he asked.

"I can't remember. Remember? Or is amnesia catchy?" JC sniggered. "Who knows? It's weird, not remembering anything. I still can't figure out where I came from, much less why I came here. Maybe I'm from Philadelphia like Sebastian thinks. I just don't know."

Hearing JC refer to Sebastian by his first name, Casey cringed. "Are you glad you're here?"

The sound of JC's sweeping stopped. Casey, with his back to him, detected JC was resting. Casey gave him credit. JC had kept up with Brother Micah's harsh demands and he deserved a break.

"Life here's a lot different," he answered. "It's like being in the military."

Casey felt a sneer stretch his lips. "How would you know, if you don't remember your past?"

"That's what makes it all so weird. I don't. I can feel it. I don't go for the cold, that's for sure. I guess I can remember hating it. I wish I could janguio in someplace like Puerto Rico."

"Why there?"

"I don't know. Warmer there this time of year. I can remember things like that. I can still read and write. I haven't forgotten how to breathe, you know."

Delores scavenged the floor, her tail low. She seemed to shun the newcomer as much as Casey had tried to. The hound had taken an immediate liking to Casey his first day at the abbey, but not to JC. Did she sense Casey's qualms about JC, or did she have a set of her own?

Casey dried a hand and slipped her a piece of cheese from a tray that Brother Micah hadn't a chance to cover and store in the refrigerator. Her strong jaw cracked as she chewed the treat. JC began sweeping near Casey by the sink. Tension stewed in their small space.

Turning back to the pot scrubbing, Casey said, "I suppose it's tough getting used to things here, especially in winter."

"The meatless meals are the worst. But Brother…. What's his name? The fat mamao."

"Brother George?"

"Yeah, Brother George told me that I should appreciate what I got here, and reflect on the suffering of Jesus, and all that."

"He's right, in a sense. We all have to face the challenges of abbey life. Part of why we come here is to suffer alongside Christ, to immerse ourselves in prayer and work. *Opus Dei*, they call it."

"That's another part I hate," JC said. "All this churchgoing, ten times a day. And going to bed at eight and waking at three in the morning. Crazy. And no TV or video games. How can you go without all that?"

Heat built up under Casey's tunic. Another one of those moments. He needed to find solitude, to pray for strength and self-restraint. He longed to take his siesta. Longed for Sebastian.

Brother Giles rolled into the kitchen, his wheels sending a discordant screech into Casey's ears, before Casey could answer. He wheeled straight up to JC. His silver beard seemed to pull on his terse mouth. Casey looked over his shoulder and gaped at them.

"You listen up, young man," Brother Giles said, wagging his long, gnarly finger at him. "You don't defile the Church or Our Lord. The Lord suffered for your sins so you could go to Heaven. You can at least pray to him seven times a day. Is that asking too much?"

Casey couldn't help but notice the veins snaking along Brother Giles's neck as he wheeled round and took off as fast as he'd come. Old Brother Giles had an uncanny strength for a man his age. Perhaps he'd honed his muscles from his many hours ironing and sewing the sacramentals they sold to summertime guests, or from pushing his wheelchair, since he disliked using the motor.

In the wake left by Brother Giles's wheelchair, Brother Lucien stood at the kitchen doorway, a sour expression staining his face. "The father would like to speak with you," he said to JC, with an unusual listlessness to his English accent.

Shrugging at Casey with a downturn of his mouth, JC leaned the broom against the counter and followed Brother Lucien out the door.

– VII –

SMOKE curled from a cone of juniper incense on the sideboard. He savored the aroma, the scent of Colorado itself. Another gift from the inhabitants of the surrounding villages. An entire case of it. Handmade by the Ute Indians. The incense signified an endless bounty. A burning desire. The smoke coiled with the sophistication of most of the gifts bestowed on the abbey by various citizen groups and individuals. His favorite of these he'd left on the round table by the fireplace. The bottle of red wine waited alongside two tall stemmed glasses, in addition to a tray of chocolate truffles, a gift from a Monfrere candymaker.

He was waiting. Anxious for his orders to be carried out. He'd instructed Lucien to fetch him, and he would arrive shortly.

"Bring him to me," Father Paolo had told him a handful of minutes before, as Lucien had stood before him expectantly. "Tell him I wish to see him."

Lucien had ogled him. "But is he well enough?"

He was becoming more obstinate than Brother Sebastian lately, Father Paolo lamented, remembering their minor exchange. "He's been working alongside Brother Micah, ran about the abbey as if he were a visiting bishop for nearly the past week. Brother Jerome tells me he's in perfect health. He's well enough, you can be sure."

"You wish to see him in private?"

"Yes, of course, in my office. Alone. That is my wish."

Lucien's face had fallen with a lassitude Father Paolo had taken for jealousy. The growing wrinkles around his eyes and mouth had deepened in the glow from the freshly lit fire. Father Paolo had disregarded the flush blooming over his underling's cheeks, which accentuated his blue eyes. He had no time for challenges from his charges. His word, ordained by St. Benedict, reigned inside the abbey.

"Go bring him to me," he had said, lowering his voice to punctuate his command.

Lucien had moved for the door, mumbled over his shoulder, "Yes, Father. Anything you wish."

And that was the way the father liked it. His word above all others—with the exclusion of the Almighty, of course.

His heart beat with anticipation for Lucien to follow through with his instructions. Soon the door would open, and Lucien would announce JC. Another minion to add to his flock.

He had waited long enough for their private face to face. The young man had lived under their roof for nearly a week, functioning as one of them. Father Paolo had watched him. He'd fit in well thus far. Worked as well as any of the young postulants and novices that had crossed his path—no more hard-working, no less lazy. Eager to please, though a bit inept, as were most from his generation. He loved how the handsome postulants tried so hard to please. So desperate to be accepted, even when unsure of their vocations.

Father Paolo's heart leaped when he heard Lucien's gentle rap on the door. He inhaled, his right hand pressed to his chest to ease the heavy breathing. He savored how the excitement made him retrace his youth. A lovesick youngster, squatting by the arbustos at Vila de Seda's Catholic youth center. He cleared his throat.

"Enter."

Lucien's face was dimmer than when he'd left. Dark with protectiveness and unease. *No need to fear, my love,* he wanted to tell him. More urgent matters demanded his attention. Poor Lucien would have to wait.

"Brother JC is here, Father," he muttered.

Father Paolo waved Lucien out the door. "If you will leave us," he said to him. "I would like some time in private with our guest." He eyed JC, standing nervous and pitiful by the cabinets. "Brother Lucien, please assist Brother Hubert with the laundry."

Lucien hesitated, nodding in obedience only when Father Paolo glared at him. He left without shutting the door, a small mark of defiance. In the corridor, his sandals clicked against the balls of his feet, fading as he turned for the laundry room.

"Come in," Father Paolo said to JC once certain Lucien had gone. He grinned to the point his cheeks lifted his glasses off his eyes.

JC fully entered the abbot's private office as if taking his first steps. Surrounded by yet additional new things, JC appeared more vulnerable than when he'd first flashed open his black eyes in the infirmary. Good. The father delighted in the helplessness of his postulants.

"May I pour you some wine?" he asked after he shut the door. "It's from one of the finest vineyards of Portugal's Trás-os-Montes region. Chaves, near where I lived as a boy, a small village not even on a map. The ladies of the Monfrere auxiliary bring us cases in autumn before the snowfall. They are kind to know of my homeland and to consider that I might long for the wines from there. Truth be told, I prefer California's dry white wines. There are so many restrictive winemaking laws in Portugal. In the United States, winemakers have no archaic regulations to hold them back. How I admire California's earthy Pinot Gris. But I accept the ladies' gift with gladness in my heart. Sweet as the red wine they send."

The ruby liquid resonated like the cadence of a lute being tuned as he filled each of the long-stemmed glasses. Father Paolo raised his glass, the wine glistening against the fire. JC stared, as if mesmerized for a moment by the play of colors from the dancing flames, and then he pivoted his head, gazed around, leery.

"I don't like wine," he said. "I never really drank that stuff."

"Tastes sweet, with a hint of cinnamon. You may enjoy it. I've seen how you devour Brother Micah's cinnamon rolls. Goes wonderfully with the chocolates." Father Paolo snickered at JC's quick head shaking. A pity the youth of America never acquired a taste for vinho. The way they drank milk.... He chuckled inwardly, remembering his first reaction when he'd beheld how Americans quaffed cold milk from tall glasses, as if they were guzzling water. At first he'd been disgusted, but soon he'd grown to find the habit charming. "Perhaps you are too down to earth," he said to JC. "Your quaintness is something to admire, yes?"

JC continued to peer around, his hands locked over the front of his scapular. Father Paolo needed to calm him. He was ranting on too much, showing his own nervousness. JC, young and impressionable, sought guidance from a strong figure. Still, Father Paolo feared he might be a tougher nut to crack than even young Brother Casey and Brother Rodel had proved.

"Would you care for something else?" he asked him, keeping his tone upbeat. "Ale perhaps? I can call back Brother Lucien and have him fetch you a mug. Cold from the cellar." Another gift from benefactors. "Or perhaps a cold glass of milk? I can only offer the kind made from powder, I'm afraid. Because we're shut off from the world during winters, we cannot receive fresh deliveries until the spring thaw. I'll furnish you with whatever you wish. Will music please you? I don't listen to rock and roll, but I do enjoy jazz."

"No, that's okay. I'm good." He finally stopped gazing around and pinned his dark eyes on the abbot. "What do you want?"

Father Paolo flinched from his vulgar frankness. Another aspect of Americans he'd had to acclimate to when he'd first arrived as a young priest, sent abroad to help the ailing parishes of a secularizing United States. "I'm not after anything," he said. "I only wish to make you more at home here and to check on your well-being."

"I'm doing good, I guess."

"You have an interesting accent," Father Paolo said, lifting the glass of the ruby-colored wine to his lips. He sipped, allowing the sweet liquid to evaporate inside his mouth before even swallowing. "Resembles Brother Sebastian's," he said after he lowered the glass. "Do you come from Philadelphia also?"

"How am I to know? I can't remember anything."

"I apologize. I'm not trying to trick you. We here at the abbey only wish to help you."

"I'll be okay. Once the snow clears up, I can get back off the mountain."

Father Paolo set down his wine glass with a thud. "But the roads aren't cleared until April, sometimes May. It's February. I'm afraid you'll be with us for quite a few more months, unless you call for the authorities to come get you in a helicopter or snowmobile. We were almost about to do it too, but then you recovered so rapidly and you're doing so well."

"How did I get here then? I must've hiked in. I can hike back out."

"And look what happened. You nearly killed yourself trying to reach us without proper attire. You're likely to die if you venture out again. Please, take a seat and relax."

JC stood stiffer than a post. His mouth, molded with firm, thick lips, puckered and flexed. He seemed to study the abbot. Father Paolo kept his stance, lifted his wine glass at chin level, the sleeve of his tunic corrugated by the elbow.

"Were you fibbing when you said you have no complaints with life here?" he said.

"I like it okay, I guess. I'm just confused."

"Confused how and why you came to us?"

He nodded. "That and everything else. I don't even remember my name."

"Brother Jerome tells me you'll remember soon enough. It's only a matter of time. Don't fret. And is it really so important to know why you came here? Perhaps God wanted you here, so here you are, and that's all that matters."

"You talk like Sebastian."

Father Paolo suppressed a cringe at the incessant way American youth called their elders by their Christian names. "Brother Sebastian is a wise man," he said, smiling. "I'm glad you've found friends here among us."

The fire snapped. JC stood unmoved. They had spoken one on one before, but only in JC's cell or the infirmary, exchanging a handful of words. Never alone in his private office, struggling with conversation. Father Paolo realized he might have been premature to ask for JC. His wish might have to wait. Gaining JC's confidence would take time. Perhaps weeks. He gestured toward one of the Bergère chairs by his desk for him to sit. This time, JC dropped his head and obeyed the father's request.

Inhaling, Father Paolo took his authoritative place behind his desk. With the mammoth oak desk between them, JC seemed to loosen up. The father said, "You look good in our attire. Do you feel contented in your tunic and scapular?"

JC scanned the length of his body. "I feel kinda silly, to be honest. But at the same time, it's comfortable."

Father Paolo couldn't help but chuckle. He set his wine glass aside and leaned back in his chair. "They are practical for our needs here at the abbey. A symbol of our vow of poverty and devotion to God."

JC's eyes fixed on the wine on Father Paolo's desk. The abbot grunted to recapture his attention. JC turned to him, his expression blank and expectant.

"Have you put much consideration into your religious beliefs?" he asked JC, wishing to focus on the mission at hand, which was to influence JC to remain at the abbey. He pressed his fingertips to his chin. "Do you recall attending Mass where you're from?"

"Nope." JC shrugged and snickered. "Maybe I'm Jewish. In America, it's hard to tell."

An icy yet burning sensation froze Father Paolo's face. Yes, he knew that, with circumcision, telling a Jew or Muslim from the rest of the pack was difficult. Father Paolo squirmed in his chair, straightened the front of his scapular.

"The brothers say I'm probably Catholic because I'm Latino," JC offered.

"Never mind what the brothers say. Do you feel a connection with God here?"

JC lifted his eyes toward the portrait of Pope Benedict XVI hanging above the father's desk. "I don't know. I'm not really sure." He flushed. "I… I think it's nice what you do here. Having such strong faith is good, right?"

"Of course it is." Father Paolo surprised himself by his harsh tone, and he smiled to mollify the frightened look that eclipsed JC's face. "Faith is all that guides us, here and everywhere," he said softly, resting his folded hands atop his smooth desktop. "Don't you think faith is what brought you to us through all this snow and wind, so high up in the mountains?"

JC's eyes fell to the red carpet. "I guess so. I wish I could remember."

Father Paolo fluttered a chuckle. He took a sip of the wine, tasted the sweetness lingering on his dry lips with a swipe of his tongue. "When your memories return, I'm sure you'll realize that you were meant to be here with us, perhaps forever." JC's anguished expression brought a wider grin to Father Paolo's face. "Don't worry. We won't keep you against your will. I'm merely hopeful. Perhaps too much."

"Everyone's been really nice to me. It's not that I'm ungrateful. Don't think that I am."

Father Paolo leaned back in his chair. He almost wanted to cup his hands behind his head in exuberant victory. Replacing JC's fear and standoffishness with subservient shame had come easier than he'd anticipated. Perhaps he'd underestimated his influence.

After a moment of luxuriating in his triumph, he stood from his desk and positioned himself before JC. Heat from the fireplace warmed him. He sipped his wine, cleared his throat, and set the glass on the desk with a light scrape.

"We enjoy having you here, Brother JC," he said. "You've given us reason to practice our Trappist tradition of caring for the sick, downtrodden, and wayward visitor."

"Am I all that stuff?"

Expectant, Father Paolo sat on the edge of the desk and allowed his tunic to spread fully and his arms to lay open by his sides. "We all need a helping hand from time to time. Love comes the most easy when we allow it. It's more difficult to receive, sometimes. Don't you think?"

JC looked directly into the abbot's eyes. Hot blood pumped under Father Paolo's tunic and steamed his neck. The young man was perhaps used to seducing his wants even more than Father Paolo. He most likely lived a promiscuous life in the city, leaving a cordon of brokenhearted girls (maybe even young men) in his wake. A fledgling lothario reared itself behind those dark eyes.

"You do like it here among us, don't you?"

JC licked his lips and gazed toward the smoldering incense on the sideboard. "I guess. It's been okay. I'm kinda getting used to all the quiet. The work, I don't mind. Getting up so early has been tough."

"I admit I had difficulty adjusting to the early mornings here myself. But faith in God stirs us to overcome hardship, just as our Lord had to."

Father Paolo reached for JC's hands. In typical acquiescence, JC allowed the father to hold them and gaze into his palms. His brown hands were strong. Exquisite. No longer any sign of frostbite. He'd done hard labor in his short life. The nails were chipped, and grime wedged under the cuticles. A mechanic perhaps. The hands of a passionate soul.

"You do not fear work, I can see," he said. "You know more about hardship and dedication than perhaps you realize. It's that zeal that drove you to us despite so much wind and snow."

JC's lower lip dropped. He murmured, as if thinking aloud, "I… I hadn't really thought of it that way. Maybe I am supposed to be here."

With the gentleness of a mother laying to rest her baby, Father Paolo placed JC's hands into his lap, his fingertips brushing his scapular, where underneath the fervor of a young man desperate for guidance and love simmered.

He released his hands and rose before him, stretching his short frame to look its tallest. Best when his underlings were seated so that he could tower over them. JC stood about five ten.

"I would like to help you with your Latin and chanting, if you'd allow me," he said, comprehending that JC would have to be coaxed from his shell. "It will take you away from some of the tedious work here. Chanting is important to us at Mt. Ouray."

"No more working with Mike?"

"Brother Micah?" The father chuckled. "Not if you no longer wish to."

"That sounds good to me."

"I'll teach you the Latin and how we intone the canticles. We'll enjoy ourselves. Twice daily, while the others are at their work stations."

"Okay by me." JC cracked a toothy smile. "Anything you want."

Perfect. He mirrored JC's grin. Just the way he liked it. Whatever Father Paolo wanted.

– VIII –

Sebastian inserted the coffee bean onto the s-clasp with the pliers, affixed it to the adjoining bean, and reached for a cross. Brother Eusebius sat beside him, his hands working with the same steady speed. Sluggish, but purposeful. On the other side of the sacristy's wall, the murmured voices of Father Paolo and JC oozed from the abbot's private office.

Sebastian tried to pretend that he could not hear. Always the same. The slow mumbling, followed by a moment of hush and the uneven chanting. Father Paolo had begun accompanying JC's chanting lessons with his cello, as if they were staging a duet. After a week of the private instruction, everyone in the abbey had grown used to the whispering sounds, the flowing music, the erratic chanting. If God had given JC talent, it was not in singing.

Neither Sebastian nor Brother Eusebius spoke of the partnership between JC and Father Paolo while they toiled inside the sacristy. He and Brother Eusebius barely shared a glance, their wordlessness expressing a thousand misgivings. Sebastian recalled the same scenario when Father Paolo had taken postulants Rodel and Casey under the sweep of his tunic sleeve.

The past few days, he'd begun to smell cigarette smoke drifting from the abbot's office whenever he conducted private lessons with JC. He had no idea where the father had gotten the cigarettes. Maybe an odd gift from a benefactor. He probably kept them handy for whenever he might need them. A carrot on a stick.

He dropped the completed rosary into a palm-sized purple sack, made of cheap Chinese velvet imprinted with the abbey's name and emblem—the Cross of St. Benedict—and pulled out a handful more beans and a string of silver wire. While beginning a new rosary, Sebastian watched Brother Eusebius from the corners of his eyes. His broad shoulders had seemed to ride up higher and higher during the past week. Now they met his ears.

Sebastian squashed the impulse to talk to him. He'd love to get his take on JC, his memory loss, Father Paolo's interest in him, and a host of other issues trapped behind the abbey's walls. Brother Eusebius's taciturn nature had transformed into a fortification of its own.

Surrounded by the tall shelves and somber solitude, the smell of dust and mildew augmented Sebastian's melancholy. He supposed the long, snowy winter was tricking him into dwelling too much on the other side of the wall.

Neither strange nor uncomfortable sounds emerged from the private office. Merely chatter, chanting, and choppy music. Often a chuckle or "aha" from Father Paolo, amplified for encouragement, startled Sebastian. Yet it was the prolonged silences that disturbed him the most. Oftentimes lingering for several minutes. The same when the father was with Casey. By the expression that tightened the lines around Brother Eusebius's mouth, Sebastian guessed he too found the pauses disconcerting.

Sebastian was almost relieved when Brother Lucien entered the sacristy. Lifting his eyes from his lap work, Sebastian allowed his mind to focus on the brother's pained expression. The stranger's presence had evolved from one of wonder to caution for them all.

Brother Lucien made like he was searching for a storage item by the shared wall. Sebastian noticed his right hand freeze in the midst of reaching for a box of toilet paper, his tunic sleeve draped over his shoulder. A moment of quiet from Father Paolo's office passed. To Sebastian's relief, more dull murmurings flowed soon after, along with a quick rise in Father Paolo's cheery voice, then the settling back to further singing and cello playing.

Distress carved itself into Brother Lucien's pale face. He failed to budge. Seeing him in an unmoving state of reaching made Sebastian's own arm ache. He needed to lessen the tension building in their small space, to hear a voice, any voice, even his own.

"Are you looking for something, Brother Lucien?"

The brother shook his head, forced a tight smile, and brought the box of toilet paper to his chest. Scurrying from the storage room, Brother Lucien left more discomfort than what had hovered over their heads before he'd come.

Sebastian recalled running into Brother George in the sacristy two days before. He'd retrieved an armful of supplies for the bathroom, including toilet paper. They couldn't possibly have run out since—even with an added boarder. Brother Lucien had not needed any bathroom supplies; he had wanted to eavesdrop on the abbot and his latest charge, hoping for a better earshot than what the administrative office might provide. A few times, Sebastian had been tempted to press his ears against the wall and snoop himself. But decorum—and Brother Eusebius's presence—had fixed his bottom to his seat and his fingertips to his rosary beads.

For the first time since taking their seats that morning, Sebastian and Brother Eusebius exchanged stares. The muted voices from Father Paolo's office picked up. A flush germinated over Brother Eusebius's dark features. Sebastian mirrored the brother's movements and returned his eyes to his bead work.

He swallowed a desire to throw his head back and laugh out loud so that Father Paolo might hear from his side of the shared wall. He was embarrassed when Brother Eusebius noticed his grinning and finally spoke to him.

"What amuses you, Brother Sebastian?"

His voice, so resonant and deep, startled Sebastian a moment. "Life, I suppose," he said, shrugging.

"And our young visitor?" Brother Eusebius went on.

Sebastian took the cue and opened up to the sober brother. "It's so strange, it's almost humorous. I do feel pity for him. He's so lost and confused with his memory still sealed."

Brother Eusebius's ebony eyes narrowed. "Is that all?"

"He's got street smarts, no doubting that. He'll be okay."

"I still don't condone all this ogling, like a prize hog at a county fair."

Sebastian clutched the rosary he was beading. What might he say? Brother Eusebius always exhibited a cunning way about him without overt forthrightness. "Yes," he said. "I worry over that." Then he grew heated under his tunic. "You're not concerned about Father Paolo, are you?"

"It's not just him," Brother Eusebius said with a sharp sting to his voice. "The others too. I'm not blind. I've seen how everyone fusses over the stranger."

Astute as the middle-aged man from Georgia was, Sebastian never gathered if Brother Eusebius took him for a homosexual. Most people never figured Sebastian for gay, or so he assumed. He figured people had regarded him as a lifelong bachelor. Some of the brothers couldn't hide their sexuality even if they tried. Like Brother George and Brother Rodel. Perhaps even Brother Hubert.

And Casey?

Father Paolo and Brother Lucien's relationship had a hushed acceptance in the abbey. No one ever spoke of it. Sebastian had them pegged his first week as a postulant. And by the passing of his first month, whatever doubts he'd still held had vanished.

Sebastian supposed some of the brothers might have weakened with one another. Sebastian had himself once, what seemed so long ago. It had been his third week at the abbey. He'd grown nervous and unsure about his new station in life. While the others were choring, Brother Micah had approached him in his cell, expressing worry over his obvious despondence. After a few moments of talking and finally making Sebastian at ease, Brother Micah had knelt before him where he sat on his bed, slipped up his tunic, and taken him into his mouth.

Shocked, Sebastian had tried to stand and push him off. But Brother Micah had held him firmly by his thighs. Soon Sebastian's struggles had abated. He'd allowed pleasure to erase his uneasiness.

He'd given in to the sensation of release, to a physical bliss that had taken his mind from indecisiveness and fear. He had seen it coming too. From the first moment he'd stepped out of the van from Telluride's small airport, Brother Micah had showed him extra attention. The same kind that Sebastian had shown Casey when he'd first arrived.

Sebastian remembered Casey's first day as a confirmed postulant, and watching him amble up the walkway from his cell window. The cells faced the front so that the monks might spot incoming guests. The design dated as far back as when the first reformed Trappist brotherhood established a monastery in Soligny-la-Trappe in Normandy, six hundred years ago. The sole passenger that day, Casey appeared bright yet unconvinced. Sebastian was glad to see him return after his summer retreat. He'd brought freshness inside the abbey's stone cold walls.

He hadn't wanted to lapse with Brother Micah. For days afterward, Sebastian had tried to avoid him. Refused even eye contact. Eventually, guilt had persuaded Sebastian to confront him, and he'd apologized for being austere, and then said that he didn't want for anything further to happen between them. Brother Micah had seemed to accept Sebastian's words, but Sebastian had detected a quiver to his bottom lip.

They remained friends after Sebastian's talk, although their conversations came a bit strained whenever speech was permitted. No animosity lingered. It was almost as if the encounter had never happened. Sebastian could barely picture it in his mind without questioning if it had been a dream, or someone had recounted the experience to him.

During the long hours alone fashioning rosaries, Sebastian had been tempted to confess his secrets to Brother Eusebius. Not only about his homosexuality and his sole interlude with a fellow monk. About his other secrets too, the ones that had steered him to Mt. Ouray and its secluded fortress, surrounded by an impinging sea of spruces and aspens. Secrets he'd hoped would disappear like smoke from a dampened incense cone.

As Sebastian watched Brother Eusebius's shoulders rise up even higher and his lips pucker to the point he feared he might spit, Sebastian remained firm mouthed.

"And in a house of God," Brother Eusebius went on, gripping his pliers as if he were about to hammer nails into a wall. "I've overlooked the past nonsense. I turn my cheek with Brother Lucien and Father Paolo. I understand there are those who enter the abbey who shouldn't. I have no say in that. But it's difficult to bite my tongue when even the abbot swoons over someone we know nothing about."

Sebastian worried Brother Eusebius's anger might escalate. He shared some of his qualms, but wanted to quiet him. Muffling a snicker, he said, "I don't think it's so bad."

"It's bad, it's… it's… I must guard my tongue."

"I see your game, Brother Eusebius," Sebastian said, squaring his shoulders over his lap work, still hoping to lighten the mood. "You're trying to stir up more excitement in your dull days here."

"That's not it at all, Brother Sebastian. I know you well enough to recognize that you agree with my concerns."

Brother Eusebius had resided at the abbey nearly twenty years, longer than most. He was the youngest "old timer" at Mt. Ouray. Sebastian took comfort in that. An outcast inside the abbey, yet Brother Eusebius knew more about the heartbeat of Mt. Ouray—and the world—than anyone Sebastian had ever spoken with. Sebastian chose to be honest with his friend, more than at any time in the past.

Without giving away too many of his thoughts, he said, "Does it bother you that much, Brother Eusebius, being around so much of this at a monastery?"

Brother Eusebius wrenched a few s-clasps, and rested his large, callused hands in a fold of his black scapular. "When I converted to Catholicism as a teenager and chose to attend the seminary, I have to admit I was a bit taken back by the… well, sometimes overt displays of interests some of the priests had for the students and each other. Sometimes it was all too clear. Other times subtle enough to never know for sure." He shrugged. "After a while, I figured seminaries and monasteries are similar to prisons."

"That's a harsh comparison."

"But accurate. I've seen a lot here during the past twenty years. There's a gentle, good quality to life inside a monastery. But men are human. It's inevitable that they might wish to fulfill certain needs. And on top of that, the Catholic Church attracts that type of man. I know. I can see. Being an oddity even among oddities, I can see, Brother

Sebastian. Not so much for the obvious. A man who finds a woman a divine gift, why would he choose the life of a monk, surrounded only by other men? Devotion to God? That's what attracted me."

Brother Eusebius always had a distant glint to his dark eyes, yet they were focused and penetrating. He kept to his bead work all throughout his diatribe. The weightiness of his words must have stewed inside him for some time, before even JC's inexplicable arrival at Mt. Ouray. Sebastian was unsure if he should cap his mood or let it erupt. Brother Eusebius was more than an "oddball," as he often described himself. Mentally, he stood apart from most of the brothers. No surprise that Sebastian had forged a closer friendship with him than he had with any of the other monks. Except perhaps for Casey.

"Would you be so shocked if I confessed I've had a few temptations too?" Brother Eusebius went on. "Oh, not what you're thinking. During the summers when guests arrive, I've had to turn away from a lovely woman at times. I'm unashamed. I'm a man. But I've stuck by my vows of celibacy all these years. I'm an oddity here, but in a funny way. That's what makes it easier for me. I have fewer temptations."

Surprised by Brother Eusebius's sudden frankness, Sebastian held his breath. Only after he felt a slight dizziness did he realize the need to inhale. Stale but reinvigorating air entered his lungs.

"Twenty years is a long time," he said. "I've been here almost four." He gazed toward the sacristy door, beyond which the abbey functioned, akin to any industrial institution. It had a heartbeat and breath that at times sighed loud enough to shake a winter's worth of snow from the mountains.

He hadn't really reflected much on his own intended vow of celibacy. He'd gone without most of his adult life. Years before entering Mt. Ouray, he'd turned his back on romance and love, the way he had his city. Once or twice a year hardly made for a vigorous sex life. Little he had to sacrifice when he'd chosen the monastic life.

Then Casey had arrived. And the stirrings commenced anew.

"I must confess," he said in a whisper, "whenever I think about the years to come, I become nervous that I won't be able to honor my vows."

Brother Eusebius clutched a half-finished rosary to his chest. "You, Brother Sebastian?"

Had he divulged too much? What did it matter now? Within the solitude of the sacristy, a confessional where, with no one to hear or to judge him but his confessor and God, he might seek penance for the thoughts that had taken over his prayers. Thoughts of Casey Galvan, alone in his cell at night. Only twentysomething. What did Casey understand he'd given up? The veiled-off sacristy, like a latticed barrier, offered Sebastian courage to continue.

"I have my moments," he said. "Like you said, men are human."

Turning back to his beadwork, Brother Eusebius said, "All we can do is take life in the steps of Jesus when he carried the cross to Calvary. The Way of the Cross is why we garner strength in prayer." He chuckled. "Now here I go, sounding like Father Paolo. But it's true, in many ways. Going without gives us strength. There's something powerful in abandoning material and physical desires. Yes, leaving things behind indeed strengthens us."

Prickly chills raced along Sebastian's arm when Brother Eusebius uttered those last few words like a thunderclap. What had leaving his world in Philadelphia meant for him? Had it made him stronger or weaker? Sebastian wished to change the subject. "All I keep wondering is how and why our guest got here," he mumbled.

"He does frighten me, and I'm unsure of the reason," Brother Eusebius said. "He has those eyes, like looking into a fire pit with the remnants of cold embers. The fire is long gone, but you can see that something had burned there."

"He's not an escaped convict. The father has already checked for that."

"Maybe he's committed a crime without detection. Making his way here in all that snow and wind, he'd have to have a good reason to escape something."

The hushed voices of Father Paolo and JC oozed through the wall. "Or find something,"

Brother Eusebius bit his lower lip. The veins on his neck thickened into thin copper cables. Together, they continued their toil without words until the clock's call for Sext ushered them to the chapel.

– IX –

AFTER the passing of several days, Sebastian realized the chanting and the cello playing from Father Paolo's private office had stopped. He had grown so used to the sounds, he couldn't recall exactly when they had ended. Perhaps at that precise moment, or days before. He sat in his cell reading Scripture during siesta, wondering if the others had noticed.

Jealousy plagued the brothers. Perhaps even Casey, who still had a difficult time remaining near Sebastian without turning away. Brother Eusebius had deciphered the brothers' gapes, drooping lips. He'd understood the longing and lust in those expressions. Brother Eusebius had acknowledged his own covetousness toward the pretty female patrons who visited the abbey during summertime. They had enticed him with their flowing hair, healthy complexions, stylish and tight-fitting clothing, smelling of jasmine and other fine perfumes bought from fancy department stores.

But Sebastian did not desire JC, not in the same way the abbot possessed him or how Brother Eusebius had alluded the others did. His beauty captivated him, but only as one might gaze upon a garden blossom.

"You can appreciate the splendor of a rose without plucking it," Brother Giles had once told him when he'd returned to Mt. Ouray to stay. For what reason the older monk had spoken those words,

Sebastian never comprehended. Perhaps sage advice for a contemplated lifetime behind abbey walls.

The father had even given JC a statuette of the Virgin Mary, a gift reserved for postulants and established brothers. Sebastian had noticed it on the wall shelf inside JC's cell the last time he'd interviewed him. The story went he'd dropped it when the father had handed it to him, nearly breaking off the head. The plush carpeting in the abbot's private office saved it from smashing to pieces. Sebastian had experienced it in civilian life. Gifts to entice, lure, mislead. The misuse of power for one's own gain.

The father's possession of JC had made it difficult for Sebastian to interview him. With his curiosity about how and why JC had come to their fortress mounting, he'd wanted nothing more than to sit with him for hours, chiseling away at his mind until it cracked open like a piñata full of information. But his inquisitiveness would have to die on the vine like grapes in a cold snap, for by Sunday morning, he learned JC's visit would soon end.

It was after breakfast, while the brothers lined up outside the chapel for Lauds, waiting for the abbot to lead their way in, when JC, against the silent custom, announced his plans.

"You guys should probably know," he said, his voice ricocheting off the walls. He wore his street clothes without his cowl, which had the brothers gaping. "I already made it clear to Father Paolo. Being cooped up here is getting to me. I plan on leaving now that those storms passed. I won't bother with calling the forest service or a helicopter to come for me since it costs too much and they'll ask too many questions. I'm going to borrow some snowshoes and hike out down the road. You've been real cool and all that, but I need to take off."

"When?" Brother George whispered.

"Sometime next week, I hope, after I figure out more where I'm going and what I'm going to do."

"But you don't even remember where you're from," Brother Rodel said. "Or even your name."

"What difference does it make? I'd rather be lost and confused down there than up here."

"What about why you came?" Casey asked. "You had to have a reason to come here."

JC yawned. "If I ever find out, maybe I'll come back."

Brother Jerome screwed up his forehead. "How did the abbot take your decision?"

"He got kinda mad. Said I'm wasting all my talent. He thinks I'm a real good singer. But I told him I'm not cut out for all this monk stuff. No offense."

"It'll be near impossible for you to make it all the way to Monfrere," Brother Hubert said, fixing his glasses over his big red nose. "You'll have an all-day hike in this snow."

"Maybe I'm an expert, like Sebastian said. Who knows? Don't worry. I'll be out of your way soon."

They sealed their mouths when Father Paolo made his way down the corridor, the train of his lengthy cowl sweeping across the terracotta floor to hush them. His hands were tucked inside the cowl's folds, and his eyes remained fixed to the floor. He glimpsed at no one—not even JC in his shameful street clothes—when he turned for the chapel's entrance. Normally he would nod them along. That morning he entered without gesturing for them to follow.

The brothers looked confused. Sebastian cleared his throat and motioned those before him to head in.

Inside the chapel, the father conducted service as if it were any other Sunday. The brothers chanted the *Rosa vernans* and the psalms. All except JC. This time, he refused to sing. His defiance proved his intention to leave the abbey as soon as possible.

Sebastian was unsure, but many of the monks' chants sounded louder than ordinary, their voices pushing against the wooden beams and opening the ceiling to the dawn.

The brothers' enthusiasm for JC had waned; Sebastian was certain of that. The abbot's possession of him had steered him from their grasps. Unofficially, he was off limits. And JC's own alteration, one that had changed from a complacent awe to a restless indifference to abbey traditions, left the brothers avoiding him, rather than whisking him around the abbey in the manner they'd done after he'd first awakened.

According to a few of the brothers, he'd even muttered curses while others were around to listen, although Sebastian had never heard them. Clearly, the stranger lacked the religious fortitude that Father Paolo had imagined.

"He called me a fat loco," Brother George had grumbled two days before while they'd plated their breakfasts and JC slept. Steam from the fried potatoes had coated his eyeglasses. "No one has ever ridiculed me inside the abbey."

Sebastian still craved to solve JC's mystery, but perhaps it was best if he did leave by next week, taking with him his secrets, no matter how dangerous it was for him to descend the mountain. Sebastian raised his chanting voice to match those around him and decided he longed for nothing more than to return to their normal, humdrum abbey lives. Forget that they had ever discovered JC lying unconscious in the blizzard.

The abbot ended service with, "We praise you, God," and the monks responded with an elongated, mellow, "Amen."

The morning pressed on, and the day left Sebastian frazzled and yearning for the privacy of his cell. He watched the clock between morning work and Compline for the hour to strike seven thirty so he could take care of his personal needs and retire for the night. He was tired of the whispers, and although the brothers seemed happy JC was about to leave them, his rash decision left a lingering agitation.

Alone in his cell at last, he sat at his desk under a single lamp's light and listened to the flute notes flowing from Casey's room three doors away. Upon the emergence of another Grand Silence, he had allowed Casey's music to seize him and carry him away. He knew he should spend his solitude in *lectio divina*. What difference did one more daydream make?

Guided as if by God's hand, he stood from his desk and stretched his lanky form over his lonely bed. With his eyes fixed on the ceiling, Casey's music called to him, mesmerized him. The young novice spoke to him through the finger holes of his instrument. Playing just for him. His tune sounded as glum as Sebastian's mood.

Where had he heard that melody before?

Claps of thunder accompanied Casey's gentle flute playing, along with the incessant winds blowing off the San Juan Mountains. Above the rattling of his windowpane, the squeaking of Brother Giles's wheelchair emerged somewhere in the corridor. Sebastian suspected he was using the bathroom to drain his catheter.

He longed for the spring thaw, when his work responsibilities shifted to more manual labor outdoors and his muscles would ache again, beyond the rawness in his fingers from stringing rosary after rosary in the stuffiness of the sacristy each day, and he'd forget what the abbey's walls trapped inside. In warmer days, he'd trim the large lawn with the ride-on mower, take turns weeding the gardens with Brothers Hubert and George, allow the soft breezes to carry away his indecision and worries. And in the autumn, splitting the hundreds of cords of logs they'd purchased from a local wood provider for their three wood-burning fireplaces, preparing for the long winter.

That was when he understood abbey life the most. When God smiled upon him from above the perpetually snow-covered peaks. Winters often brought dubious wonderings. Had the abbey life been right for him? Should he have left everything behind in Philadelphia, so much of it unresolved? Would he one day profess before the abbot?

He squeezed his eyes to let Casey's somber music weave through his head and relax him. Then it stopped. More thunder broke above the unremitting winds. He waited. Casey must've settled in for the night. Father Paolo did not permit music playing past eight thirty, when Retire officially fell over Mt. Ouray.

Pulled into a ball, Sebastian succumbed to fitful dreams of unfulfilled tragic lovers and raging forest fires that chased him through the night.

"BROTHER JC has left, just like he promised," Brother George whispered to the brothers in the corridor outside their cells upon Rise the next morning. "I knocked four times and he never stirred. So I peeked. He's not in his cell."

"Are you sure?" Sebastian took two steps to JC's assigned cell next to his own, and looked inside. The bed was made, and what few possessions he'd brought with him—the yellow knapsack and his thin parka—were gone. The room appeared completely cleared out. Vacant. Returning to the others, he said, "Has anyone looked for him?"

"I searched the bathroom and the kitchen, even the pantry where we found him before," Brother George said. "He's nowhere."

"Where could he have gone off to this time?" Brother Rodel said.

"He said he was leaving," Brother Micah said.

"Good riddance, that's what I've got to say," Brother Jerome grunted. "He was a busybody. Just the other day I caught him in Brother Augustine's cell, looking about like he wanted to take something. He said he'd mistaken it for Brother Sebastian's and that he kept getting turned around. I think he was looking to rob from a feeble old man."

"Why would he want to speak with Brother Sebastian in his cell?" Brother Micah asked.

"I was helping him try to uncover his memories," Sebastian mumbled.

"Uncover memories?" Brother Lucien snorted. "Is that all?"

"He wasn't quite how I expected him," Brother Giles said from his wheelchair, where he wrung his hands over his lap. "Not at all what I expected. Quite a disappointment. And imagine I considered giving him a sacramental to wear around his neck."

Brother Lucien locked his arms across the front of his cowl. "I heard him ask the father for money yesterday after Mass. I didn't hear the father's reply. I was afraid to ask him if he'd given him any, he's been so sour lately."

"It would've been the Christian thing to do, regardless of how badly he's behaved among us," Brother Rodel said.

"I still don't believe he's gone so soon after telling us he was leaving," Brother George said. "He told us he wanted to wait until next week."

"It *is* next week." Brother Micah grimaced. "It's Monday. He's gone, you can be sure."

"Why would he leave in pitch darkness with all that blowing snow?" Casey said. "I saw him retire to his cell last night. Why wouldn't he wait, like he said?"

"I'm glad he's gone. I'm glad," Brother Jerome repeated.

"At least he worked hard," Brother Rodel said. "You have to give him credit for that."

"What's all this chatting?" Father Paolo strode down the corridor from the bathroom, his eyes screwed up into fierce slits behind his glasses.

"Brother JC has already left, Father," Brother George said. "We were discussing it. Forgive us for speaking during the Grand Silence, but we were concerned."

"There's nothing to be concerned about. He's gone. We knew he was leaving."

"But in the middle of the night with all this wind?" Brother Eusebius shook his head.

"It didn't stop him from coming," Father Paolo growled. "Keep quiet now. Let's remember who and where we are. Come, it's time for Vigils."

They marched behind Father Paolo to the chapel, and when JC failed to show for Vigils, Sebastian suspected it was true. JC had left for good. The brothers seemed to sigh a collective relief in their chanting, knowing that they no longer had to worry about whether JC might turn on them. A mere three weeks before, they'd embraced him as a welcome change to their dull abbey lives. But at breakfast the brothers seemed to fall into a strange malaise. Brother Micah was in a snit about the mess everyone had been leaving in the kitchen. Brother Hubert took ill and refused to eat. Brother Eusebius grunted and sighed. Brother Rodel retreated deeper into his world. Brother Lucien and Father Paolo remained distant in his office. Sebastian, too, wanted only to plate his food and disappear. No one dared utter JC's name.

After the Eucharist, Sebastian peered out the front door and along the footpath toward the parking lot. Under a wan sun that crested the mountains, the winds continued to rage. The back and sides of the abbey revealed the same whipped cream smooth landscape. Seemed the mystery of JC culminated even in his absence. Sebastian shook his head, staring into the white expanse.

Sebastian decided to put the ordeal behind him and accept that he'd gone. For good. Swept away by the whistling and rushing winds off the San Juan Mountains. Father Paolo had confirmed his departure. That was that. No further need to think of him, the father had said. A strange illusion had punctured their serene winter, with no trace of him coming or going. He'd entered and departed their lives the same way.

Sebastian and Brother Eusebius toiled in the sacristy with less tension budding around them. Their industrious hands filled velvet sack after velvet sack of the brown-beaded rosaries, ready for the abbey's gift shop come summertime. Sebastian kept his ongoing wonderings about JC to himself.

The abbot's private office on the other side of the shared wall remained silent. One time Sebastian heard Brother Hubert's voice, later, Brother Lucien's. Typical, since they both provided the occasional administrative function for the abbey.

For siesta, Sebastian retreated to the library, where he gazed out the arched window. The winds had settled, leaving a clear enough view of the snow-draped spruces and aspens. And Mt. Ouray loomed in the distance, a faint outline under the milky white canopy of sky. The first time in more than two weeks he'd been able to see it reach heavenward.

Try as he might, lingering speculation on JC continued to paw at his brain. Why would he have departed down the mountain before daybreak after he'd said he wanted to wait and decide his destiny?

Despite everything, Sebastian prayed he had found a safe passage. Yet his departure seemed unimaginable. Most likely he wouldn't have survived another attempt to win over the elements. The Rocky Mountains gave only one chance. He should probably suggest Father Paolo inform the authorities to search for a body in the morning.

He was about to imagine hiking the mountain in such harsh conditions when someone pulled a chair out next to him. Sebastian could not help but grin when he shifted to see Casey sitting beside him, his eyes, brown and droopy like Delores's, shimmering in the subtle sunlight.

"Am I disturbing you?" Casey asked.

Sebastian was surprised how much his grin grew as he shook his head. "Not at all. I'm glad to see you. You've been keeping yourself scarce. What have you been up to, Casey?"

"Daydreaming, mostly."

He chuckled. "I thought only I did that."

"I do it too often, I'm afraid. Sometimes my prayers turn into daydreams, and the guilt chews me up."

"Hard to tell daydreams and prayers apart at times, I suspect. Don't worry over things too much. I'm sure God understands the musings of our minds."

The sound of Casey's chuckles, the gentle ringing of a Sanctus bell, brought a delightful shiver along Sebastian's neck. He suppressed the urge to simply lay his hand over Casey's, which rested on the oak tabletop.

Sebastian turned back to the window, hoping to suppress the unexpected heat in his lap. The landscape outside seemed to glow brighter.

"I wanted to apologize if I've seemed evasive," Casey said.

"Things have been crazy around here, that's for sure," Sebastian said, facing Casey again. "All of us have been preoccupied."

"With JC, you mean?"

Sebastian nodded. "He brought us excitement and confusion."

Casey rubbed the tabletop with his fingertips, making a subdued squeaking noise. "I suppose it's good he's gone. He made me feel strange." Then he looked penetratingly into Sebastian's eyes. "Had he done that to you?"

Sebastian stretched over his chair. "I was mostly curious about him. Still am, to be honest. He's unlike anyone I've ever met. A living and breathing mystery."

"I guess many of us felt that way."

Casey's voice, suddenly faraway and dull, forced Sebastian to sit straighter. He peered at him, deciphering his mood. He had sat next to him, cheery and submissive. Now a cloud eased over his features, grayer than the ones outside. Yes, there was envy behind that shadow. His rich brown eyes confessed as much. But was it for Sebastian or JC?

He wanted to clarify his statement when Casey stood with a skid of his chair on the floor. "We probably shouldn't be speaking. I'll see you later at dinner."

Sebastian watched the flow of his tunic mold around Casey's physique from his quick exit. Resembling JC in many ways, Casey embodied a strange mix of intrigue and melodrama. A result of their generation, perhaps. Reared on unrestrained mawkishness, which pushed them to extremes, like hiking along precarious mountains in the dead of winter.

Casey wasn't that much younger than Sebastian. Thirteen, fourteen years. Sebastian too had been raised in the post-modern culture with its fondness for fantasy and sentimentality. But the real world—one filled with violence and death most see confined to their televisions—had shaken Sebastian long ago. Romantic ideals had left his heart in the fury of fight or flight. He no longer worried about love. But he did care for Casey, more than he ever imagined he would when he'd first encountered him last summer.

He continued to dwell on both Casey and the oddity of JC into the evening. By Retire, the quiet of the abbey had never penetrated his ears so heavily while his thoughts compacted one on top of the other. To appease his nerves, he went to warm a cup of cocoa in the kitchen before concealing himself in his lonesome cell for the night. Brother George had just left the kitchen with an apple, leaving him and Delores alone. The pour of the milk, the strike of the match to the gas stove, the puff of the blue flames filled him with a hushed calm. Weren't those some of the gentle reasons why he'd chosen the life of the Trappists?

He adjusted the flame, set the kettle on the burner. He scrunched his nose when Delores's scratching at the walk-in freezer disrupted his tranquility. "You can't have anything from there, old girl," he whispered. "It's all frozen. I'll get you something."

She continued to scratch and whine while Sebastian retrieved a dog biscuit from a cupboard. He'd never known her to refuse a treat, but she did that night. He clenched the biscuit in a fist and watched her fuss by the freezer door. He remembered the last time she'd scratched and pawed—at the pantry door, when they'd found the nude stranger cowering in a corner.

Sebastian dropped the dog treat on the counter and opened the freezer. A blast of cold, dry air hit him in the face. He expected Delores to scamper away from the chill. Instead, she bolted inside and ran straight into a corner. Large paw prints marked the frost on the cold thermal flooring.

She scratched and snarled, glancing at Sebastian with big brown eyes. Sebastian bent over her, trying to understand what she saw. The one light in the freezer shone mostly in the center. He stepped back to allow the full light to shed on the corner. Boxes of frozen veggies and fruits stacked one on top of the other. He could discern nothing that should interest Delores. Sebastian sensed someone at his back. He glanced over his shoulder at Brother Hubert, standing by the freezer door.

"What's she fussing at?"

Sebastian chuckled, and his breath exhaled in thick, misty clouds. "I don't know, Brother Hubert. She's acting silly."

She continued to scratch at the floor around the boxes. Strings of snot and saliva coated the area. Amused, Sebastian yanked her back and peered between the crevices. Delores panted beside him, running in small, tight circles, her large tail tracing a wide arc in the air. The thick thermal walls muffled her barking and whining.

"Calm down, girl. Calm down."

Turning his head from side to side to get a better look, he fell to a crouch. Flanked by more stacks of boxes, an elongated object wrapped in thick green trash bags leaned against the frosted metallic walls. Sebastian pushed and pulled the boxes farther apart. His enchantment evaporated when something about the package struck him as eerie. He edged nearer. Delores barked.

The package could not be frozen meat. Theirs was a fleshless order. What else could be that size? He hadn't recalled seeing it before.

He elbowed the hyper Delores back. Standing, he reached for the trash bags and began to tear a hole at the top to see what hid underneath.

Blood pounded in his ears.

Nothing prepared him for the horror, or for the high-pitched wail emitted by Brother Hubert behind him.

Under a frozen cowl hood, caked and coagulated blood from a gash wound on the left temple streaked along the blue face. The white of his eye emerged, and Sebastian nearly fell backward. He continued to tear at the plastic wrap with trembling fingers to expose more of the surreal contents. His single heart-shaped diamond earring caught the freezer light, and the sharp and sudden flash cut into Sebastian's eyes with the ferocity of a solar explosion.

– X –

SEBASTIAN could not shake from his memory the horrible ordeal of carrying JC's rigid remains into the infirmary for a haphazard medical examination. According to Brother Jerome, JC had been bludgeoned on the left side of his head. But that probably wasn't enough to have killed him. His body was riddled with frostbite. Even the eyeballs. While wrapped and unconscious in trash bags, his icy tomb had sucked life out of him.

He'd been inside the freezer for at least eighteen hours. Some time the night before, JC had faced his horrible death. When Sebastian had found him, dressed in a white cowl (hard to the touch, like plaster), Sebastian could not deny the sick irony. They had found JC outside in the snow much the same way.

Sebastian had to admit, Father Paolo's swift actions following the haphazard medical examination were justified. He'd called the brothers from their cells and corralled them in the corridor. Their sleepy expressions evolved into gaping horror once they heard what had taken place inside the infirmary while they'd slept.

"Do you remember seeing anything the other night?" the father demanded of them.

"I was playing my flute then," Casey said. "After that, I fell asleep and didn't hear anything until Brother George woke us for Rise."

"I took Brother Augustine to the bathroom after Retire," Brother Hubert put forth with a shrug and a look of shock on his face that matched the others. "I did hear Brother Casey's flute playing, but I hadn't seen anything strange along the way. After that, I'd slept soundly."

"I saw Brother Hubert, just as he said," Brother Rodel added. "I was looking into the corridor right at that moment, and I hadn't seen anything strange either. Brother JC's cell was still sealed. Everything appeared calm, and nothing woke me."

"Brother Eusebius and I met in the kitchen just before seven thirty, if I recall," Brother Micah said. "We were getting hot cocoa and saw nothing peculiar."

"I can attest," Brother Eusebius said. "I noticed nothing unusual."

"I was in my cell reading and turned in at the proper hour of eight thirty," Brother Jerome said. "I heard and saw nothing."

"Nothing." Brother George shook his head. "I… I… went to get something to eat earlier, I think, but…. Nothing."

"I slept like a baby," Brother Giles grunted.

"I hadn't seen anything, Father," Brother Lucien said.

Sebastian pulled in his lips. "I wish I knew something that might help."

Frustration carved on his ashen face, Father Paolo ordered each of the monks to return to his cell "immediately and until further notice."

Father Paolo held back Sebastian and Brother Jerome while the others sealed themselves in their cells. He escorted them to his private office, where they sat mute, staring at the ruby carpet in disbelief. Small orbs of light from the lamps stained the walls.

"He's dead," Brother Jerome mumbled toward his gnarly toes. "Someone actually murdered him."

Only when Brother Jerome had uttered the word did the realization of what they stood in the midst of sink into Sebastian's mind. The sharpened axe of reality.

Murdered.

He'd seen it before. Many times. Too many times.

At first, Sebastian had considered that JC might have slipped in the kitchen, and someone had discovered him unconscious and made the rash decision to wrap him in trash bags and leave him in the freezer to keep the body from rotting. The guilty monk feared coming forward, embarrassed by his dim-witted actions. Yet the lack of blood splatter on anything inside the freezer or the kitchen rendered that scenario unlikely. Unless whoever was responsible had taken great pains to clean up the scene. Or transported him from another part of the abbey?

"Is there any other explanation at all?" Father Paolo asked, staring at them with pleading eyes and wringing his vein-covered hands over the top of his shiny mahogany desk.

"I... I don't know," Sebastian said toward the carpet.

Brother Jerome shook his head. "Who would do such a thing? I can't imagine. I've never heard of it. Not in my entire life, outside the abbey or inside."

Father Paolo launched himself from behind his desk and paced, leaving dark prints along the plush carpet from his sandals, which clipped and clapped against the balls of his feet. Sebastian followed him with his eyes, his mind racing with disbelief. For the first time since his arrival at Mt. Ouray, he feared for his other brothers—and feared them.

Should they be standing guard at the cells, making sure the culprit didn't escape? But where would he go with another raging snowstorm barricading them even from reaching the guest cottage? Were they really trapped inside with a desperate killer and nowhere to run?

"We'll have to call the authorities." Sebastian's words rocketed from his mouth in a firestorm. That was the first action he'd wanted to take. Unlike the other times, he refused to wait for the abbot's instructions. "What other options have we? As soon as the storm clears, authorities can helicopter or snowmobile in and investigate. We should've called them while he was still alive, regardless of what he wanted."

Father Paolo stopped pacing and glared at him. "No," he said. "It's impossible. We can't have law enforcement traipsing around here.

We can solve this… this… whatever it is. Once we have who's responsible apprehended, only then will we contact the proper authorities."

"I believe that's wrong," Brother Sebastian dared to say, and he formed tight fists in his lap. "You heard Brother Jerome. There's been a murder. With all due respect, Father, this is out of our hands."

"I've made my decision."

"What about JC?" Brother Jerome asked.

Father Paolo studied the two men, as if wondering which one of them might have bashed whatever instrument over JC's head and attempted to conceal the crime. "For the time being, remove him from the infirmary and put him back in the freezer," he answered without further uncertainty. "Wrap him in the plastic bags we found him in. Keep him away from the food, of course, just in case."

Sebastian and Brother Jerome gaped at each other. The tremor Sebastian noticed flowing under Brother Jerome's tunic sleeves seemed to travel through his knotty fingers to Sebastian. He clasped the armrests to steady his arms and legs.

"That's ghastly," Brother Jerome muttered. "I don't know if we should do it."

"We must, Brother Jerome." Father Paolo returned to his chair behind his desk. "The body will preserve there."

The body. Too easily the words had fallen from Father Paolo's thick lips. The young man had arrived at the abbey known only to them as "the stranger." In time they'd begun to refer to him as "the visitor" or "the guest." Later, after learning his name might be JC, the brothers had commenced calling him "Brother JC," as if he'd belonged to them. Now, barely a month later, the abbot referred to him as "the body." A body in need of storage. Sebastian nearly cried out at the appalling absurdity.

"You have any other suggestions where we might store it without venturing out into this blizzard?" the father said.

Brother Jerome lowered his eyes. "I can think of no other place, Father."

"Then I expect you to obey my orders. Do it before I allow the others out of their cells for Vigils. I'll send Lucien to help. Brother Jerome, you clean the infirmary. Have Brother Hubert launder any soiled sheets."

"What about his clothes?" Sebastian asked, numb. "We had to cut them off him."

"Bundle them up and stuff them inside with his wrapping."

Sebastian and Brother Jerome sat speechless. Minutes later, they followed through with the abbot's demands without words. They rewrapped JC in the same trash bags, as if he were a life-size doll. Brother Jerome appeared nearly sick, and, like Sebastian, the former doctor had seen many bodies in his day too. But the circumstances were much different. A murder had taken place inside their abbey, not out on the heartless streets. Afterward, Sebastian and Brother Lucien carried the body to the freezer. They stored it where Sebastian had found it and shut the door with a resounding thud.

Behind the gloom of a new storm, the morning awakened. During Vigils the chapel remained dim. No sunlight streamed through the stained glass windows and illuminated the crucifix hanging on the high altar. The monks' voices barely rose above the howl of the wind. Not even Brother Jerome, who always chanted louder and fuller than any of them, raised his shaky baritone beyond a raspy whisper.

Sebastian noted the vacant and deadened stares of his brothers; it looked as if none had returned to bed, knowing what stirred among them. They'd shared the same expressions at the impromptu assembly Father Paolo had called in lieu of breakfast. He'd ordered that they fast for the morning, considering the dreadfulness that had befallen the abbey.

They sat on the hard wooden chairs and continued to gaze blankly, waiting for the father to address them. The fireplace at the end of the dining hall stood cold and empty, the gaping, murky mouth of an ogre.

The abbot muttered a Latin prayer and scrutinized each one from his chair on the other side of the table. "If you struck out in a fit of rage without forethought or by provocation in self-defense, come forth and let me know," he said. Only the wind smashing against the arched windows parted the silence that lingered. Enlarged eyes darted from one brother to the next.

"He can admit his guilt without worrying about standing out among his brothers," the father went on. "Whatever he says will be kept in strict secrecy between him and me. He has my word. No one will or needs to know his deed."

"It's not true, it's not true," Brother George wailed.

"It is true, Brother George," the abbot barked. "And unless you have something to confess, keep your mouth sealed."

A few of the brothers dared to raise their eyes and ogle the father and their fellow monks after Brother George's outburst. Which of those peering eyes appeared the most guilt-ridden? Sebastian hated the new emotions that coursed along his weary limbs.

Casey remained frozen on his chair. His shimmering au jus-colored eyes reflected the sorrow and fear in everyone's faces. Sebastian wanted to comfort him. They had not shared a word since he'd emerged from his cell.

Brother Giles gazed at his lap, his withered hands demonstrating that uncanny strength as he clutched the wheels of his chair, as if he only needed one word so that he could take off, hide away from the others, never face any of them again.

Sebastian sympathized.

"We will continue our day as any other," the father said. "God, now more than ever, will demand it from us. Prayer could not prove more potent. I will expect that you remain inside the abbey. There's no way off the mountain, not in this blizzard. If anyone attempts to leave, I'll call the authorities. They'll hunt you, if you don't die first. I will wait for a confession in my office. Go now and prepare for Lauds."

Father Paolo had stated a simple order, but one that filled Sebastian—and the others too, by their looks—with sickness and dread.

Go about their day as if nothing had happened. Pray. Work. Wait for whoever had killed JC to step forward in secrecy. Or if he chose to run, hear news of his being chased like a fox in a hunt.

The father's lecture seemed to have unleashed profound emotions in the brothers. During Lauds, the Eucharist, and Terce, Brother George failed to hold back his weeping. Even the hyperspirited Brother Giles appeared forlorn, his good cheer having evaporated along with the smoke from the votive candles in the transept. The brothers glued their eyes to the pulpit where Father Paolo sang the psalms, ignoring the echoing, choked sobs of Brother George and the repeated heavy sighs from Brothers Rodel and Micah.

Had any one of them yet come forth? When would they know?

Work with Brother Eusebius passed as any other work period, as if nothing had happened. Only that morning the rustle of the coffee beans and the clink of the silver wire resided heavy and tedious inside Sebastian's head. They kept to the tradition of silence, with more relish than ever.

"It's hard to believe. Hard to believe," Brother Eusebius finally uttered moments before the call for Sext. "Must be some kind of accident."

Sebastian said nothing. No words came to mind to speak.

Midday prayer passed, and the brothers lined up to take their leave from the chapel, dipping their shaking fingertips into the holy water, crossing themselves as they exited, continuing about their day as if Sebastian hadn't found JC's body in the walk-in freezer. A painful parade of numbness and bewilderment.

Later in the kitchen, where they served themselves lunch (despite missing breakfast, Sebastian hardly had an appetite), they exchanged no words, no glances. The stillness stretched before Sebastian. He fed Delores and patted her big head like he had a thousand times before. As if nothing had changed in their lives. As if the sky hadn't opened up and unleashed a horror upon each of them.

The absurdity seemed surreal.

Brother George dropped his serving spoon and sobbed again. "Did he fall? Is that how he died? Please, tell me he fell and didn't die by one of our hands."

Sebastian gazed at him with pitying eyes. He allowed a slight smile to nudge his cheeks. Brother George wiped his tears while

Brother Hubert patted his shoulder, much the same way Sebastian had stroked Delores's head. Brother George returned to heaping food on his plate. Despite his anguish, the portly brother's appetite seemed little affected.

No one knew if anyone had yet confessed to the abbot. Sebastian figured Father Paolo would update them without betraying anyone's identity. So far, the father had taken his lunch and retreated back to his private office without comment. Casey began again to help Sebastian plate his tray, pour his coffee, butter his bread. Sebastian supposed, with JC out of the picture, Casey could go back to the way things were. Yet his eyes never lifted to meet Sebastian's gaze. He exuded shame, as did they all.

In whoever's guilt, they carried the sin among them all. Buried deep in their breasts, the burden of the crime dwelt inside each of them. Disgrace for the horrible acts of a fellow monk, a fellow human being, gripped Sebastian.

He grew increasingly aware of the brothers observing each other as the day stretched ahead. Passing one another in the corridors, their furtive glances held onto one collective thought: Which one of the brothers was slinking off to the abbot's private office to confess his sin?

Dinner taken together in the dining hall lingered more brutally than an impending train wreck. Sebastian could not wait to free himself. But the awkwardness failed to cease. When the brothers met again for Vespers… and Compline, during the singing of the *Salve Regina*, their eyes continued to dart above their psalmodies and around their cowls. Would Father Paolo inform them someone had confessed? When would the snow lift and the authorities descend on their private retreat like the Marines on Okinawa, to escort the condemned man to prison?

But just before retiring for the night, with both relief for his solitude and puzzlement still percolating inside his mind that the crime remained unsolved, someone rapped on his cell door.

Sebastian opened the door a crack. He suppressed a sigh of displeasure at seeing Brother Lucien. He'd hoped Casey had snuck from his cell to unload his grief on his shoulders. "What is it, Brother Lucien?"

"Father Paolo needs to speak with you."

"Now?"

"He insists." Brother Lucien's face looked gray and aged. "He says right away."

FATHER PAOLO was seated behind his heavy desk, his eyes unblinking, when Sebastian stepped inside the dimly lit office. He had on only one desk lamp, and the fireplace ran cold. Brother Lucien left them alone with a numb thud of the door.

"No one has come forward," the father said bluntly, without greeting him or lifting his eyes from his glowing desk lamp. "No one. No confession at all. Has anyone said anything to you?"

Sebastian shook his head. "We've all been sealed tight. Stunned by the events, I suppose."

"I provided everyone ample time to admit to striking JC and dragging his body to the freezer. Whoever is responsible might have asked God for forgiveness and he feels that is enough. I was hoping to have someone locked away in his cell without question by now. That's why I've called for you at this late hour, Brother Sebastian."

Sebastian swallowed. "What help can I be?"

Father Paolo's frown elongated the lines around his mouth into wide arches. His black irises, glistening behind his eyeglasses, pumped cold blood into Sebastian's heart. What was he alluding to? He couldn't be thinking what Sebastian feared he might.

"Sit, why don't you?"

Reverting to an obedient child, Sebastian took baby steps to one of the large Bergère chairs and eased into it. He clasped his hands together atop his lap, waiting and wondering. He felt almost nude without his scapular. He'd left it hanging over his desk chair in his cell when Brother Lucien had knocked.

Father Paolo crossed his arms over his chest. A smirk lifted his ashen face. He looked down at Sebastian with fast blinking eyes, licked his lips. Sebastian gripped the armrests, his mouth dry.

"I can assume you're not guilty, correct?" the abbot said after an agonizing minute, almost playfully.

Unsure how to respond without coming across as sarcastic, Sebastian said, "Of course."

The father sighed, and he refolded his hands over the desktop. "Your secret has been kept with me for all your years here."

Sebastian squirmed, twitched. Sweat built up on his palms. The padded armrest felt itchy under his grip.

"I will not tell the others about your well-guarded secret. I haven't after all this time."

Sebastian tried to utter something, one word that might confirm life still breathed inside him. All he could do was vibrate his heavy lips. The father had him cornered.

Father Paolo of course knew about his bygone life outside Mt. Ouray. He had come clean when he'd first entered the monastery as a postulant. The abbey conducted extensive background checks before permitting anyone to reside among the brothers, anyway.

"I never held you accountable for why you came to seek prayer in God's house. I can understand your wanting to flee all that crime and corruption. It must have been horrible."

"Why… why are you raising this now?"

The abbot's smirk lengthened, deepening the shadows around his mouth and nose and turning his eyes into mere slits. "The Philadelphia Police Department's loss is our gain. At least for the present situation." He leaned back in his chair, clasped his hands below his chin in his signature posture. "It's in your blood. You've already snooped into why and how Brother JC had come here. An investigation into his death won't be any different."

Sebastian's eyes widened, and his heart fluttered. Trepidation clenched onto his limbs, held him in a death grip, a suspect apprehended by a hypergregarious police officer. A man much like

Sebastian had once been. A life that seemed so remote, led by someone else. Yet it had only been four years ago.

Hard to imagine that existence now. So much had transpired. A stark difference from his current position, wearing a white tunic, black scapular, and worn leather sandals, compared to his world of five-hundred-dollar suits and silk ties and a badge.

That past life as a sergeant with the Homicide Unit of the Philadelphia Police Department, digging up crumbs of every hideous murder dropped in his lap, couldn't be farther from his routine at the abbey. He'd once believed detective work defined him. Before big city bureaucracy and a grandiose media forced him out.

There was no doubt, though, that ever since he'd carried JC into the abbey after Casey had spotted him lying in the snowbank, his investigative instincts had recharged into a powerful machine he'd feared unable to control. Each time he'd contemplated the young man, he'd wanted to interrogate him, relive his past inside the twenty-fifth district's "interview room" on Whitaker Avenue. Never in a lifetime of years had he envisioned JC would become a murder victim too. And inside a monastery. His monastery. Mt. Ouray. A place where he'd hoped to leave the nonsense and violence of the city behind.

He wanted to turn from the abbot's face, realizing that putting the past entirely behind one was more improbable than pushing back the Rocky Mountains. Life's experiences stalked its former stewards, regardless of where they tried to hide. Somehow his had found him and reared again, a rabid wolf shaking him in its clutches, ready to force a pay up.

Yet the spasms in his throat signified something more. Father Paolo's insinuation had aroused him. Enthusiasm for the chase, the taste of a good hunt, sprung up inside him. He never could leave behind the desire for uncovering motives and culprits. Even for crimes as ugly as murder.

Brother Sebastian and Sergeant Harkin were the same man, and always had been.

"We will keep your investigation into who killed Brother JC between us, of course," the abbot said. "I'm certain you can uncover clues without detection. I know you're dying to."

He allowed the words forming inside his mind to accumulate on his tongue before speaking, wanting the father to understand him without ambiguity. "I will do as much as I can, if you feel it's important enough, but in the meantime, I still believe the authorities should be notified—"

"I won't change my mind on that issue," the father spat. "I'm putting the entire investigation into your hands. That's that, Brother Sebastian."

"But, Father…."

"I won't have a scandal hanging over my head," he said. "We must and will take matters on ourselves. We're a religious order. No one wants to learn of such ghastly events."

"Won't the authorities find out at some point anyway?"

"If we can solve the case ourselves, we can hand him over to the police when the time is right without worrying about fanfare. The media has a small attention span. They like news timely."

Sebastian realized the abbot was right on that matter. He swallowed and gave the impression of a nod.

"Keep JC's murder sealed inside our abbey," the father reiterated, "and I will permit you to pry into his death. I find that a suitable compromise, don't you?"

"How will I go about it?"

"I would think this would be one of your easier jobs. No one can come or go. All suspects are trapped within our walls."

"Won't the brothers figure out what I'm doing?"

Father Paolo sighed toward the cold fireplace. "I'm more aware than anyone of the channels of gossip that rove our corridors here. I'm the abbot. There will be talk. What matter? Let them know if you wish. They understand your inquisitive nature. Tell them you're investigating out of your own morbid curiosity, with the abbot's consent. You can keep your former police job and all that happened in Philadelphia hush-hush. I won't tell them. I haven't all these years."

"It could be dangerous for us here. Perhaps one of the brothers has fallen mentally ill, suffers from cabin fever or something, or has developed rage issues."

"Can you think of anyone who fits such a ludicrous description? Our most recent postulant is Brother Casey. This is his first winter here." The abbot grinned. "Do you think he's the one who lost his mind and killed Brother JC?"

"Never," Sebastian stated with a firm chin. "It couldn't be him."

"And it couldn't be you or me or Brother Lucien." The father flushed. "Lucien was with me during most of that night, going over administrative matters."

"Yes, Father."

The abbot stood, palms flat on his desk. "My decision is firm. If you choose to disobey, let me remind you of the ramifications for those who defy an abbot's command, stipulated by St. Benedict in his *Rule*. Shall I go over them?"

Sebastian understood well enough. Whoever listened to the abbot listened to the Lord. St. Benedict's fifteen-hundred-year-old text left no room for uncertainty. "…as the master gives the instruction, the disciple quickly puts into practice the fear of God."

Sebastian had lived by such codes his entire career, codes he'd been threatened with if he'd dared to break the mold, or was even perceived to. No people endured more stringent canons rammed down their throats than those in law enforcement. Rules piled one atop the other that formed the foundation of the police department, heralded through layers of power. Governing parties, the media, captains, and those on the street. Each distinctive. All applied with equal severity.

Inside the confines of the abbey, Sebastian also understood St. Benedict demanded mutual obedience. At some point, a truer compromise would have to be forged between him and the abbot.

For now, he acquiesced. "No, Father Paolo," he said into his shiny eyeglasses, "you do not need to clarify the consequences of disloyalty to me."

Father Paolo's voice softened. "I know I have assigned you a burdensome task, but it's not beyond your ability to bear the weight. Trust in God, and you will see an easy path to whoever has brought us disgrace at Mt. Ouray."

"Yes, Father."

"I'm glad we understand each other." He held out his hand for Sebastian to take. "Think of it as a gift I've given you. You can exercise your inquisitive nature without worry of my censure. Now go get some sleep. You'll need it."

When Sebastian left the abbot's private office, Brother Lucien was sprawled over a chair in front of one of the computers, snoozing like a well-fed armchair quarterback. Had he heard what had transpired between him and Father Paolo before nodding off? Was he merely pretending to sleep?

Already, Sebastian tasted the detective skills ripening on his tongue.

– XI –

THEIR vocal cords were loosening. The passing of twenty-four hours had allowed time for JC's awful death to settle in like a fog over the San Juan Mountains, and the brothers had acclimated to their new station—a faintly glowing world of murder and suspicion. In the absence of initial shock, another round of excitement had emerged. They sensed no one had come clean about the murder; the abbey grapevine would have coughed up something by now. It was in the air, a bad stink. The silent order could no longer seal their lips. Casey listened to his fellow brothers bantering while they plated their breakfasts. He found himself caught up in the speculation as much as any of them.

"Nothing like this has ever happened here. Not in the abbey's fifty-year history."

"Not too long ago, a visitor fell and hit his head, Brother Jerome," Brother George said, matching the brothers' hushed tones. "Slipped on the stone walkway out front after a drizzle. Died instantly." He placed a fat finger to his downturned mouth. "I think his wife sued the abbey, but lost."

"Brother Hubert once told me about the monk who fell down the steps in the cottage house. I forgot when. He was carrying soiled guest towels." Brother Rodel cringed. "Horrible to think."

"It was about twenty years ago," Brother Hubert mumbled.

"It's that curse," Brother Micah said, squeezing a spatula while he flipped over more fried potatoes before the stove. "The Dalakis Curse."

"There's no such thing as curses," Brother Eusebius said. "Accidents happen and people die. Doesn't mean a curse. The honorable Brother Thomas Merton, a Trappist monk like us, was electrocuted in a bathtub in Thailand while listening to a phonograph. Which reprehensible curse had struck him?"

"But this was no accident," Brother Lucien said.

"I must believe maybe it was," Brother George said, piling his plate with scrambled Egg Beaters and corn mash. "You should've seen poor Brother Augustine's face. Even he looks shaken, and he can't see or hear any better than a cave cricket."

"It's the curse. I sense it," Brother Micah reiterated.

Casey too had wondered about "the Dalakis Curse." Almost embarrassed he'd believed that the legend of black magic by the previous landowner might explain JC's death, he'd shaken himself and concentrated on obeying Father Paolo's dictum. Stick with the abbey routine. Help in the kitchen whenever requested, stay abreast of incoming discernment inquiries and prayer requests, keep wood stocked for the three fireplaces. *Ora et labora.* Prayer and work.

Only for a brief moment, when the reality of the unfolding events had seemed impossible to comprehend, did he entertain the fantasy of curses. Often magic made the most sense when logic failed to offer credible explanations.

In turn, Brother Sebastian had pushed his way into Casey's head. Casey had tried to maintain a civil disposition around him. Now, with JC—he gulped—out of the picture, he wanted to sit beside Sebastian again. Act as if nothing unpleasant had ever arisen between them or the abbey.

He wasn't among them that morning when the brothers, realizing Father Paolo might skip breakfast, had shifted their silence into soft chatter about JC's death. Sebastian had plated up before the others, ignoring age-old custom that the eldest monks serve themselves first. Casey hadn't even the chance to help him plate his food or pour his steaming black coffee. Trancelike, he'd shuffled about the kitchen. He'd glimpsed from brother to brother before walking off with his tray.

The odd circumstances of JC's death seemed to lie heavier upon Sebastian's shoulders than the others, like the way a knight might carry a lance in hopes of saving a kidnapped damsel. Was Sebastian mourning his lover?

"I'm sure there are no such things as curses," he said, reaching for a cold muffin and trying his best to keep his head clear of inane fantasies—whether diabolical hexes or handsome monks. "Deuteronomy says, fathers shall not be executed because of their children's sins, and children shall not be executed because of their fathers' sins. A curse, therefore, makes no sense."

"What makes you think God had a hand in this?" Brother Giles wheeled to the beginning of the food line and refilled his plate. "Perhaps a dark energy grabbed the hand of whoever did this."

Brother George gasped. "Brother Giles, you shouldn't say such things. God's hand is in everything."

"The devil stalks every corridor and lurks behind every tree." Brother Giles shrugged. "Maybe the killer is unaware of his actions."

Silence punctured their soft conversation. Eyeballs darted back and forth. Each brother held suspicions. Yet only one had committed the deed of a murderer.

"That's fantastical," Brother Lucien said, shaking the brothers from their stunted silence. "You're ranting on about possession."

"How much do you really know about Brother JC's death, Brother Jerome?" Brother Hubert peered at him behind his black-framed glasses. "Are you keeping anything from us?"

The fluorescent lighting accented the red blooming over Brother Jerome's pallid face and the bald spot on his head. While waiting for him to answer, Casey tried to savor the aroma of Brother Micah's cinnamon rolls basking under the warming lights. But they failed to relax him.

"I know as much as any of you," Brother Jerome said at last.

"Are you sure it wasn't an accident?"

Brother Lucien, standing behind Brother George in line and impatient, glowered. "Someone gave him a good larrup, Brother George, accept it."

"Was he really struck on the head?" Brother Rodel asked. "On purpose?"

"I've seen it before. I saw the signs." Brother Jerome gave a succinct nod. "Yes, I'm certain he was struck on the head. Whether or not on purpose, well, that's not for me to say."

"Do you think anyone has come forward?" Brother Hubert asked.

Most of them shook their heads. "No one ever will," Brother Micah said. "The mystery of his death and his killer, along with how and why he'd come here, will be forever sealed...."

The others followed Brother Micah's gaze to the door of the nearby walk-in freezer. Casey noticed many of them visibly shudder. He, too, felt a creepiness inch up his spine while they spoke about a young man whose body they stored mere feet away from them.

"We're talking nonsense," Brother Eusebius said. "Let's mind the Grand Silence. The abbot might be in for breakfast any moment. You saw his expression at Vigils. More sour than I've ever seen. If he hears us speaking in this manner, no telling what he'll do. He'll remand all of us back to our cells."

The brothers heeded Brother Eusebius's warning. They remained quiet, plating their food and carrying their trays to far-flung parts of the abbey, where they ate in solitude. When he'd finally spooned out his portions, Casey took his tray to the cloister overlooking the garden. He sat beside Sebastian. This time, there was no need for coyness.

They ate shoulder to shoulder on the terracotta floor, uttering not a word. The radiators' cadenced humming shrouded them with gentle warmth. Outside in the morning darkness, the snowfall had settled to a steady downpour of crystal dust. With the monumental storms of the past few weeks, the shrubs and fountain were now impossible to distinguish.

Sebastian's lake blue eyes remained fixed on the darkened windowpane. He chewed methodically, swallowing with a deliberateness that somehow delighted Casey. Then he turned to Casey.

His toothy grin spoke volumes. He might have been preaching from the high altar, swathed in his flowing white cowl, highlighted in the spray of sparkling golden chalices, and gazing at none other than Casey.

At that moment, Casey knew. He belonged to Mt. Ouray and to Sebastian. Sebastian was not a test of his devotion but an accoutrement. The whiff of a scented candle in a breeze or the rainbow cast across the chapel floor by the stained glass windows. He was as glorious as all that, perhaps more.

Happily, Sebastian's blue eyes held no personal remorse. Like all of them, he regretted JC's tragic death and feared whoever had defiled the commandments, but the downturn of his mouth that cut a fine pleat below his bottom lip disclosed something more than lament.

Sebastian hadn't minced words when he'd confessed to Casey in the library that JC had mostly baffled him. "A living and breathing mystery," he'd said. He cared for JC as one might an old school acquaintance. No more.

Casey envisioned them as old men, confiding in a postulant or novice about the days past, about the "dark day" they'd found a body in the walk-in freezer. Pumping life into the legend of "the Dalakis Curse." But always—without fail—Sebastian by his side. Part of his life. His brother. Forever. Growing old together until well into the midcentury when outside, where Christianity faced a final death, they still lived behind the monastery's secluded walls. Safe and secure. He wouldn't care about the civilian world. He'd have Sebastian.

But did Sebastian share such daydreams? Did he want to remain in the abbey for the rest of his life? Casey couldn't imagine what he'd do if Sebastian ever decided not to profess his vows and leave. Casey might as well have never boarded the Greyhound bus in Hutchinson.

Casey sighed, permitted a gentle smile to crease his face. He wanted badly to rest a hand on Sebastian's thigh. To reassure him. So often he'd looked to Sebastian for hope. How strange to be the one to want to provide comfort.

He set his tray on the floor and stretched his legs, waiting for Sebastian to finish. Sebastian had spent so much of the morning brooding, his food and coffee had gone cold. Casey gestured with his head down the corridor toward the kitchen and made to take the tray from him. Sebastian smiled again, shook his head. No, he did not need Casey to warm his breakfast.

Casey wiggled his toes, protruding from his sandals, and noticed how he needed to trim his nails. He probably should have Brother Hubert, the abbey's barber, cut his hair too. Casey preferred to keep his below the ear. He liked Sebastian's close cropped, which drew attention to the firmness of his jaw and the solidity of his features. Beyond protuberances, his nose and chin seemed extensions of his face, with spirits of their own, as did his hands and feet. Yet they worked in harmony. The purposeful way he'd lift his head, like a dancer at a barre or a lion testing the air for danger.

Sebastian did that now. With his chin raised, he inhaled and licked his lips.

"Are you certain you didn't see anything suspicious the night of JC's death?"

His voice, which always sounded as if he were chewing on a mouthful of scrumptious, hearty stew, tickled Casey for a moment. Then he shook himself. "Nothing out of the ordinary," he said softly. "I was playing my flute."

Sebastian smiled. "Yes, I know. I was listening."

Flushing, Casey said, "Should you be asking me this, Brother Sebastian?"

"There's something I should share with you, Casey," he whispered, although the cavernous corridor seemed to pick up his words and carry them afar.

Casey's heart drummed against his chest. "What is it?"

"No one has come forward about JC's death."

Casey looked toward the window. "We figured."

"There's more. Father Paolo has asked me to snoop around to find who killed him."

He snapped his head around to face Sebastian. So that's why he appeared overwhelmed. The father had relegated the responsibility of JC's murder onto him. There was no need to ask why Father Paolo had asked Sebastian to investigate, as opposed to anyone else in the abbey. Of all of them, Brother Sebastian possessed the most astuteness. Sharp, bright, and authoritative in a good way. A true old-fashioned leader. One Casey could trust. The kind of mentor he'd sought his entire life. He'd make a better abbot than Father Paolo, Casey dared to think, followed by a rapid mental muttering from Psalm 95 to beseech forgiveness.

"I've seen you, Casey," he said. "The past few months, I've studied how you look at everything. You're sharp-eyed. Perhaps more than me. I could use a man like you. Would you care to assist me?"

Casey swallowed hard, drugged by Sebastian's caramel-smooth voice. "Assist? I would like that. I'll do whatever I can to help you."

"All I ask is that you keep your eyes and ears peeled."

"I will."

"I know you," Sebastian said. "I can trust you."

"Of course you can."

"I'm sure the others will find out in due time," Sebastian said. "But let's try to keep this between you and me for as long as we can."

A secret. Between the two of them. Casey's head swirled with the thrill. "Sure," he said. "But shouldn't Father Paolo notify the authorities?"

Sebastian shook his head. "He has his ways."

"I guess there's no use, anyway, what with the storms."

Sebastian gazed into the snowy garden, his food and coffee cold and forlorn on his tray. "Nothing to do about that now." He smiled at Casey. "I'm glad you're on board. But don't ask too many questions or make yourself obvious," he said with a solid nod of his poised head. "Be yourself. Keep alert."

"Yes, Sebastian. Sure thing. You can count on me."

"Good." He stood with a crack of his lanky bones. "Let's clean our dishes and head to Lauds. And remember now, you're my secondary."

CASEY sat at his morning work station in the administrative office, answering prayer requests and postulant inquiries, eying the computer across the room accessible only to Brother Hubert, and most likely Brother Lucien and Father Paolo. They used it to update the abbey's website and keep the books. And to do "research" for articles. He was compelled to help out Sebastian in more ways than to "keep his eyes and ears peeled." Sebastian had given him an important role, and Casey would rather die than disappointment him.

He might be able to find something useful on the Internet. Something on JC. Any information about the man they still knew scarcely anything about. A clue that might answer why he'd come to them—leading to the answer of who and why someone had murdered him.

Stowed away behind the door to the office, Casey stewed. Save for the occasional indifferent brush from Brother Lucien, who came and went from Father Paolo's private office, Casey was left devoid of interference from anyone. Briefly, he wondered what Brother Lucien might do if Casey were to strut to the off-limits computer and try to log on. Was there a way to access it without a password?

Brother Lucien disappeared into the abbot's office and shut the door, followed by the click of the lock. Casey stared at the door. Heat on his cheeks made him look away. Many times he'd sat in the office when the lock to the abbot's door had clicked with Brother Lucien and, more recently, JC on the other side, and he'd tried not to imagine what went on.

Typical dread tracked his thoughts. He'd come to Mt. Ouray seeking a life of contemplation and seclusion, dedicated to prayer and labor. To do what the Trappists demanded, willingly and openly. How could he imagine making love with one of his fellow monks?

He threw his head back and beseeched God for mercy, uttering a few verses of Psalm 23. The pain of love—the worst punishment man could endure.

He almost wished Sebastian had not lived among them. He'd have no physical attraction to any of the others. Then again, if not for Brother Sebastian, Casey's life at the abbey would rumble past in isolation and drudgery.

And Sebastian needed him. Sensations as glorious as the breezes in the alpine meadows had swathed Casey when Sebastian had appealed for his assistance. He was his secondary, whatever that meant. But it sounded nice. *Eyes and ears peeled.*

On the computer screen, Casey spied the corners of his mouth lift. A rose in bloom set on time lapse. He glanced over his shoulder to ensure the father and Brother Lucien remained in the private office and did not detect his impish grin. He needed to focus on work. Prayer requests demanded attention. Discerning "healthy, virile young men" begged for guidance.

The phone rang. Startled, he lifted the receiver. "Mt. Ouray Abbey at Monfrere, how may I assist you?" A woman's voice. From New Mexico. She wanted to know if they were taking guest reservations for summer. "We don't take reservations until the first of May, ma'am," he told her. "We'll be happy to assist you if you call back then." She thanked him, and he wished her, "God Bless."

While speaking with the woman, he'd toyed with the idea of whispering for help. Insisting that she notify the proper authorities on a murder that had taken place inside their abbey. But what would the father do to him once he found out? Would he be forever separated from Sebastian? Besides, it was Sebastian who'd requested help from him. In all likelihood he'd be defying Sebastian's trust as well. Best to mind Sebastian and keep his mouth sealed.

Alone in the still office, the rebellious desire to help Sebastian grew stronger. Sebastian would be proud of him if he were to find anything on JC. Perhaps he could use it to lure more of Sebastian's attention. Sebastian would appreciate Casey's ingenuity. He'd think him a good soul. Smart and forward thinking. And the quicker he learned that JC was nothing but a scoundrel who'd come to the abbey to steal from them and cause trouble and had it coming to him....

Casey breathed. He was acting worse than the vagabond he'd created in his mind.

Holding his breath, he glanced back and forth between both doors to ensure no one was coming. From experience, he knew Father Paolo and Brother Lucien would be at least fifteen minutes. He bit back his apprehension and tiptoed to Brother Hubert's computer.

Another quick glance to make sure no eyes spied him and, without sitting, he tapped the keyboard. A light clank met his ears. For a moment he worried someone might hear. He peeked over his shoulders. Still alone.

The first sight on the computer display: a box requiring a password. He tried the obvious, the name "Hubert." Unsuccessful. Brother Huber's last name, "Nusselbaum." Nope. "Mtouray" also failed to grant him access. He drummed his chin with his fingertips. What other options had he? "Fatherpaolo." Fail. "Lucien." Again, nothing.

He was about to walk off, dejected, when an idea whispered to him. Ensuring once again no one saw, he gently opened the top drawer to the desk. Notebooks, papers, envelopes, and pencils were jammed inside. He slid the drawer open wider and rummaged through the contents, stopping when his hand hit a piece of paper with scribbling on it. Odd scribbling. Different from normal English. Gibberish mixed with numbers. Casey nearly chuckled out loud.

Exactly what he'd been searching for. Passwords. He guessed the middle-aged Brother Hubert might've jotted down one for the computer in case he'd forget. But he'd written five. Casey inhaled, tried the first. Then the second. He gnawed on his knuckles, thinking of the old adage "Third time's the charm." The computer lit up, blue and alive, simulating the Rocky Mountain summer sky.

He recoiled when the computer sang out. He flinched back, expecting Father Paolo to rush in to investigate. His heart beat against his chest, and his fingers trembled when he pulled up the browser. He waited. Silence behind Father Paolo's door, save for an occasional moan. The clock above the wall cabinet ticked. He should have several more minutes to spare before Father Paolo and Brother Lucien finished whatever they were doing.

Temptation to research more than JC stalled Casey's shaky hands over the keypad. From the first time he'd met Sebastian last summer, he'd wanted to research his name, find out more about him. He often did so with the men he'd fancied back home or at college.

Unable to hold back, he typed "Sebastian Harkin." No hits related to his Sebastian appeared until he came to the second page. He pulled up one. Then another. No way was any of it true. But there it was. In black and white, sometimes blue and orange. One from the Philadelphia *Inquirer*. Another from the *City Paper*. Must be lies. Conjecture and yellow journalism.

Under "images" he found Sebastian's photograph, the one they used in the abbey's website, smiling above his white cowl. A surge of love swept Casey. Then there were other images. He was dressed differently, dressed in business suits. Captions underneath confirmed he'd worked for the Philadelphia Police Department, matching the descriptions of the articles he'd scanned. In one photograph he looked dejected, beaten. A photographer had taken it for a newspaper's front page. And there was another one of him in full uniform, smiling for a department photo.

He clicked out of the browser and reproached himself while he fumbled for the cache to remove traces of his search. He was unsurprised to find that Brother Hubert had been conducting searches for missing persons. Was he trying to impress Sebastian with his efforts to uncover vital information? Or had Father Paolo done the research? Casey was about to return to his own research on JC, when an odd group of websites left in the cache stole his attention. Sites he'd heard of but never visited.

Out of curiosity, he clicked one. He nearly dropped to his knees when a site popped up full of naked men engaged in sex. That must be what those other passwords were for. Brother Hubert, or maybe even Father Paolo or Brother Lucien, who also had access to the computer, might have created them when they joined the adult sites.

He recalled the friend of his mother whispering about her run-in with Internet porn while working for the local Catholic parish. The offending priest had forgotten to delete the website from his desktop.

Though he wanted to look away, the pictures reawakened his longing for Sebastian. One couple reminded him of the two of them— the way he'd fantasized they might look together: a tall and redheaded man with one who was shorter and dark-featured.

He was tempted to try the other passwords and view more, but knew he shouldn't. Besides, Casey wanted more than the illusion of being with Brother Sebastian. Either the real thing or nothing: it was one of the reasons why he'd figured monastic life might suit him. He could go without if need be. And he still wanted to do research on JC.

The murmur of voices from Father Paolo's office snapped him to attention. His cheeks burning, he deleted the page and signed off the computer. Safe at his desk, he flashed Brother Lucien a winsome smile when he stepped back into the main office, his scapular askew.

"Is everything all right, Brother Casey?"

"Yes, Brother Lucien. Everything is fine."

Brother Lucien left the office, and Casey cursed himself for allowing his curiosity to squander his chance at helping Sebastian. Some secondary he made. But what of his discovery about Sebastian? He needed to find an appropriate time and place to confront Sebastian and get his side of the story.

– XII –

FATHER PAOLO had not excused Sebastian from his regular abbey duties, so Sebastian waited patiently for his work period to end before he could slink off undetected and examine the abbey for clues. He spent the last two hours beside Brother Eusebius, fashioning rosaries while encased in silence. Though the hunt for JC's killer excited him, it also repulsed him. He had to live with an escalating distrust. With each speculation of who had killed JC and how and for what reason, he must accept that he brushed shoulders with the killer each day—standing in line to plate his meals, seated or standing at the pews for Mass and the seven prayer stations, and now, working side by side with one of his best friends inside the abbey, Brother Eusebius.

He wanted to gaze at him, to use his skills and decipher his thoughts from the movement of his eyes, the twitch of his mouth. Sebastian eyed the flex of his hands while he toiled. Steady, committed to his task. Brother Eusebius had expressed contempt for JC—but many of them had. Difficult for Sebastian to forget the burning behind Brother Eusebius's dark eyes when he'd confessed his loathing of the sexual dalliances that took place under their noses. Could those hands, which worked with such dedication to fashion rosaries, kill a man?

All the brothers fell under suspicion—all except for the feeble Brother Augustine. Eeny, meeny, miney mo. Which one had done it? To the innocent brothers, Sebastian, too, was a suspect. Even more reason to keep quiet about his snooping. They'd accuse him of dishonesty and concealing his own tracks.

Pleased with the quiet of the sacristy, Sebastian allowed his mind to ruminate over JC's death and the possibilities while his hands worked analogously to Brother Eusebius's. Reliving his stint back at the PPD, he made a mental checklist of feasible scenarios, pieces of the puzzle he might have overlooked.

Odd he'd found JC wearing a cowl, with his street clothes underneath, along with his sneakers. JC had foregone wearing the Trappist garments days before his death. No reason why he'd have worn a cowl in the middle of the night when no one would have even seen him. The blood pattern on the inside of the cowl indicated the killer might have dressed JC after he'd bludgeoned him. Streaks of blood went from the neck to the waist, along with a spot on the inside of the hood that matched the wound on his left temple.

He clutched a completed rosary, one he'd been working on for most the morning. Normally, after two years of practice, he'd finish an average of three rosaries each work period. The feel of the coffee beans, the bite of the cross in his palm brought a reality to their ordeal.

In the name of the Father and of the Son and of the Holy Spirit... I believe in God the Father, Almighty, Maker of heaven and earth....

He prayed the rosary the way he had when he'd worked cases back in Philadelphia. Many of his fellow officers, most of them Irish, Italian, Puerto Rican, Polish, uttered Catholic prayers for guidance.

A quick glance at Brother Eusebius, and Sebastian realized he'd mumbled aloud. He opened his mouth wider to apologize, but Brother Eusebius had begun to join him in prayer. He too had clasped a near-complete rosary to his chest and recited the Apostles' Creed, followed by the Our Father.

Their prayers fizzled, and they continued their toil in silence. After work, Sebastian popped into his cell and dug among the contents of his small chest of meager possessions. He pushed aside the pocket Bible he'd carried with him during college, the Flyers baseball cap he sometimes wore when he worked outdoors in summer under the harsh mountain sun.

He found it, still secured inside the small box where he'd stowed it when he'd left the police force four years ago. He took it out and lifted it to his eyes. The faint light filtering through the window glinted off the stainless steel.

Many of his fellow officers had worn St. Michael pendants around their necks. And always made the sign of the cross instinctively when a call dispatched them to investigate another homicide, usually one per day in Philadelphia. Clenched in his fist, the medal magnified the resolution to conquer a brutal world.

The reality of the situation tapped him on the shoulder. JC had been murdered. Inside their abbey. By one of his fellow brothers.

Without any further delay, he draped the chain around his neck and slipped the medal out of sight inside his tunic. The cold chain sent a shiver along his spine. Too much time had lapsed since he'd relished the tickle against his chest.

Sebastian was more than a Trappist monk, a fellow brother. He now donned the garb from his past. A homicide detective. Suspicious of each of them.

By Retire, Sebastian had the quiet of the abbey to search for something useful. While everyone was tucked inside their cells, he walked the corridors, looking for a probable path the killer might have taken when he'd moved the body to the freezer. Obviously, the body had been moved. He suspected the crime had taken place inside JC's cell. But who among them possessed the strength to have carried him from there to the freezer? Only himself, Casey, Brothers Micah, Lucien, Eusebius….

What if he didn't act alone? Had two brothers carried the body into the walk-in freezer?

He tried to engage his old investigative and profiling skills. Did JC bring out desires in one of the brothers that would cause him to murder? Which one of the brothers had been ready to snap? If that was the motive, who might be next? Casey was the youngest—and by far the most attractive. Did they have a sociopathic serial killer on their hands? Someone who'd succumbed to the harsh, isolated winters high in the mountains and was looking to strike again?

Little intelligence had been obtained from the slipshod medical examination Brother Jerome had conducted. Brother Jerome had admitted he had scant forensic experience. But Sebastian, focusing on the laid-out body of JC, had understood what he'd gazed at. The killer had struck JC's left temple with some kind of blunt instrument, causing him to pass out, and then carried his body into the freezer, where he'd eventually asphyxiated or froze to death. The blow was dead on, no scraping or cutting. A solid hit with level force from a wide swing. Sebastian wanted to see more. Persuading the abbot to allow another medical examination might prove more difficult than the investigation itself.

He walked down the long corridor outside the cells, acting as if he were heading to the bathroom in case any of the monks were to emerge and ask why he prowled about. Their doors were closed tight, including JC's former cell. He opened the door, half expecting to find JC's ghost sitting on the edge of the neatly made bed. Although he shared a wall with JC's cell and hadn't heard a commotion the night of his murder, the attack might have come swiftly and been nearly soundless. Plus, there had been a storm that night. Glancing around for what seemed the tenth time, he hoped a clue that he'd missed before might jump out from hiding.

Faint moonlight cast a muted drabness on the already bland, tiny room that smelled of the familiar mildew, with a lingering hint of sandalwood. It looked untouched from when he'd last gazed inside. The wall shelf sat empty and pitiful. The chair pushed snug under the desk. His mind wandered, churning, deliberating. He shut the door tight and slinked away.

His feet carried him farther into the abbey. He searched for a blood trail, markings along the corridors. Any signs of unusual scuff marks. Probing for clues, reliving his old steps through the rougher sections of Philadelphia's northeastern neighborhoods.

He found himself looking into the kitchen. Brother Micah had scrubbed the counters and the chopping block, set upon the back wall, and the dinner pots and pans were stowed away and he'd shut off the lights for the night. Everything exactly as it should be.

Sebastian opened the walk-in freezer. Cold air bit at his exposed toes. The floor was covered with tracks. All with the same sandal sole pattern, yet different sizes. More than Brother Micah—who, as the abbey's cellarer, would have reason to walk in and out of the freezer— had tramped about. Even remnants of Delores's paw prints crisscrossed the floor.

The crime scene had been horribly corrupted. Captain Terry Reems back in Philadelphia would've chewed him out for disturbing the integrity of the scene. But his mind, fastened on the perspective of a monk's when he'd discovered JC's battered body, hadn't registered normal investigative protocol.

Spreading frost coated the trash bags that cocooned JC. He remembered carrying JC inside from the snowstorm and washing him and enveloping him in blankets while he was still unconscious. He had wanted to augment his body temperature. That no longer mattered.

Before replacing him in the freezer, he had placed JC's bloody cowl in a bag and taken it to his cell, where he'd examined it numerous times, but without modern forensic technology at his disposal, the blood markings meant little, other than JC had most likely been killed before he was wearing the cowl. He had to work primitive. Or, as Captain Reems used to call it, "slogging lean."

He scouted around JC's body. Perhaps the creepiest crime scene Sebastian had examined—and he'd examined many. He laid a hand to his heaving chest, where underneath his tunic hung his St. Michael medal. His increasing breath came in thick bursts of hoary steam. He gazed around. Nothing in the freezer spit up any more clues than the last time he'd checked.

Because the body had frozen, he and Brother Jerome could not definitively determine an exact time of death from hypostasis or rigor mortis, but there was little doubt the killer had struck when everyone was asleep in their cells during the night, sometime before the call for Rise.

The killer probably wanted to conceal the body temporarily, and then once he had the opportunity, toss it someplace undetected. Maybe even the incinerator. Killers loved incinerators and dumpsters. But why hadn't the killer taken the body there directly? In a fit of desperation, the killer had wrapped the body and shoved it in the freezer until he could clear his mind. Or maybe he knew well enough that a human body could not disintegrate in temperatures less than fourteen hundred degrees Fahrenheit.

Sebastian closed the freezer door and peered around the kitchen. He switched on the light, waiting a good few seconds for the fluorescent bulbs to flicker to full brightness. Everything looked in its proper place. Brother Micah made sure his kitchen remained spotless and tidy. If any clues had remained, they'd been long scrubbed away.

Sebastian held his breath. He stepped closer to the magnetic wall strip that held Brother Micah's knives. He'd seen the knives so often, he hadn't thought to look. He'd even used them himself when asked to help prep meals. They lined up in order, except for a single strange gap.

But what did a missing knife have to do with JC's murder? The killer had bludgeoned him with a yet unknown object. He placed a finger to his head and scratched to pull blood into his brain. Throat clearing behind him forced him around.

"What are you doing?" Brother Micah said, peering at Sebastian.

"I was just thinking of getting something to help me sleep, some warm milk or hot cocoa." Sebastian forced a smile, tried to look nonchalant.

Brother Micah smiled back. "Can I make something for you?"

"I've actually changed my mind. But thank you for asking." He nodded over his right shoulder. "Did you know you're missing a knife?"

Brother Micah screwed up his eyes and inspected the knife strip closer. "You're right. My fillet knife is gone."

Sebastian had been right. "I know how you prize your kitchen utensils. I hope it didn't break. When was the last time you used it?"

"A few days ago. Saturday, I believe. I sometimes use it to peel apples when I make applesauce. I find it easier to control than the peeler, which was designed for righties. I didn't break it. I don't recall anyone else using it. And I emptied the dishwasher firsthand."

"Maybe it'll turn up."

Brother Micah stood motionless, his unfocused eyes on the wall of knives. "The ladies' auxiliary in Monfrere gifted it to the abbey two summers ago," he said. "They're very expensive, from what I gather. Made in Massachusetts. A two-hundred-year-old manufacturer."

"Perhaps you can order another one. A single knife can't be that expensive."

"Yes, I suppose I could."

"Should I shut the light off, or are you staying to get whatever it is that brought you into the kitchen?"

Shaking his head, Brother Micah smiled like an impish boy. "I've changed my mind too."

"Then I'll walk you to your cell, Brother Micah."

"Certainly, Brother Sebastian."

Sebastian bade Brother Micah good night by his cell and returned to his own, where he sat at his desk in the dark. The howling winds outside only seemed to jumble his head. He pulled his blinds shut and put his face in his hands.

On Saturday, Sebastian ventured into the basement, where the brothers incinerated their trash during the winter. In summer, a service hauled out the garbage they couldn't compost. The thin smokestack, the most visible edifice after the bell tower and which they used only during tourist season, puffed dark clouds into the wintery sky whenever they burned their garbage once a week—Saturdays.

Sebastian had volunteered to cart the trash down in the service elevator and burn it for an excuse to rummage for clues. JC had been killed Tuesday night. Had anyone tried to discard vital evidence before the Saturday burn?

"Brother Sebastian."

Sebastian glanced up right before opening the primary chamber, the flashlight he'd concealed inside his scapular squeezed in hand.

Casey approached him. "I followed you here. I wanted to speak with you alone."

"Do you have news about JC?"

"I went onto the computer in the administrative office, the one accessible only to a few others. I found the security password hidden away in a desk drawer."

"But I asked you to stay out of trouble."

"I had a perfect opportunity, so I took it."

"Did you find anything?"

Casey shook his head, his eyes downturned and his cheeks darkening. "Not before Brother Lucien came. Unfortunately, I can't access that computer anymore. Someone already changed the security password. Do you think it's the killer?"

Two mice scurried past them and into a dark recess. *Need to get Delores down here*, Sebastian thought, scratching his head. "Father Paolo probably detected someone using the computer and he changed the password, that's all."

"I don't think I cleared out the cache to cover my tracks, I'm afraid. Or maybe they always change the password on a recurring basis. That would explain why Brother Hubert would have to write so many. But I can't find any new ones left in the desk like last time. I can recheck later, if you want."

Sebastian peered behind Casey's shoulder toward the elevator shaft. "That won't be necessary. I doubt they'd leave the passwords lying around again. Father Paolo's too edgy about anyone on the outside finding out about JC."

"I can almost understand why," Casey said, carrying on Sebastian's reflective tone. "Imagine what the publicity would be like if the media learned a murder took place inside a monastery. Journalists can be vicious hounds. They'll twist the truth and turn it into a worse scandal than it already is, making it into nothing but entertainment."

Sebastian examined Casey's features, obscure in the basement's murky lighting. There was something all-knowing in those chocolate brown eyes of his. "That's very true," Sebastian whispered. "Very true indeed."

"I'm sorry I couldn't have been more helpful."

Sebastian set aside his flashlight. "You've done fine, thank you. In the meantime, you can help me rummage through the garbage bags before I torch everything."

Casey scooted closer. A strange, excited grin stretched the smooth skin around his mouth. "You think someone might have wanted to burn evidence?"

"Exactly. Now you sort those two bags, and I'll look through these. Careful, now."

For several minutes they dug among the trash until Sebastian sighed and wiped the sweat from his brow. "Nothing here. What about you?"

"Just garbage. Lots of potato skins and apple peels and coffee grinds." Casey shook his hands free of the grime.

Sebastian scanned the flashlight at the trash by Casey's feet. "You're right. Looks like common garbage. Let's check out the incinerator. There might be something left behind from the last burn."

"But JC was murdered on Tuesday. We don't burn trash until today."

"I wondered if I had smelled smoke Tuesday night. I'm thinking someone might have come down here in the middle of the night. Do you recall smelling anything?"

"I wish I did."

Sebastian recalled his strange dream the night of JC's murder. He'd seen Casey playing the flute by a cliff above a tree-filled gully, a bright angel surrounded by the dark clouds racing above. Then he realized the dark clouds were billows of smoke, and a raging forest fire had snuck up behind him. He remembered the stench of smoke, so real he could taste it. The abbey's three wood-burning fireplaces never created such an odor, even when lit simultaneously. The incinerator, when torched on Saturdays with the low air pressure of a cold winter day, often did. Had the smell of someone lighting the incinerator filled Sebastian's dreams?

With a quick flex of his wrist, Sebastian aimed the flashlight inside the chamber. The brothers had burned much garbage throughout the winter. Mounds of ashes and charcoal chunks stood as relics to discarded moments in time. The frugal brothers burned mostly foodstuffs, cardboard boxes, and a meager amount of paper products. He roved the flashlight along the bottom and into the back and around the edges, where the less burnable trash piled up. The incinerator was still warm from the last burn, which Sebastian believed had been Tuesday night.

"When I found JC in the walk-in freezer," Sebastian said, his voice echoing inside the chamber, "he was wearing a cowl over his street clothes. Why would he be in a cowl in the middle of the night? His jacket and knapsack are both missing from his room."

"You think the murderer tried to burn them to make it look like JC had left like he planned?"

"I hope to find out."

Sebastian also hoped to find whatever blunt instrument the killer had used to strike JC on his left temple, along with the missing fillet knife. He glanced over his shoulder at Casey standing watch. He paced, peered around the corner toward the elevator and stairwell, wrung his hands. More nervous than Sebastian. Perhaps he shouldn't have enlisted his help. Too much for him to handle.

But Casey he trusted. That's why he'd asked him to be his secondary. Too bad he could no longer access the computer. Maybe Sebastian should talk to the abbot about that. He did request he look into JC's murder. Computers proved instrumental in any good, modern investigation.

Sebastian shoved his head deeper inside the chamber, almost as if he wanted to suffocate those troublesome notions. Stink of soot and cinders and rancid garbage made him turn up his nose.

A strange thrill exalted him. The hairs on his nape stood erect. He wanted to pull Casey closer in a sudden rush of good feeling. Someone had murdered a guest of theirs, yes, but only Sebastian had the gifts to solve the riddle. He searched and prodded and penetrated, like he had for eight years before being forced out of the PPD. But he understood his expanding confidence, not the horrendous crime, tickled him.

"Grab me that poker."

Casey handed the poker to Sebastian, and Sebastian raked among the ashes and debris to see what lay underneath. He pulled closer to his view a strange looking half-dollar-sized object. He laid the poker aside and stood to get a better look at the object in the light.

"What is it?"

"A buckle of some sort," Sebastian said. "Partially melted, but clearly a buckle. Made from tough polyurethane. Hard to burn. Not to mention poisonous."

"You think it's the buckle from JC's knapsack?"

Sebastian grinned at Casey. "That's my guess. I can't think of anything else. But who knows how long it's been buried in there. Could be from anything."

He scavenged through more of the debris. "Here's something extra." He pulled out a thin, slinky object about two feet in length.

"It's a zipper, looks like," Casey said.

"Long enough to fit a coat about the size JC wore. Not sure what all this means, other than it confirms my suspicions." Glancing back inside the chamber, he said, "Doesn't seem to be much else here. We better head back upstairs before everyone thinks we've fallen in."

Casey and Sebastian loaded the primary chamber, after which Sebastian secured the loading door, struck a match to the firebox, and stepped back to watch the flames fill the chamber.

They met again at lunch, a quick passing in the corridors, at dinner, and then after Vespers in the laundry room, where Brother Hubert trimmed their hair. Afterward, Casey shadowed Sebastian into the bathroom, the way he had dozens of times before. So much had transpired between them with the investigation, it seemed odd to Sebastian not to speak to him during those times. Swathed in a knowing manner, they grinned at each other more than usual. Hidden secrets prowled behind those furtive smiles. Did Sebastian dare add more?

He stood by the shower stalls and turned, flushing, as Casey moved to slip out of his sandals. From his acute peripheral vision, Sebastian watched him uncinch his bathrobe and pull it off his shoulders. He shifted his gaze when Casey turned back from hanging the robe on the wall hook.

He'd seen it before. The boxer briefs that Casey liked to wear under his monastic garb. The kind that, on the appropriate wearer, might accentuate the curve of the thighs, the subtle muscles of the hamstrings, the roundness of the butt cheeks. Casey was one of those people.

The sheer tautness of the white fabric against Casey's backside stole Sebastian's breath. And when Casey stripped off his underwear and hung it over his robe, the sight of his exposed backside drained spit from his mouth.

Sebastian looked away again and waited to hear Casey crank on the jet behind him. By the volume of the rush of water, he could tell that Casey hadn't bothered to pull the curtain shut like he normally would. He was watching Sebastian. Spying on him. Waiting.

Sebastian could linger no longer. He yanked off his bathrobe, balled it on the bench, and stepped inside the stall directly opposite Casey. He, too, dared to leave the shower curtain open, but kept his back to Casey. Hot ringing in his ears converged with the first blast of warm water across his shoulders and back.

He stretched his legs and arms, his hands busy lathering his body. Finally, he opened his eyes over his right shoulder, looking toward Casey. Sebastian's instincts proved true. Casey was staring, ogling him. Sebastian rotated fully, met the force of his gaze, a pair of headlights blinding him.

Water fell over Casey's newly trimmed hair and ran along his chest and across his sinewy stomach and pelvis. Keeping his eyes glued on Sebastian, he lathered himself with the soap. His flesh glistened, imitating the most luxurious silk. Suds slid along his arms, chest, legs.

Sebastian fixed on Casey, waiting to see which one would flinch first. An impassioned standoff ensued.

Steam built up around them. New blood filled Sebastian. He did not try to conceal his partial arousal, should Casey see through the mist. Sebastian wanted to reach across the way and touch his sleek flesh. His hand trembled by his side. Soapy bubbles tickled his chest. He was aware of his lengthening shaft. He kept his eyes fastened on Casey, whose form fluctuated with the expanding steam.

The muted scrape of someone's sandals on the bathroom floor stole away their attention. Casey jumped first, drew shut the curtain in a spray of soap and water. Sebastian rinsed quickly, shut off the jet, and covered himself in a towel.

Brother Eusebius was filling a sink basin with water. His toiletry bag sat on the counter below the mirror. Acting nonchalant, Sebastian dried off by the bench while Brother Eusebius shaved. Sebastian, sensing Brother Eusebius was staring at him in the mirror, threw on his robe and scurried off for his cell.

LATER, during Retire, Sebastian lay in bed, eyes wide open. His mind stayed glued to Casey and what he'd seen of him earlier in the shower.

For the first time in many weeks, he loosened the belt on his tunic and submitted to his own touch.

– XIII –

CHANTING voices filled the chapel. Crying out to Heaven. Beseeching for peace, for an inward understanding of all that embodied pure knowledge.

A week had passed since that horrible day of finding JC's body in the walk-in freezer, and Ash Wednesday descended over them like a faraway truth pushing against dreams. Harsh, cold winds outside shook them from their stupor. Confusion and suspicions grew.

Sebastian studied their faces, eyes, body language. Even old, crippled Brother Augustine, whom Brother George had wheeled to the chapel for the special Mass. One of them held onto a singular notion: Guilt. But none imparted anything more than incredulity. Casey showed signs of shame—his head low, eyes slightly closed and mouth drooping. But certainly his expression came from what had occurred between them in the shower room on Saturday, not from the guilt of a murderer.

Sebastian didn't share his shame. Maybe he experienced regret that things couldn't go further. Or frustration that he'd opened himself to vulnerabilities, the ones he'd hoped to keep capped forever. And disappointment that he might have dragged poor Casey into the same arena that he loathed whenever Father Paolo misled naïve postulants. But not shame.

He didn't wish to speak to Casey about what had happened. He didn't like to share his feelings; his actions spoke for themselves. And now Lent sat upon their shoulders, ushering in a new level of austerity, a new season of self-restraint. He and Casey had exposed themselves to each other in the shower room in an act of finality before the going without. Their personal Fat Tuesday—played out on a Saturday afternoon with a slap of rushing water and hazy steam.

Father Paolo read from Scripture. The Lord's message enveloped Sebastian. On the police force, he'd used the power of God to pull him through the ugliness of crime—and the loneliness of his personal life. He'd hope and pray. Was there a way to vindicate JC's death and perhaps save the brother responsible?

In some ways, prayer had become a habit. He'd been doing it since he was a boy. God could not abandon him now, after he'd devoted so much of his life to asking for guidance. Not when the abbey needed him more than ever.

Why had JC uttered the name Manny?

Did the misplaced fillet knife factor into the crime?

Had the killer snatched it to kill again?

What object had he used to strike JC? Had he smashed it over his head in a fit of rage, disgusted with JC for his rude behavior, like the rest of them? And where had he discarded it? There were few hiding places in the abbey. Not even the incinerator could conceal hard evidence.

Yet the most anguishing reflection on Sebastian's mind was this: No one had come forward to claim responsibility a week after his crime. A Trappist, even if he'd lost control in a blinding rage, must know the importance of renouncing his sin before God and his fellow brothers. Unless....

Unless the brother was a sociopath and lacked the normal human conscience needed to understand the severity of his crime. Sebastian had stared into the eyes of psychopaths before. None of the brothers exhibited the empty yet piercing expression of a madman. Implausible.

The more Sebastian pondered, the less anything made sense.

God, come to my assistance; Lord, make haste to help me.

Sebastian uttered the prayer, hoping to find clues in it. The verses did not come to him like music. This time, they inched up inside him, stalagmites cleaving to his soul. Sharp and empty.

Perhaps God frowned upon the abbey—frowned upon all abbeys.

Frowned upon him.

But his God was a merciful one, not vengeful. Wasn't he?

"The Dalakis Curse." He wanted to holler out loud, let his moans carry to the rafters. He'd heard the silly rumors his first week as a postulant.

The former owner of Mt. Ouray's land, Mrs. Dalakis, had suspected her late husband of dabbling in black magic and worshipping demons, and the story was told of an evil that lurked on the abbey's grounds.

Because of Sebastian's faith, he'd never fallen for monsters and goblins. Wickedness resided in the hearts of men. Diabolic murderers inside abbeys came about by human action alone. People created their own wickedness. Unless mental illness stalked them. Mr. Dalakis had probably fallen victim to cabin fever. Lost his head and began seeing visions of witches and devils.

Had that happened with JC's killer? Had one of them snapped, hallucinating that JC was some kind of devil that had arrived mysteriously at Mt. Ouray to harm them? Had he heard bodiless voices whispering for him to murder?

Or perhaps a heated battle between good and evil was playing out inside their abbey. God versus Satan, the eternal conflict waging onward. And the brothers, trapped for the winter, stood helpless in the midst of the perennial death match.

The coming prophesy, as Revelation proclaimed. Satan, released from his prison, unleashed upon mankind. Shot from Heaven on the back of a lightning bolt. JC had been sent to Mt. Ouray—once the possible site of black masses and satanic rituals, and eventually the final blows—for that sole purpose. "It will happen exactly as I've intended, exactly as I've planned...."

Seated next to him, Casey seemed to notice Sebastian's quiver. He glanced above his cantorum. Sebastian wanted to smile at him and reassure him. He knew he shouldn't. Not during the Eucharist. Not on Ash Wednesday.

The father read the Proclamation: "We are therefore Christ's ambassadors, as though God were making his appeal through us...." And afterward he chanted Psalm 51: "...wash away all my iniquity and cleanse me of my sin."

The brothers chanted in refrain: "Create in me a clean heart, oh God."

On and on they chanted the psalm, until the abbot stunned them by breaking protocol. He stepped before the pulpit, his cowl flowing around him in a rush of brilliant white, and, after clearing his throat, stated in a pained voice, though one without hesitancy: "Use this season of Lent to ask God to forgive you of your sins, and ask that he walk with you when you, who acted alone in murder, step forward. I implore you. A week has passed. Do it now, in God's house, before your brothers who see you as Jesus, in greatness and in sin. Stand up and announce yourself. We will embrace you. Now is the moment to save your soul."

The brothers stirred. Glances grew stronger, changing into gaping stares. When no one made to move—not even a flinch to come forward—they turned their eyes away from one another. Sebastian kept a close watch on them. Which one displayed the look of a killer?

Brother Eusebius stood tall and solid, his hands clenching and unclenching by his sides. Brothers Lucien, Micah, and George shook as if Father Paolo had flogged them. Brothers Jerome and Hubert cast their eyes to the floor, shaking their heads. Brother Giles, stiff in his wheelchair, pursed his lips. Brother Rodel twitched, mumbled prayers. Casey, the sole one among them who stared directly at the abbot, embodied the most innocence in Sebastian's eyes. He wasn't prejudiced, was he? And Brother Augustine sat slumped in his wheelchair, oblivious to the gravity of the moment.

Silence in the chapel whirled around their heads, underlining the fierce winds outside. Someone cleared his throat. A low sob broke from

Brother George. A minute passed. Then another. Head bowed, the father returned to the pulpit. Without another spoken word, he raised his hands and sang the Prayers of the People and led the monks into the corridor.

From there, they went about their chores and responsibilities, devoid of food save for bread and water. Sebastian cared little that they fasted on Ash Wednesdays. He had scarce appetite anyway.

Somber puzzlement hovered over the brothers. They walked about with heaviness upon their shoulders. Sebastian wanted only to crawl into bed. More and more he questioned his reasons for coming to Mt. Ouray. Older brothers discouraged postulants from seeking monastic life as an escape. But three solid years inside the abbey had taught him that almost all of them did.

Brother George, although he would've had a tough go of it in the modern world with his puerile attitude, might have had limited choices. Brother Eusebius's devotion appeared sincere. Brother Rodel, who he was certain was also homosexual, seemed the most likely of the postulants Sebastian had seen come and go in his short years to preserve into middle age.

Casey? What had driven him, so young, to seek the secluded life of a monk? Sebastian never questioned his devotion—no one had a grasp of the Latin and psalms better than he. Had he chosen the perfect vocation?

Sebastian had fantasized about Casey long before their time in the shower. Each night he crawled into bed, he'd see Casey's nude body, its tautness hard to conceal beneath his tunic. And after he'd shut his eyes, Sebastian chased him in his dreams, naked and yearning… then Casey would turn the tables and become the pursuer.

Sebastian had opened a door when he'd asked Casey to be his secondary. He held onto no misconceptions of his motives for forging a partnership with him. He'd done it once before, during a triple homicide, when he'd involved a young officer he knew lacked the experience. Eventually, Officer Julio had become uncomfortable with Sebastian's attentions and excused himself from the case. He kept his distance from Sebastian from that point on, and by the end of the month had requested a transfer.

Sebastian had never experienced such inner humiliation.

But Casey embraced Sebastian's interest. They shared a new level of intimacy. That had become clear during their "dance" in the shower stalls, their nakedness in full view for each other.

And as the first week of Lent came to a close and still no clues pointed to who had killed JC, Sebastian took solace in the one earthly dependability in his life: Brother Casey Galvan.

THE hurried slap of sandals on the terracotta floor grabbed Sebastian's attention where he sat by the cloister garden eating breakfast. Casey stopped in front of him.

"You told me to keep my eyes peeled," he whispered. "Well, I noticed something. It's probably nothing, but much better than what I had to offer you last time."

"What is it?"

"In JC's old cell. Will you come look, while everyone's occupied with breakfast?"

Sebastian left his tray on the sideboard in the entrance foyer and followed Casey. Before opening the door, Casey peered up and down the corridor. Sebastian matched his stealthy posture and tiptoed inside. Casey switched on the light, and they glanced around. Everything looked the same as the last time Sebastian had checked.

"Do you notice anything?" Casey asked.

Sebastian focused. Then all of the sudden he brightened, eyes fixed on the wall shelf. "The statue of the Virgin Mary."

Casey nodded. "It's gone. I remember Father Paolo gave him one. It was the stir of the abbey. Brother George said he was shocked he'd given him a statuette before he even committed as a postulant. JC had placed it on his wall shelf, I saw it once when I brought him clean sheets."

"I saw it too," Sebastian said, still gazing at the empty wall shelf. He mentally kicked himself for having failed to notice earlier. "What made you look in here?"

"I was searching for clues."

Sebastian couldn't help but chuckle. "Good job, Casey. Very good indeed."

"Do you think the killer was angry that Father Paolo had given it to him, and after he'd killed him he took it?"

"It's quite possible. Or maybe it had fallen during a struggle. At least this gives us reason to believe JC's cell might be the scene of the assault."

Sebastian dropped to his hands and knees and checked the room for the tenth time, sweeping his eyes under the bed, reexamining the closet, scrutinizing each nook and cranny. Casey, eager to help, scurried alongside him like a raccoon foraging for roots.

Like the other times, they came up empty. Not even blood splatter. If only he could get his hands on luminol. Sebastian wanted to reexamine JC's body to confirm what he now considered, that the killer had used the statue to knock JC unconscious. Signs of the statuette—paint flecks or ceramic pieces—might still be imbedded in his scalp. Frozen in place. That would require some persuasion of the abbot.

Meanwhile, Sebastian fastened on one objective, and that was to find the missing statuette. He and Casey used the time they should be engaged in *lectio divina* to split up and search the abbey, all the while trying to look casual to the occasional brother they passed in the corridors. Certainly God would not mind that they neglected studying Scripture to search for an important clue to a murder.

After nearly an hour, they both met in Sebastian's cell. By the look on Casey's face, he hadn't had any success finding the statuette either—or what remained of it.

"Don't fret," Sebastian told him with a counterfeit smile. "A good investigator keeps looking until he's exhausted each lead."

Throughout the day, Sebastian tried to squeeze some strength from his own words. With the gnawing revelation of the statuette missing from JC's cell still fresh, he realized that to meet his goal, he needed to employ his true investigative skills: conduct face-to-face interviews with his fellow monks.

Whether or not his brothers grew apprehensive of his actions, Sebastian did not care. He had wanted to sit down with each of them, one at a time, for days. No reason to hold back. He was tired of the sideways glances and unrelenting assumptions.

The best technique would be to poke his nose within inches of theirs and demand they confess. But Mt. Ouray was not the "interview room" of the twenty-fifth district. He could not assail his fellow Trappist brothers with such drastic tactics. Gentle nudging would serve his best interest for now.

"Can you think of anything that might explain JC's murder?" Sebastian asked Brother Giles while he gave the illusion of helping him tidy the entrance foyer, taking a much-needed morning off from crafting rosaries. Sebastian, tucking his dust rag under his arm, lifted his breakfast tray, embarrassed he'd forgotten it.

"I'm glad he's gone from us," Brother Giles said. Spittle collected on his lower lip—lopping and swollen, as if he'd chewed on it for some time—and dribbled alongside his crumb-covered silver beard. "I pray God to forgive me, but I'm glad he's gone."

"Did he do something to harm you, Brother Giles?"

Brother Giles held the cleaning rag in his veiny, liver-spotted right hand. "I went in to check on him in his cell a few days before his death," he said, facing the long corridor that led to the cells. "I was bringing him fresh linens. The door was ajar. I didn't think anything wrong with going inside." He shook his head. "I found him lying in bed, his scapular tossed on the floor and his tunic uncinched. Doing that horrible thing. And he didn't even stop when I walked in."

Sebastian's cheeks warmed. Hadn't they all committed that sin before? "Perhaps he didn't see you."

"Oh, he saw me. Looked right into my eyes. Didn't even stop. An animal. Even in private, it's a vile thing to do."

The old-fashioned monk took things personally, Sebastian gathered. JC hadn't even professed an interest in joining the monastery.

To hold him up to a staunch conviction seemed unfair. He hadn't come to them for any purpose they understood. That mystery lay frozen inside him forever. But Sebastian refrained from telling Brother Giles that.

"So I hadn't imagined smelling something foul," Brother Giles went on with a glower. "Disgusting habit. Smoking in his cell. That's forbidden here. Where did he get cigarettes? That's what I want to know."

Sebastian almost laughed aloud at his blunder. He'd assumed Brother Giles had caught JC in another act. "Did you notice the Virgin Mary figurine in his cell?" he asked, centering on the topic he was most interested in.

Brother Giles wheeled round to Sebastian and seized his forearm with an uncanny strength, nearly knocking the tray from Sebastian's hand. "Yes, as a matter of fact. I remember turning my eyes away from him and seeing the Virgin on the wall shelf. I tried to draw strength from her. What a sacrilege. Father Paolo shouldn't have given it to him. He shouldn't have. And to think he had dropped it so crassly without any care, chipping her lovely face. The clumsy oaf." He released Sebastian's arm and gazed at the floor. "The abbot probably gave him the cigarettes too."

An hour later, Sebastian waited for everyone to leave the kitchen with their lunch trays to speak alone with Brother Micah, who stayed behind to tidy up. "Did you find your fillet knife?" he asked him.

Brother Micah wiped his hands on his scapular. "No, I haven't."

"You thinking of ordering a new one once the winter passes?"

He shrugged. "I'll see about it."

Sebastian stepped closer to him while he scrubbed the last of the pots and pans. "It's a shame. Those are valuable utensils. We have little here as it is."

"Do you wish for more?" Brother Micah said toward the sudsy water.

"I'm content, aren't you?"

"You've known for a while there's only one thing more that I want here."

Blood seared Sebastian's cheeks. Desperate to deflect one of Brother Micah's awkward and sudden innuendos, he asked, "How long had it gone missing?"

"About two weeks."

"The Saturday before last?"

"Maybe. Maybe before that."

"But I recall you telling me you'd used it before then."

Brother Micah kept his back to Sebastian. "I can't remember exactly. Now that you mentioned it, I think I lost it later."

"Didn't you say you used it to peel apples for your applesauce?"

"What is this, the Inquisition?" Brother Micah snickered lightly and softened his voice. "What difference does it make? I searched. I couldn't find it."

"You didn't mention it to anyone?"

"And why would I do that? Things get misplaced. I seemed to have lost a few dishtowels lately too. I didn't think it warranted pulling the alarm."

"Did you notice the statuette Father Paolo gave JC is missing too?"

Brother Micah pivoted his right shoulder to face him, his arms submerged in the soapy water. "He probably threw it away, knowing him. What does that have to do with my fillet knife?"

"I'm not sure. Do you think there's a connection?"

He refocused back to the pots and pans, the lapping of water heavy in the ensuing silence. "I know how this awful ordeal has been trying for all of us," he said at last. "Please, I'll help find the killer anyway I can. I really will. You can trust me, Brother Sebastian."

Brother Micah unplugged the sink stopper, and Sebastian listened to the water gurgle down the drain. "That's unselfish of you, Brother Micah. Thank you."

He had even less luck with Brother Eusebius. During the afternoon work period, he struck up a conversation with him in the sacristy, hoping to learn something. Brother Eusebius was more closemouthed than in previous times.

"Have you ever heard of anyone succumbing to cabin fever in your twenty years here, Brother Eusebius?"

"Cabin fever? No, never. We relish our solitude. That's why we come."

Sebastian's next direct question about who he suspected might have killed JC led the brother along a strange path, where he began to reflect on his own life and how he'd come to Mt. Ouray. Much of it Sebastian had already learned through the abbey hearsay, which Brother Hubert was the tiller of.

"My father didn't speak to me for years after I converted," Brother Eusebius said toward his now inactive hands. "But after I graduated with my doctorate, he started to see me as someone... well, worthy as he. You know my father was a well-to-do man, once co-chair of the Southern Association of Black Entrepreneurs."

Sebastian knew this. Again, the abbey gossip mill had carried the information from mouth to ear. Brother Eusebius had come from a well-to-do African American family of Georgia, long entrenched in education and money, a legacy handed down from his great-great-grandfather, who'd made a fortune in the iron industry after the abolishment of slavery. One of the first black men to run for congress, his headstrong zeal matched Brother Eusebius's.

"My father presumed I'd forward the family name, along with its honor," Brother Eusebius went on, dreamlike. "Before his death, he'd written me a long letter, hoping I might still. I'm his only son, you know." He sniggered. "Would've been worse for him had I turned out homosexual, I suppose. Yet in the end, same result. A son without an heir."

And he ceased at the precise point where they'd ended their last in-depth conversation about JC and homosexuality in the Church. Brother Eusebius loathed the idea of it. At least within the confines of the Catholic Church. But he'd acclimated to its indelible presence. Or seemed to have.

Brother Eusebius said no more. Sebastian refrained from asking him about the statuette. They returned to their beadwork, not another word shared between them until the following work period.

To Sebastian's surprise, Brother Jerome became the most combative.

"Why are you asking all this?" he said in the bathroom, where he'd been brushing his teeth before Retire with slapdash movements. "Are you a detective with the Pinkerton Guards? Why are you harassing me?"

"Doesn't it puzzle you, Brother Jerome?" Sebastian stood before him by the sinks, face towel clenched in hand, looking at him in the mirror. Both wore their bathrobes. "Don't you want closure?"

"Not as much as you, apparently. I only want to get back to my normal life here. To live as a monk, the way I professed some fifteen years ago. All of you young people today. You cause so much trouble in the world."

"I didn't mean to anger you, Brother Jerome. You know my inquisitiveness can get the best of me at times."

Facing Brother Jerome's taciturn stubbornness, he asked if any of the brothers had come to him seeking medical attention for cuts or bruises following JC's death. Brother Jerome shook his head.

"Been quiet in the infirmary, other than… other than that god-awful medical exam you made me do."

Sebastian contemplated Brother Jerome's lined features. JC's murder had unnerved him and the others more than he would have guessed. The days since, knowing his body was locked in the freezer, had caused Brother Jerome agony, as if he were wrapped and stowed alongside the dead man.

Brother Jerome gazed into the mirror, his eyes looking as if he saw something beyond their reflections, far from reach. "I'd lost my wife in the prime of our lives," he said. "She died from cardiac arrest at age forty-three. I have only this place and my three sons, and I only get to see them once a year, at most. I hadn't come to Mt. Ouray seeking more death."

"I'm sorry, Brother Jerome."

"There's nothing for you to be sorry about." He gathered up his toiletries and said to Sebastian's reflection, "This is the first time in many years I've wanted to leave here, and I hate that feeling." And he left with tears billowing behind his eyeglasses.

The next morning during breakfast, Brother George buried his face in his hands when Sebastian cornered him in the library, where he'd carried his tray, and asked for his thoughts on the murder. "I want it all to go away," he said.

"I'm trying to make it go away," Sebastian reassured him.

"No, you're making things worse." Sobbing, he ran off with his loaded tray before Sebastian had a chance to ask him more.

The other brothers offered up even more scant information. Brother Hubert, Brother Lucien, Brother Rodel. Even Father Paolo knew nothing of the statuette's whereabouts or of any other useful scoops.

Yet he had one last long shot to interview.

– XIV –

SEBASTIAN knocked on the cell door out of protocol, but he knew the aged monk inside could not speak or probably even hear. He hadn't uttered a word since Sebastian had lived under the abbey's roof. Brother Jerome had once told him he'd stopped speaking about fifteen years ago. A series of strokes had stolen his speech, along with his ability to do much of anything for himself.

He cracked open the door, peeked inside. Could be his own cell. Same white stucco walls, same cheap oak desk, same single window, same twin bed, same lonely shelves where most of the brothers placed the ceramic Virgin Mary and a host of other knickknacks. Brother Augustine sat in his wheelchair by the desk, his back to him. Sebastian heard his labored breathing, the only indication he lived. Sebastian announced himself and opened the door wider. He set the lunch tray on the desk and smiled at him, trying his best to do what Brother George had done for many years—provide Brother Augustine with the utmost humane treatment possible, although the abbey's eldest brother had no more understanding of a smile than he did a frown, Sebastian supposed.

Brother George had acted skeptical when Sebastian had offered to carry Brother Augustine's lunch to him. A few minutes of convincing and he'd eventually assented. Brother George, an old-fashioned monk entrenched in tradition and with an instinct to serve and nurture, had looked lost when Sebastian had taken the tray from his chubby hands and left him staring at the kitchen's tiled floor.

More than a drive to serve his fellow brother compelled Sebastian to meet with Brother Augustine. He'd already interrogated the other monks in the monastery. Several days had passed since those failed attempts, and he'd finally rallied the gumption to try his last, vain hope.

Glaucoma-riddled eyes stared at Sebastian while he tucked the napkin into the collar of his cowl. Frail and thin, Brother Augustine's Trappist garment cloaked his body like a tarp over a toddler's abandoned tricycle. Brother George still dressed him each morning (he'd found dressing him in the cowl easier than the more tight-fitting tunic and scapular), though few eyes ever saw the eighty-seven-year-old outside his cell.

They'd stopped wheeling him to the chapel for the seven stations and Mass three summers ago, when they'd assumed he'd lost his sight and hearing. Father Paolo always made sure to bring him the sacraments each day. In warmer weather they'd sometimes leave him out front to enjoy the gentle breezes flowing off the surrounding mountains, bringing with them the scents of wild honeysuckle and roses. He seemed to luxuriate in the relentless summer sunshine, which radiated off his bone-white skin.

On special occasions they'd wheel him into the chapel so that he might not be left out of the chanting or the infrequent solo concerts Father Paolo provided when he wished to play his cello for the brothers or retreat guests. Last Christmas Mass, Casey and Brother Eusebius had accompanied him on flute and their small spinet piano. They'd played "O Little Town of Bethlehem," "The First Noel," and a few more holiday favorites. A special treat for their ears. None of them knew for sure if Brother Augustine could hear to appreciate it.

After his first two strokes, the abbey had placed Brother Augustine in a nursing home for round-the-clock care. One or two of the brothers had visited their esteemed brother, bringing him flowers from their gardens to brighten his bedside. A few months later, they'd brought him back to Mt. Ouray when they'd concluded they might provide him better care than the nuns at the cash-strapped nursing home.

Sebastian sat in the desk chair next to Brother Augustine and lifted a shaky spoon to his chapped lips. "Here you go. Take this now."

The brother instinctively slurped in the corn mash. Moist crumbs fell onto his lap. Unaccustomed to feeding anyone but himself, Sebastian scooped the crumbs into Brother Augustine's mouth like he might feeding a baby.

Brother George had opened the window blinds when he'd fed Brother Augustine breakfast, and Sebastian gazed out the window while Brother Augustine chewed and swallowed. Another blizzard raged onto Mt. Ouray as the gray sky shadowed the grounds. Winds stronger than those from the past few weeks shook the windowpane. The contracting air squeezed Sebastian's head into a pressure cooker. He wondered if the storms ever bothered Brother Augustine.

His mouth trembled, as if pleading for more of the fleshless food. Sebastian turned back to him with a spoonful of cheddar cheese crumbs, aged in their cellar. Next he lifted the mug of powdered milk to his mouth. The aged brother wrapped his dry lips around the straw, his head shaking with what doctors had diagnosed as vascular Parkinson's. He took several pills per day, including levodopa, a drug Sebastian knew too well, since his grandfather had suffered from the same disease. White liquid barely filled the straw. Sebastian set the milk aside. He fed him more of the corn mash, cheese, and applesauce and wiped his mouth.

He wished the old man might speak. What stories must he hoard about his fifty years at the abbey, almost as old as the abbey itself. Did he possess the secrets to a happy life? What was it like to be sealed tighter than a safe without the means to communicate? Had he experienced "the Dalakis Curse"? Did he ever transgress?

In his younger days, had he come close to loving a fellow monk in the same way Sebastian imagined he did Casey?

He peered to his right at the wall shelf where Brother Augustine's Virgin Mary figurine sat. Father Paolo had started the tradition of gifting each of the monks with the statuette soon after his rise from prior to full abbot, according to Brother Hubert. Tall and solid, made in China, the icon exuded a celebrity-like fascination for men of the Church, often the sole female—representational or otherwise—in the lives of monks and priests. A mother figure for some. A lover for others. The perfect veneration of unsoiled purity. The Second Vatican

Council hadn't budged on that issue. Blessed Mary, leaving the Messiah without siblings, had lived and died a virgin.

The statuette appeared to be winking at Sebastian. A small chip on the side of the face had taken out the right eye. The missing statuette from JC's cell had something to do with his murder, Sebastian was sure. He'd asked everyone about it. They only knew that the father had given it to him, but hadn't seen it since the last time they'd laid eyes on it at some point before his death. Each of them had expressed disapproval for the father's actions. Had the statuette caused one of them enough angst that it had become a motive for murder?

He rested his hands, allowed a moment for Brother Augustine to digest his food. Outside, the winds rumbled. He walked to the window, near forgetting Brother Augustine. He peered out to where the long stone walkway from the parking lot led to their front door, now buried under at least three feet of snow. He could still see the groove marks left in the snow where they'd partially dragged JC's body to the barn after Terce.

Father Paolo had demanded they store the body in the barn after the second botched autopsy that Sebastian had managed to wheedle out of the abbot—and Brother Jerome. Sebastian still smarted over the lack of evidence retrieved, especially since he'd butted heads with the abbot to take JC's body from the freezer and lay it out in the infirmary for another examination.

The body, spread out on the plastic-covered cot, appeared dreamlike to him. Brother Jerome had shaken while they'd reexamined him. Sebastian had gotten used to the half-closed eyes. Despite the tissue damage (reticular epidermal burn as a result of hypovolemia) JC was still stunning, in a way. His skin had darkened. Preserved in everlasting, youthful beauty. But not even the smallest imbedded piece from the figurine showed up. Samples under a magnifying glass gave scant help.

Then, to have to haul the corpse to the barn along with Brother Eusebius.... Sebastian had felt as if he were the one guilty of JC's murder. The absurdity of it seemed to have grabbed him like the snow under their slogging boots. He relived the awkward moment when they'd dropped the body in the cumbersome snow and wind and had finally dragged it the remainder of the way to the barn.

Worst still, he sensed Father Paolo wanted him to pull back on the investigation. "Intelligent men know when to quit," he'd said right after they'd reported to him they had secured JC in the barn behind the sacks of grass seed, as the father had requested. The father was sounding more and more like Sebastian's former police captain. "Let it stew," his old supervisor would tell him under similar situations. But Sebastian didn't feel like letting the investigation stew. He needed to uncover at least one concrete lead. Something to satiate his curiosity. For his sake as well as JC's and the abbey's.

The windowpane revealed Sebastian's knitted eyebrows. Behind him, Brother Augustine's head slouched to one side as if he was napping. Was it possible? A few of the brothers, including Sebastian, had been studying *lectio divina* in their cells the day Casey had spied JC from the library window. None of them noticed anyone hiking up to the abbey the few times they'd glanced outside. *What could we see in the snowstorm, anyway?* Might Brother Augustine have seen anything? Was it possible he wasn't blind after all? Perhaps he'd witnessed JC's murder too?

Even after a half dozen strokes, Brother Jerome had said that his mind could very well be "as sharp as a scalpel." Only his body had failed him. Sebastian would give his next three days' worth of meals to know for sure. What percolated inside Brother Augustine's head?

Sebastian rotated his shoulders and probed the monk's wizened face, creased with deep crevices and marred with liver spots and moles, some protected with thin adhesive strips. His silver-coated eyes popped open. Feebly, he tried to raise his left hand, but failed. Was there a way to reach him, to get him to respond?

The brother struggled to shift his head and gaze at the tray of food. Sebastian scurried to assist him. He fed him until his head again drooped to the side and his eyes closed. Sebastian noticed grime in the wheelchair's nooks and crannies. They focused so much on the brother's personal hygiene, Brother George and the others had neglected cleaning his wheelchair.

A stain on the aluminum hand rim looked odd to Sebastian—and eerily familiar. He rubbed his fingertip over it. There was no denying what he suspected. Dried blood. But whose? Of course, the brother might have bled a number of times. Cut while being shaved or while having his nails and what was left of his white hair trimmed. Anything might explain it. If only they housed an onsite lab. Maybe Brother Jerome's magnifying glass might show a similarity between the blood on Brother Augustine's chair and JC's. Ridiculous notion, he knew.

He suppressed a sigh, remembering some of the odd banter from the brothers. "The Dalakis Curse." The devil had made someone do it. Brothers Giles and Micah both insisted a force nearly as powerful as God had possessed the killer. Might a demon have seized the frail Brother Augustine, turning him into a coldhearted killer with the strength of a twenty-five-year-old wrestler? The sardonic laughter in Sebastian's mind sent a chill along his spine. He forced a smile and shook his head.

"Would you like to look outside?" Sebastian kept his voice airy and light. "There's not much to see through the storm, but you can just make out the trees and the barn. Imagine it all in spring, not too far away, with everything in bloom."

He eased Brother Augustine to the window. The squeak of his wheels, the sole sound rising from Brother Augustine, connected the two. Dark shadows matted the snowy landscape. The brother appeared mesmerized by the storm. His gray eyes widened.

"I'm unsure if you can hear or understand me," Sebastian said, squinting out the window alongside Brother Augustine. "Bad things have taken place here the past few weeks. Brother George might've told you while he's cared for you. I respect the sagacity you've acquired over the years." He glimpsed at the brother in the windowpane, as if he were an old friend Sebastian's age. "I'll spare you the details. We had a guest, a young man about twenty. We don't know how he came here or why or where he came from. Perhaps you saw him push through the snowstorm some weeks back. Well, now he's dead. Yes, someone murdered him. Right here inside Mt. Ouray."

He observed the brother. Had his irises shrunk when Sebastian had mentioned murder? Was that a tear poised in the corner of his eye?

One of sadness or of knowledge, or merely the watering of a diseased eye? The sides of his mouth twitched. Sebastian gazed back out the window.

"Father Paolo insisted I investigate," he continued with his mock conversation. "Now I suspect he wants me to ignore what's happened, thinking maybe I've failed. I cannot do that. It's in my blood to find answers until there are no more clues left to decipher. I used to be a homicide detective with the Philadelphia Police Department. You might already know. Rumors travel fast inside the abbey. If you can hear, you'd know that I came here to escape big city corruption and crime. And now, it's right back at my feet. Almost funny, in a way."

A minor grunt emanated from Brother Augustine's dry throat. Sebastian turned to him, leaned in closer at eye level, expecting to witness a spark of life.

"Can you hear me, Brother Augustine?" He watched him. Desperate for an answer, knowing one could never come. Yet he persisted. "Is there anything you can tell me about JC's murder? Please, move something. Bat an eye, wiggle a finger. Anything to give me a clue that you understand me."

Sebastian's face soured, and he turned away his nose. The brother had comprehended not a single word. His guttural moan hadn't come in response to Sebastian's pleading. Sebastian sighed, rolled up his tunic sleeves, and wheeled the venerable monk out the door toward the bathroom, where he hoped to run into Brother George to help him change his diaper.

The sound of Brother Augustine's squeaking wheels echoed in the corridors like a scream into oblivion.

– XV –

WET towels steamed on the hearth for when Father Paolo and Lucien finished. They were naked, tucked under each other before the hissing fire, embraced in a sixty-nine knot.

Father Paolo rested his throbbing lips, looked aside while Lucien engulfed him on top. The father lifted his pelvis to meet Lucien's mouth. He wanted him to take him deeper. Lucien obliged. He never resisted the father. Even when he emitted a soft gag—the gurgle of a drowning lamb—Lucien pleased him unwaveringly.

The father came while staring into the dying fire. Lucien sat upright, wiped his mouth.

He reached for a hot towel and swabbed the father, moistening the towel in the large ceramic bowl between one or two wipes. The father wanted to take Lucien again, this time forcing him on his back. But he knew he lacked the stamina to finish. Best to lie still, allow his underling to fuss over him with the warm towel bath, which felt so soothing on his aging muscles and left a delightful scent of eucalyptus as the steam rose off his glistening flesh.

When he finished, Lucien set the towel aside and fed the fire more of the old *New Yorker*s Father Paolo kept stacked in his closet, some dating back as far as two decades. Blue flames curled from the glossy pages. Lucien stepped back. Father Paolo laid a hand on his bare shoulder.

"It's time for you to dress and retire to your cell, dear Lucien."

"If you say so, Father." Lucien dressed in his tunic and scapular and cinched the leather belt around his waist. Father Paolo dressed also, but left his tunic uncinched and the scapular balled against the round table, where he'd tossed it when he'd grabbed for the already disrobed Lucien.

"Can I get you anything else before I leave?" Lucien asked after slipping on his sandals.

Father Paolo, lifting his eyeglasses from the table and situating them over his nose, shook his head. "I'll be heading for my own cell shortly. Careful you don't wake the others. They aren't sleeping as soundly as they used to."

"Should I carry the towels to the laundry for Brother Hubert?"

"Leave them for now. Good night, Lucien."

"Good night, Father."

He realized he'd hurt Lucien by not kissing him on his cheek the way he often did before he'd leave. He did not feel like it that night. He'd already spent a half hour locked against his body. Though he enjoyed the physical contact, he needed a break from him. They'd been spending too much time together. Once Lucien had satisfied him, Father Paolo longed for solitude. To think.

He paced his office, letting his fingertips brush the top of his mahogany desk with each passing. The cello in the corner by the fireplace appeared in his eyes with every sharp spin of his heels. The same cello avô had given him for his fourteenth birthday. His grandfather had saved for years to purchase it from the owner of Vila de Seda's sole fado bar, where lonely peasant women sang in exchange for companionship.

Whenever he needed to relax, he'd play it—or whenever he wanted to relax someone else. He had massaged the strings for JC. The strange young man had no interest in Bach or Dvorak. He'd stared at the cello as if it were an alien creature without legs. Never even heard of the great Portuguese cellist Guilhermina Suggia. No musical appreciation. No taste for fine vinho.

No understanding for the elegance of lovemaking.

JC had rejected him. Flat out. He had a bad track record the past few postulants. Was he losing his touch? Perhaps he needed to update his repertoire. Youth of today lacked any admiration for the finer things in life. Perhaps that's why the older Brother Lucien had been an easier procurement.

But, like Father Paolo, Lucien had come from Europe. Europeans understood life's nuances. They appreciated the subtle tuft of a newly lit candle, whereas Americans delighted in the roaring of engines. The thirst for the big and physical had soared them into outer space, yes. Did they value the feel of fine leather under their bones, sitting before a blaze that came from a stone fireplace rather than the backside of a rocket ship?

That demand for the tangible, to dissect and explore, had led Brother Sebastian to insist on a reexamination of JC's body. To their surprise, the father had allowed it. He'd had a long day on the phone with superiors in Denver and hadn't wanted to deal with "Detective Harkin's" hankerings. Little difference it had made. The second autopsy had proved futile. Something about scant evidence showing up under a magnifying glass. All the better.

Then Brother Micah had badgered him to have the body kept out of the walk-in freezer.

"I don't want it returned there," he'd cried, standing before Father Paolo's desk while Brothers Sebastian and Jerome conducted the autopsy in the infirmary. "Please, Father, you must have it stored somewhere else."

"We have nowhere else to put it," the father had said, shocked at the brother's bold insistence. "The body must be kept preserved and hidden. Where else but the freezer?"

"Every time I go in there to get something to prepare for a meal, I see it in the corner, the trash bags covered in frost. It's horrible for me to be in the kitchen each day, and for the other brothers who help me from time to time. I've prayed for strength, but I don't think I've gotten any. I don't want it put back there. Please, Father, once they are done with it, have them take it away for good."

"But where, my dear brother? I can't think of any other solutions."

Brother Micah had seemed to ponder. His eyes, red and moist, had burned holes into the carpet. "Can't we store it in the barn?" he'd finally said, looking beseechingly at the abbot. "It's freezing outside. Out there, it'll preserve just as well as in the walk-in freezer."

Brother Micah had sparked a wondrous idea. Splendid, indeed.

And so the father had made it happen.

Mid-March had already arrived. The snowstorms continued, but spring reared around the corner along with the first signs of snowmelt. The warmer days of April brought out the forest service workers to clear the road, trailed by the villagers below, eager to see if the monks had fared well during the harsh winter. They were already calling two, sometimes three times a day to reserve rooms in the cottage house. Denver's bishop had already expressed eagerness to visit along with his entourage. They'd descend upon the abbey like locusts.

In the past he'd greeted them with open arms, his wide tunic sleeves flapping in the spring breezes. He'd looked forward to the slew of new summer retreatants coming for their discernments. Fresh men, young and old, arriving at Mt. Ouray. He had a growing list of interested postulants who'd e-mailed the abbey wanting information.

In a few months, a choice flock of new pickings would stand before him. He always knew which new arrivals to handpick too, and encourage them to come back in the autumn as postulants. Strength of character was important, of course. They needed to preserve. But a youthful man with an uncertain glint in his eyes charmed Father Paolo. One requiring guidance and understanding. New blood for their world.

Casey Galvan had been one such retreatant. Father Paolo had persuaded him to return to the abbey after his first visit. He'd been a tough nut to crack. No doubting his sexuality. But from the first day, Father Paolo had detected the burning fire in his belly for only one of them—Brother Sebastian.

The father's envy had faded to shrugs. He could live without Brother Casey's big brown eyes gazing upon him, or the subtle feel of his smooth flesh stretched over taut muscles. He had his beloved

Lucien, and on rarer occasions, Brother Micah. But how much time had sprinted past since their last tryst? Two years? When he, Lucien, and Brother Micah had enjoyed each other's combined bodies by the fire. Brother Micah, constantly anguishing over trifling matters, had aged far quicker than any of the other monks.

And there was young Brother Rodel. Always cowering behind his scapular hood. At first, Father Paolo believed he wouldn't preserve. When he requested to take his final vows after only a year, the father had been stunned indeed. Thus far he seemed a perfect fit for Mt. Ouray. Little doubt he'd remain at the abbey for the remainder of his life.

But the body of JC left a schism between him and his new challenges wider than the Red Sea. Word of a murder might keep them away in droves. Scandals had a way of repelling even the most insensitive of people. He'd seen it happen to monasteries before, both in the United States and Europe. The Church ushered in new abbots or priors and monks, shuffling them around to keep the protracted claws of the media and law off their backs. The FBI had only last year sealed the doors to a monastery in Louisiana.

He could not have that happen to him. Not after his dedication and effort to achieve this position. And he was so close to reaching the title of Dom. Besides, the Church and the community looked up to him. A scandal would disillusion them.

He lit a cone of incense, as if to mask the anticipated stink of a rotting corpse. He stood still and watched the smoke coil toward the ceiling. The incense eased his anxiety. He could lose himself in the subtlety of the wisp of smoke and the scent of juniper. He paced again.

Night after night, he'd lost sleep over what might befall him and his abbey should the world discover their awful secret. While the others had tossed and turned away the dark hours, he'd paced the cold floor of his cell barefoot, or returned to his spacious office with its opulence and sat snug at his desk to think.

Brother Casey had already dallied on the "off limits" computer, most likely on Brother Sebastian's request. Those two were more entwined than English ivy and oak. Brother Hubert had been lax in letting his passwords lie around for easy viewing. Luckily, he'd caught it in time and cleaned the cache and created new passwords, hidden away from nosy brothers.

The chance that Brother Casey had uncovered the porn sites little concerned the father. With everything going on at the abbey, his occasional venture into Internet porn—and most likely Brother Hubert's and Lucien's—was a minor infraction.

Someone in Pennsylvania had already reported a man missing matching JC's description. The family had traced his travels to Denver on a Greyhound and another bus line to Telluride, where his cell phone and credit card trail had reached a dead end. Where those two items were now, Father Paolo had no idea. Certainly it would not take the family long to find them and track his movements to Monfrere, where someone might have recalled seeing him. Maybe a villager had picked up JC hitchhiking in the snow. There was no mention of why he'd left home.

He stopped pacing in midthought and clutched his desk to balance himself. The fire smoldered. Their winter wood supply had dwindled and they had resorted to using old magazines and rolled-up paper bags. March, the season of Lent, was always like that. A time for austerity and waiting.

He pulled back the velour drapes and gazed out the darkened windowpane. Outside, windswept snowdrifts piled higher and higher. God's fortress kept them safe for now. But spring's warmth and brightness perched beyond Mt. Ouray's lofty peak. What would the world find on their abbey grounds once the days lengthened and the snows melted?

April in the San Juan Mountains often arrived fiercer than January. But it also could land gentler than a bunny's hop. They needed to work fast. He must square away the matter of JC's body before the eager feet of outsiders came faster and in larger numbers, their nosiness awakening with the butterflies and wild roses. He fretted that forest rangers might come by once the storms ceased, as they sometimes did, to check on them.

The father had overheard the gossip in the corridors that grew with verve each day.

"Didn't you hear Brother Jerome? He said it was a blunt force trauma. That means someone hit him."

"Do you think so, Brother George?"

"The minute I saw that boy lying in the infirmary, I knew he'd be trouble."

"We all feel that way now, Brother Giles."

"Brother Eusebius did it."

"Oh, but Brother Lucien, why would you say such a thing?"

"He's not even a real Catholic."

"What's that supposed to mean?"

"He's a convert. Didn't you know?"

"I think I remember Brother Hubert telling me that once. But that doesn't mean anything. I think it makes him more pious, in a way. Isn't Brother Hubert a convert too?"

Father Paolo's sneaking up on them would scatter them like mice. He'd stand his ground, grinning over his power. Certainly he must insist they keep their mouths shut, even among each other, and maintain focus on *Opus Dei*.

Their predicament demanded great care and shrewdness.

If he must, he'd place them all in solitary confinement indefinitely. Accuse them of guilt. Use threats to get them to comply with his wishes.

He let the curtain dangle back in place, strode to his desk. He leaned back in his chair, brought his hands under his chin with his elbows resting on the armrests. Inhaling the perfume of incense, he closed his eyes. The gears of his mind churned and ground.

A homicide had taken place inside their abbey. Yet it wasn't as bad as one might think. Brother Jerome had concluded the point-blank blow to JC's head hadn't killed him. The rash decision to wrap his body in plastic bags and conceal him inside the freezer had caused his death. Brother Sebastian had said authorities would charge the culprit with either manslaughter or "criminal negligence." He had googled both terms and found Colorado law rather sensible on the matter. "Manslaughter," a class four felony. Many cases had resulted in the defendants spared from serving any jail time. "Criminal negligence," a class five felony, mandated even lesser consequences.

Brother Sebastian, their in-house expert, had affirmed the killer had acted without premeditation, probably a result of "mutual combatants," he'd called it. He'd seen it many times. The father had used this information to comfort the brothers. JC's death had been a mistake, after all. Nothing more severe than a suspended sentence waited for the responsible party.

But none of that mattered now. Yes, Brother Micah might have inadvertently solved all their troubles.

Rather than burying JC's body in the spring, the way he'd considered, they could toss it into the forest, waist high with snow. It would look like an accident. A crazy hiker had gotten lost and died from exposure. Occurred often in Colorado. In a sense, that's exactly what had happened. If it weren't for Brother Casey's sharp eyes—those big hazelnut eyes—they'd never have found JC. Officials would have declared his death the result of hypothermia. No questions asked.

That was the best plan. Dump the body in the forest before the April snowmelt and the guests, and act as if they had never found him. Conceal the truth—regardless of the class of crime. It was for their best interests. His, the abbey's, and his fellow monks'. Perhaps even JC's.

No counterforce wielded the might to impede his resolve. The others would have to abide by his orders. He was the abbot. His word echoed the word of God.

His largest obstacle would be Brother Sebastian. He needed to think of a way to bury the issue without alarming him. The others remained as obedient as Abraham. But Brother Sebastian—he demanded answers. Father Paolo had misjudged his determination.

Father Paolo had already dropped a few hints for him to stop the investigation, but he knew Brother Sebastian's steadfastness well. Perhaps he'd been wrong to have insisted Brother Sebastian investigate. He'd unleashed a mountain lion on them rather than the snooping house cat he'd expected.

Brother Sebastian's detective skills had sharpened since he'd brought him into his office that day and solicited his help. Slick and methodical. Overly so. There must be a way to force him to stop without incurring his rancor. Or worse, forcing mutinous resentment.

The father had appealed to his vanity by asking him to solve the crime. He'd use the same tactic to persuade him to quit.

If that failed to accomplish his objective, then he'd employ a more direct approach. One Brother Sebastian couldn't refuse.

– XVI –

SEBASTIAN was headed to his cell after lunch to dress for None when a hand laid upon his back startled him. He jerked around, smiled. "What can I do for you, Brother Rodel?"

"I didn't mean to scare you, Brother Sebastian," he whispered, glancing up and down the corridor. "But can I speak with you for a moment in private?"

"What's it about?"

Brother Rodel led Sebastian into his cell and shut the door halfway. "I think you should stop," he said, maintaining a soft voice.

"Stop what?"

"The investigation. Everyone knows about it. Word is Father Paolo asked you to look into Brother JC's death, and you've been asking everyone many questions. Please don't do it anymore."

Curious, Sebastian analyzed the diminutive young monk's face. Had Father Paolo put him up to persuading him to ditch the investigation? But Brother Rodel's beseeching appeared heartfelt. Always a worrywart, he had cautioned Sebastian about many issues in the past, real and trivial.

Sebastian supposed being the youngest of eight siblings had made him extra guarded. He'd come from a strict Catholic upbringing in the Philippines. "Dirt poor," Brother Hubert had disclosed. Brother Rodel had so many official names Sebastian couldn't remember all of them—Rodel Roberto Aquino Lubiano, or something like that. He'd once told Sebastian that, as a male, his family had expected him to either enter the clergy or the military. Two brothers had joined the U.S. Navy, one an officer stationed in San Diego, the other onboard an aircraft carrier in the Persian Gulf. Yet a third brother had enlisted in the Australian Navy.

His diaspora family, scattered across the globe—the United States, Britain, New Zealand, Australia—couldn't have been more proud of his choosing the monastic life, Brother Rodel had told him in passing last summer. Including his five sisters, all of whom lived abroad, like their brothers. The money the children sent home to their widowed mother in the Philippines allowed her to live like the village princess.

"I'm worried for you," Brother Rodel pressed. "For all of us. What if the killer wants to do more harm? If you keep quiet, maybe the bad seed will leave everyone alone and he'll return to where he belongs after the spring thaw."

"Someone should investigate, don't you think?"

Brother Rodel fell into a trance and peered toward the tiled floor. "Can't we go back to our normal lives, as if JC had never come here?" He looked again at Sebastian, imparting an uncommon self-determined expression for him. "JC's death is irreversible. Let's leave it alone, please."

Sebastian scoffed at Brother Rodel's dramatics. Surely he was overreacting. But Brother Rodel clung to his fight.

He fixed his eyes on Sebastian. "We've lived together, day in and day out, for nearly two years. Don't you trust me? It's best if we put it all behind us. I don't want you to look for the killer."

Sebastian licked his dry lips. "Would it be so horrible to uncover the truth?"

"Do you really want to know, Brother Sebastian? Are you prepared to learn who among us killed JC and stored his body in the freezer?"

Sebastian stared deep into Brother Rodel's oil-black eyes. Persistence and urgency swam in those dark irises. And so did fear.

Swallowing hard, Sebastian said, "Please, tell me, Brother Rodel, is there something you know? Did you see anything the night of JC's murder that might pinpoint the killer?"

Brother Rodel shook his head vigorously. "We're in danger here, Brother Sebastian. I can feel it. Please, I beg you. Stop the investigation. Stop before another one of us gets hurt."

WANTING to discard the uneasiness that lingered in his bones from his strange encounter with Brother Rodel, Sebastian decided to take advantage of a break in the storms and take Delores outside for a stroll. He smiled when Casey came into the entrance foyer, where Sebastian was pulling on his boots.

"Good thing I caught you walking by," Sebastian said to him. "I was about to take Delores out. Why don't you strap on the old snowshoes and come along?"

Casey's face brightened. "Do you think Father Paolo will allow it?"

"It's our free period. We can do what we please. Look outside. The storms have finally passed. God beckons us."

Casey gazed at him, his brown eyes wide and wondering. Like a boy about to skip school. "Let me get into proper gear. I'll meet you and Delores out front. Ten minutes, okay?"

Fifteen minutes later, Casey, dressed in snow pants and parka, strolled onto the front walkway that Brothers Eusebius and Micah had cleared earlier. He sat on the top step and fastened the hand-me-down snowshoes onto the boots someone had gifted to the abbey. Delores danced in circles around Sebastian and bit at the snow, barking in anticipation of their hike.

"Where should we go?" Casey asked, struggling to stay limber in the hip-high snow as he wobbled forward with the aid of an old pair of ski poles Sebastian had left by the snowshoes.

"We'll find out once we get there."

"I doubt we'll get too far in this."

Sebastian chewed his lower lip to keep from grinning too widely. He felt freer than he had in many months. First time since September of last year he'd gone on a day hike. And how pleasant to leave his Trappist garments behind. Nice to have his feet in something more substantial than sandals. He and Casey kept on their scapulars to shield their faces from the cold with the hoods, and his heavy snow pants allowed him the freedom to kick up his legs. Casey laughed when he nearly fell backward.

It took a good few minutes before they could acclimate to distributing their weight so they would not sink up to their waists. Heated under the heavy layers, Sebastian smiled at Casey's quick grasp of snowshoeing.

Up to their knees, they pushed on toward the surrounding forest. Delores stepped in the small gullies created by their snowshoes and snapped at the snow chunks spit up from their frames. Tightly packed trunks of birch, aspen, and spruce filled Sebastian's vision. A wondrous grid of thick and thin brown pillars. Comfy in his winter gear, Sebastian felt he might hike through the forest until he reached the ends of the earth.

Casey stopped to catch his breath. "Good to get exercise and fresh air, but this is some effort."

With his ski poles held wide, Sebastian exclaimed, "It's fabulous."

For the moment, Sebastian permitted himself to act silly. He needed to nourish the child inside him. Perhaps God had sent Casey into the entrance foyer for a reason—so that Sebastian could ask him to tag along with him on a hike. To traipse outside on a clear day and inhale the invigorating mountain air. He wanted to fling decorum aside, join the warblers and wrens in their chatter and singing. Release the stress and pressure.

The more Sebastian glanced at Casey in his snowy getup, the more he was glad Casey stood on his side. The clever Casey had proved a good investigator with the realization that JC's Virgin Mary figurine was missing from his cell. Casey had as much reason as any of them to kill JC. But Sebastian refused to believe it. He'd never pictured any of his fellow brothers capable of rash violence. Casey especially was too sensitive, in an intelligent way. Sebastian hadn't defied the abbot when he'd solicited Casey's help. Notwithstanding temptation, Sebastian had never once reported the crime to an outsider.

Delores sniffed the remnants of animal tracks and droppings that dotted the hardened snow. Sebastian recognized they belonged to deer mice. Everything popped out from hiding after the eternal blizzards. Above them, sparrows gathered in tight bands in the tree branches and created a canopy of avian chanting. Casey reached into his pocket and flung them crumbs. They scurried from the trees and pecked at the snowy ground.

Sebastian grinned. "Is that why you were late meeting me outside, to get bread from the kitchen?"

"The search for food is difficult with all this snow," Casey said. "I thought I'd help them out."

A blast of wind cuffed Sebastian's ears. He pulled his hood lower over his face and glanced between the white tree branches toward the sky. Cumulus clouds edged the western side of twelve-thousand-foot Mt. Ouray, which jutted above the white awning of trees to the north. More snow would fall by evening. He stomped closer to Casey, who gazed around at the golden dapples of snow.

The canons of the abbey, fortified by St. Benedict's fifteen-hundred-year-old *Rule*, receded into the distance the farther they hiked. Sebastian let his spoken words carry up and along the snow. Loud and full of vigor. He wanted to scream until the snow shook from the trees. What were those words that crossed his mind like a marquee? Who had he meant? God or Casey? Perhaps he loved both equally.

"It's amazing, isn't it?" Sebastian said, steam curling from his mouth.

"I'll say." Casey echoed Sebastian's enthusiasm. "Look over there, how the snow on the trees makes a nice tunnel. Let's hike under it." The crowns of the spruce trees, joined at the tops and bent in a fixed curtsey from the heavy snowfall, created a frozen ballet of white.

Sebastian instinctively ducked his head. Snug in their "snow grotto," he mounted his sunglasses on his head and peered around. The encompassing snow absorbed their voices and Delores's barks. A comforting seclusion cloaked Sebastian. As if he and Casey were the only two people left on Earth.

Matching Sebastian's youthful zeal, Casey reached his gloved hands for the branches of the trees and laughed. But when their eyes met across their snowy tunnel, Casey's laughter faded. His grin eased into a rigid, tight line. Points of moisture sparkled in the corners of his eyes.

"What is it, Casey?" Sebastian whispered.

"I don't know how to say this, but out here, secluded from the others... I feel... I feel that I should."

"Well," Sebastian said, "then let's hear it."

Casey inhaled, and he looked away toward the far end of the tunnel. "I know about you being a former homicide detective with the Philadelphia Police Department, and that's why Father Paolo asked you to investigate JC's death."

Sebastian released a burst of silver steam from his nostrils and clenched his gloved hands by his sides. "I figured you'd learn soon enough," he said. "Everyone else has, I suppose. Did Brother Hubert tell you?"

"Guess he hadn't gotten around to it yet. I've only been here a few months." Casey's cheeks, already pink from the rigorous hike and the cold, blossomed brighter. "I found out on my own. When I was searching on the off-limits computer for information on JC. I googled your name. I'm sorry. I couldn't help it."

A man much like himself, Sebastian realized. "Don't feel bad. I'd probably do the same myself had I been in your place." Sebastian lowered his hood to get a clearer view of Casey. "Did you have time to read the details?"

What Sebastian hinted at was history, yet it surrounded him like the snow in the forest. Walls of it. But he wasn't going to allow it to suffocate him. He had nothing to hide. Not really. Not anymore.

Casey flashed his eyes back on Sebastian. "A little."

"What do you think?"

"Does it matter what I think?"

"Yes." Sebastian waited, thinking. He hadn't lied. Casey's opinion of him counted a great deal. "Yes," he repeated with a firm nod and renewed conviction to his voice.

"I think they were unfair to you. If what they said was true, then...."

"Then what?"

"Then you wouldn't like me much, would you? I mean, I'm Latino. My biological dad's parents are from Ecuador and my mom's from Mexico. And you're such good friends with Brother Eusebius and so kind and considerate to Brother Rodel when others grow tired of his bashfulness."

Casey's gentle and naïve words pleased Sebastian. He never worried much about how the outside world judged him. It was when his colleagues had abandoned him that he'd hurt the most. Even his family had shown unease whenever he'd come around after the "scandal." Sure, they'd comforted him, insisted they didn't believe the news reports. But having him gone had been easier for them just as much as for himself, hadn't it?

"Whatever happened to proving guilt?" Casey said.

"It doesn't always work that way."

Casey shook his head. "Who are they to think they can do that? People always see so much ugliness in human souls. Why do they always have to assume everyone but them is evil? Why can't they accept that people make mistakes?"

"You mean like with JC?"

Casey flinched, and Sebastian could see through his mittens that he clutched his ski poles tighter. "I saw how you were with him," Casey said. "You liked him too. You couldn't be all those horrible things they said about you. You were kind to JC, treated him like a brother." Casey eyed his snowshoes. "Better than I treated him."

Sebastian sighed toward the white ground. "Some people need angels and devils more tangible than ours here at Mt. Ouray. It doesn't hurt to sell a few more newspapers and win the ratings war along the way."

"They're bullies, that's what they are."

"Don't let it get to you."

"I find it condescending."

"So do I."

"But how? You're not like me. You're white."

He wanted to shout he *was* like him. Shouldn't they both state it outright? No one would hear but Delores and the birds and the trees. He knew Casey had to be. Certainly Casey had pegged him. After that time in the shower, they had de facto, literally and figuratively, exposed the truth to each other. Why continue the pretense? Why not shout with the full thrust of their lungs: "I'm gay!"

Sebastian shuffled closer to him, balancing himself above the snow with the ski poles. "I never liked JC the way some of the others did, not in that sense."

Another deeper flush streaked Casey's face. "I grew to realize maybe you didn't. I'm glad."

Sweet tunes from the sparrows enhanced the splendor of Casey's words. Sebastian cocked his ears toward the birds' crooning, wanting to lose himself in their airiness. Delores puffed billowy breath by his side. He stroked her muzzle. Should he mention what had happened between them in the shower room? Best to let it wash away. What was there to say, anyway?

Instead, he asked, "Why did you choose life inside a monastery, Casey?"

Casey shrugged. "Why do any of us? Always intrigued, I guess." He snickered. "When I was a kid, for fun I used to watch Mass for shut-ins on TV."

Sebastian shared his laughter. "I envied the other altar boys who got to hold the Communion paten under people's chins."

The fluttering birds carried away their chuckles. Sebastian said, "Are you glad of your decision?"

"Yes."

"Do you ever worry you might not preserve?"

"I used to think about it all the time, but not so much now."

Sebastian smiled at his candor. "I suppose I worry sometimes."

Casey's eyes widened. "But don't you want to profess?"

"Even couples on the verge of marriage wonder if they've chosen the right mate." Sebastian tried to chuckle again, but this time his throat constricted. "We're only human."

"The thing is," Casey began, his gaze far along the snow cave, "I... I think about my life here often, and how different it might be if... if you, maybe some of the others, weren't here anymore. I guess that's why I resented JC. I was afraid he might snatch my family." He stared at Sebastian. "You're my family. I never really had much of one other than you."

"We love each other here like brothers," Sebastian said, shifting his eyes from Casey's earnest gaze to the icicles hanging from the spruce trees. An image of Casey naked in the shower flashed across his mind. He shook his head. "That won't stop, no matter what." When Casey remained silent and brooding, Sebastian lowered his sunglasses and said, "We better head back. It's getting near the afternoon work period."

Red faced, Casey moved toward the abbey, and Sebastian and Delores followed tight behind him. Snow crunched under their heavy snowshoes and fell in between the tree branches in a shower of diamonds. Silent save for their heavy breathing, they focused on the path ahead. They stopped once outside the snow tunnel to catch their breaths.

Distant, steady rumbling pulled Sebastian from his persistent meditations. Casey glanced up, and Delores lifted her snout, testing the air with her mouth partly open. She barked when two bright specks grew closer among the maze of trees, along with the roar of engines.

Two men on snowmobiles came to a stop a few yards from their feet. Sebastian recognized their parkas as belonging to the forest service, although their faces were unfamiliar. Heat from their engines distorted the landscape around them. "Hi there," one of the rangers said above the din of idling engines. "How goes things up here?"

"Hello there," Sebastian said, grinning nervously in return. "What a sight you are. We haven't seen a stranger since—" He halted, realizing the first lie perched on his tongue "—since for a while."

"We were taking advantage of the break in the storms and thought we'd stop up here and see how everything's going with you fellows."

"Did you have a chance to stop at the abbey?"

"We were about to, but noticed your fresh snowshoe tracks and followed them instead. Winter treating you all right?"

"It's been fine." Sebastian held back Delores from getting too gregarious with the rangers. "Any exciting news?"

"Been a quiet winter thus far, if you don't include the storms," the second ranger said, lifting his goggles above his blue eyes, which sparkled against the white landscape.

"Sure has been a lot of snow," Sebastian said. "A beautiful day today, though. Nice change. How far in you headed?"

"This is the end of the line for us," the first ranger said, glancing over his shoulder. "We'll need every ounce of octane we got left to make it back into Silverton."

"We can give you some gasoline if you need. You can stop in at the abbey for some hot cocoa while you refuel."

"No thank you, Brother. We should head back right away if we're to beat out that snowstorm coming in from the west. We'll have plenty of fuel for the trip back. We just wanted to make sure you're doing well up here. Don't stay out too long."

"Thanks for stopping by. Come back and see us when spring arrives."

"We'll do that. Good day, Brothers."

"Good day."

In the silence left in the wake of their growling engines, Sebastian stared at the snowmobiles disappearing into the outlying trees, and sighed. Two shrinking plumes of snow coalescing into a single point of light. He'd worried the rangers might mention a missing man fitting JC's description and ask if they'd seen him. He was relieved when they hadn't.

The quiet that lingered hobbled Sebastian. He sensed Casey studying him. Why hadn't Sebastian said anything to the forest rangers? Why hadn't either of them shouted they needed help? Told them that the winter hadn't treated them kindly, that it had held them captive, like Father Paolo, who pointed a figurative gun at each of the brother's heads. Why hadn't he screamed for them to call in the state police?

Yet Sebastian had resisted giving away what was stowed in the barn, not too far from the fuel he'd offered to the rangers. His breathing had relaxed when they had declined his offer. With the scent of unleaded gasoline lingering in the cold air, Sebastian realized that Father Paolo's stubborn refusal to notify authorities had ceased bothering him many days before. At this stage of the game, Sebastian wanted to discover the truth of JC's murder on his own, without the snooping of outsiders.

His stubborn pride made him cringe with shame, and he worried Casey disapproved of his inaction. Still, a shivering anticipation, the same sensation he'd experienced while hard on a case back in Philadelphia, delighted him.

Reluctantly, he looked Casey's way. His mouth was tense, but a sparkle lingered in his brown eyes. Casey had followed Sebastian's lead in keeping his mouth shut. Perhaps Sebastian's word meant more to him than Father Paolo's. He cherished that idea as they retraced their tracks to the abbey.

– XVII –

As THE forest rangers earlier in the day had predicted, a fresh snowstorm blew over Mt. Ouray that night. It fell heavy and wet, beating downward on the already hoary landscape, splashing against Casey's cell window. In the darkest hour of morning he lay supine in bed, allowing the blizzard to underline his thoughts about his snowshoeing adventure with Sebastian.

Sebastian's refusal to tell the rangers about JC hadn't disturbed him as much as he'd have expected. He'd understood his covertness, in a way. They were ordered to keep their mouths shut. Yet Casey sensed Sebastian might have refrained from divulging the truth even without the father's stern instructions.

Detective Harkin. Strong and purposeful, unburdened by indecisiveness. That was Sebastian's way. He smiled. They had shared a moment together. More tender and intimate than when they'd ogled each other in the shower stalls. Another sturdy pillar had been erected to fortify their communion. Casey had known the moment Sebastian had asked him to hike with him and Delores.

He stared at the dark ceiling, quivering. Good feelings had evaded him for quite some time. Lingering doubts he'd had about his vocation seemed sucked under the doorframe and carried away by the abbey currents. No need for a physical interlude. They had each other. Extraordinary brothers. For the rest of their lives.

And that's all that mattered for now.

He sat upright. Someone lurked outside his door. He recognized the same rustling from a few minutes before. It wasn't coming from the storm outside, he was certain. This time he refused to disregard it.

He tiptoed to the door and cracked it open. Faint light from the subdued corridor lights cut into his eyes. He waited, listening. He opened the door wider and peered around. A wispy breeze brushed his cheeks, followed by the flash of a shadow from his side vision. The hushed slap of bare feet on the terracotta tiles receded farther into the abbey. Someone was hurrying away. And whoever it was had intentionally left off his sandals so no one would hear his prowling about.

Casey slipped on his sandals and stepped into the corridor. Should he awaken the others, see which one among them went missing? It was past midnight. Let them sleep. He'd find whoever skulked in the abbey late at night.

Careful to avoid making any noise, he followed after the shadow. Several paces down the corridor, near the cloister garden, he perceived murky movement out of the corner of his eye. An outline fluctuated. Was it the radiators causing heat distortion? A subtle bending of nothing?

Like a feline, he tiptoed toward it. Another sound behind him jerked him around. Near the kitchen. More slapping of feet on the tiles. Then silence. He stopped, waited for the shadow's next move. Creepiness kneaded its way over Casey's body. Footsteps again. Quieter. Casey inched to the sound's location.

Someone shut a door. Casey slinked to the kitchen. He peered inside, vigilant in case the shadow might be waiting to jump him. Conjuring more courage, he stepped fully into the kitchen and looked around. Nothing but the glint of stainless steel and the leftover aroma of baked bread.

A few feet from the kitchen entrance was another door that led to the generator and incinerator. He scurried back to the corridor, placed his ear to the cold door and listened. He began to open the door, but froze. The hinges screeched. An echoing explosion wrapped in silence.

The shadow couldn't have gone in there. Casey would have heard the same eerie, high-pitched sound. Had the shadow taken the service elevator? No, that was even noisier.

Slowly, he shut the door and peered over his shoulder. Worried his sleepy eyes might be playing tricks on him, he followed what he guessed was movement coming from near the sacristy. With less conviction, he slumped along the wall, holding his hands before him should he need them in self-defense.

"The Dalakis Curse." He shook the image of ghosts and goblins from his head. They didn't exist. Couldn't exist. No matter how sick and twisted the past owners had behaved, summoning demons onto their turf for some diabolical summit, God did not permit earthly hauntings. "Man is destined to die once, and after that face judgment," Scripture stated. He hoped recalling the passage might calm him, but he also remembered Apostle Mark, who warned of the "unclean spirits" that dwelt side by side with man.

The looming slap of bare feet further curdled his blood. The sound moved closer, to his right, his left, receded. A long shadow slid across the corridor, blocking his path. Growing longer as Casey stared in alarm. The game had changed. The shadow no longer wanted to avoid Casey, but sought to reach him. In a switch, Casey had become the prey.

His increased heart rate sounded like a dozen drums thumping inside his head. He paid scant attention to the mouse scurrying across the corridor for the kitchen, and he slipped inside the sacristy and shut the door.

Shaking, he listened for any rustling in the corridor. Everything went silent. The windowless storage room kept out the ruckus from the blizzard. Gloomy shadows prowled in every corner. Smells of dust and musk hung heavy. Casey detected the scent of Sebastian, who'd spent many winter hours in the sacristy crafting rosaries. That same hard-worked odor he'd relished his first day as a retreatant last summer. The whiff of honest labor that had rushed to meet Casey's nose when Sebastian had escorted him to the cottage house.

The faint light under the door dimmed. Someone was standing on the other side. Was the stalker whispering for him to come out? The knob jittered. This was no work of his imagination. Casey flinched backward. He ducked lower behind a column of boxes and inhaled more of Sebastian's scent for strength.

Millimeter by millimeter, the door creaked open. Abruptly, it shut. Light under the doorway brightened. Bare feet slapped recklessly against the floor, fading farther into the abbey.

Casey exhaled and brought his hands to his sides to keep himself from gnawing on his knuckles. He waited for his heart to stop beating in his ears before he had the nerve to open the door.

Delores stood outside, wagging her tail and panting. Casey patted her head. "Good job, girl," he whispered. "You scared off the stalker." And he traipsed back to his cell.

Cocooned in bed, he wished Father Paolo permitted locks on the cell doors. Not until that moment had Casey feared for his well-being inside Mt. Ouray.

BY NEXT morning, Casey had shaken off the prowler. He took comfort in Sebastian's being close by. Though they could not speak around the other brothers, a smile or nod from him while passing each other in the corridors or the canonical hours reassured Casey.

Father Paolo had not requested Casey work in the administrative office in more than two weeks. Casey suspected his banishment had something to do with his snooping on the "off-limits" computer. He spent most of his subsequent work periods sweeping and scrubbing the corridors or helping Brother Micah in the kitchen.

He was washing the breakfast bins for his morning work assignment when he slapped the soapy water in a sudden revelation. Brother Micah, cutting open a box of frozen onions for tomato soup, pivoted his shoulders to gape at him. Casey minded him little.

He finished the dishwashing as quickly as possible, then excused himself to sweep the corridors. He spent most of his time outside the sacristy, moving the broom near the same spot where he'd run to hide from the stalker the night before, while waiting for Sebastian to open the door and appear.

Nearing Sext, the door swung open and Sebastian and Brother Eusebius stepped out. Sebastian smiled at him, and his eyes asked, "What are you doing?"

Casey fluttered his eyelids in response.

They waited another hour for siesta to begin before they could convene alone in private. Casey found Sebastian reading in the library.

Sebastian closed the book (Casey noticed the author on the spine, Conrad Baars) and slid it aside. "What has you so excited?" Sebastian whispered with a grin.

"I was thinking, and it just came to me. Before… before JC died, I had a short conversation with him in the kitchen. He mentioned something about Puerto Rico, about how he wished he was there, about liking the warmer weather. He used a lot of unusual Spanish slang. At the time I didn't think much of it, but now I'm wondering. Do you think he's from there?"

"Might be. Certainly looked Puerto Rican. And he did use a lot of slang."

"He also mentioned his age to be twenty-one. Does that mean JC might have lied about his amnesia?"

"Not really. From what I know, and from what Brother Jerome has told us, you can remember bits and pieces without knowing why."

"Even he had said that. Makes sense, I guess."

"About the only thing."

Casey gazed out the window, where the slim sun rays cut through the gray clouds and shrouded the forest in a hazy yellow mist. He still cursed himself for wasting prime investigative time during his access to the administrative office. He figured the abbot or Brother Hubert had conducted research of his own, but neither was likely to share whatever information he'd learned. Casey wanted to state his suspicions about why the abbot would want to keep them in the dark, but he didn't want to come across as sour. He had never told Sebastian about the cached porn sites he'd found on the computer either. What difference did it make to their investigation?

He also balked at mentioning the overnight stalking. Sebastian might call him off the case if he worried for his safety. For now, the investigation operated as a glue to hold them together. United for a singular cause.

Casey mirrored Sebastian's warm smile and placed his hand alongside his on the tabletop. With all his might, Casey tried to will him to toss caution aside and grasp his hand. Why not? Theirs was a religious order based on affection and kindness. Fidelity was of the utmost importance.

"Will any of this be useful helping us find the killer?" he asked.

Sebastian cast his blue eyes to his lap.

"What is it, Sebastian?"

"Father Paolo asked me to stop the investigation. Flat out. Once and for all. But I disagreed with him, I'm afraid. I can't see how we can ignore any of this. Someone will find out sooner or later."

"What did you tell him?"

"I said I understood his position but that I would most likely continue to explore possibilities into his death."

"Was he too upset?"

"We left on amicable terms. We'll see." Sebastian stood with a dull skid of his chair. "We best get ready for work. We'll chat later. In the meantime, though, Casey, why don't you back off yourself? I don't want you getting into a mess either."

"As long as you're on the case, I'm on the case."

Sebastian chuckled. "Just stay out of trouble. I'll see you at dinner."

Half an hour later, Casey was ready to help Brother Rodel clean the radiators when Brother Lucien tugged on his sleeve and insisted Father Paolo wished to speak with him. Bewildered, Casey left his scrub brush behind and followed Brother Lucien to Father Paolo's private office.

The father was standing by the round table before the lifeless fireplace, sorting through papers. Brother Lucien bowed out of the office, and with a wide grin, Father Paolo approached Casey.

Casey's legs trembled. He hadn't been called before the abbot alone since he'd first entered the abbey as a postulant and he'd tried to seduce him with wine and chocolates and flickering candles.

This time, no wine or chocolates sat on display, and no candles illuminated the office.

The abbot stood in front of his desk, his hands folded behind his back. His tunic rustled against his ears as he moved to scratch his neck. Casey scrutinized his expressionless face. The glint in his glasses concealed his eyes. No way to judge his intentions.

Finally, the abbot leaned against his desk and locked his hands across his scapular skirt. After Casey obeyed his offer to sit, Father Paolo remained standing.

Casey gripped the armrests of the Bergère chair and tried to ignore the juniper-laced air that stung his eyes. He focused on the father's woven fingers, short and fat with veins pumping thick blood. Was he finally going to receive the lecture he'd feared for invading the off-limits computer? Did it have to do with his running about the abbey late at night? Or something worse?

Father Paolo peered at Casey above his wire-framed eyeglasses. Moistened lips glistened against the sole illuminated lamp. "Brother Casey," he finally spoke, "I have news for you. You might dislike what I have to say, but I beseech you, remember the words of St. Benedict. 'Carry out the superior's order as promptly as if the command came from God himself.'"

Casey exhaled. "What… what is it?"

He barely heard Father Paolo's response, spoken toward the ceiling as if Casey weren't even in the room. The abbot's Portuguese accent blurred with the drumming in his ears. Listening to the father, he blinked back the hot tears accumulating in the corners of his eyes and barely breathed. Casey wanted to shield himself, as if the abbot had chucked his words at him like ice-glazed snowballs.

When the father finished talking and dropped his eyes on him with an odd leer, Casey sat numb. Speechless. Holding his breath. He feared moving even his fingers, which still gripped the fabric-covered armrests, for that would mean that he wasn't trapped in a horrible nightmare. One move, one miniscule flinch, the release of a single breath, and that would prove he was wide awake, and everything the abbot had uttered was real.

Father Paolo excused him. Somehow Casey managed to pull himself from the chair and nod a salutation to the abbot. Outside the private office, he scurried past Brother Lucien, who he could sense stared after him. He headed directly for his cell without wanting to notice any of the brothers shuffling through the corridors. He even brushed off Sebastian's reaching out to hold him back.

– XVIII –

SEBASTIAN sat on his bed, pondering. Regardless of Father Paolo's latest order to end the investigation, JC's murder continued to stump him. Weak agglomerations of events and suspicions led him nowhere closer to the truth than that first night when Delores had sniffed out JC's body inside the walk-in freezer. Sebastian deduced the attack hadn't stemmed from an intimate rage. If that were so, the killer would have bludgeoned JC numerous times, rather than once. Unlikely that JC had become lovers with any of the brothers, although he was unsure how far his relationship with Father Paolo had gone. Whoever had struck JC had done so in a singular flash of fury. An anger mounted from fear, envy, and perhaps delusions.

Puerto Rico. He realized JC most likely was Puerto Rican, or at least partly. During their interviews, JC had used several Spanish slang words known within the Puerto Rican community, and his manner was familiar to Sebastian. Many people from the Caribbean island lived in his former Philadelphia neighborhood and had worked by his side at the PPD. In fact, Philadelphia comprised the second largest Puerto Rican community in the continental United States after New York City, reaffirming what Sebastian had suspected when he'd first listened to JC speak after he'd awakened from unconsciousness. JC and he came from the same city.

Strange coincidence. But Philadelphia had a large exodus rate. He'd run into ex-Philadelphians often, of every ethnicity and race.

Even a few cottage guests the past few years had once called Philadelphia home.

But how did any of that factor into JC's death?

Sebastian examined the two mysterious objects in his palms: the buckle and zipper he'd found nestled among the debris in the incinerator. The zipper, gnarled and brittle to his touch, nearly crumbled in his hand. He laid that aside and turned over the buckle, hoping different angles might reveal its secrets.

He shook his head and returned the objects to the plastic bag where he stored them in his chest. Worthless. Without proper forensic tools, he could gain little knowledge from them. But his instincts told him they had once belonged to JC's knapsack and coat.

More than ever he wanted to tear apart each of the brother's cells, dig and dig until he unearthed the missing link. The one shred of evidence that would crack the riddle. Who cared if the courts declared whatever he found inadmissible as evidence? At least he'd know. How was he to get a search warrant nine thousand feet in the Rockies in the dead of winter, anyway? Especially on top of the abbot's latest stubbornness?

They were at *lectio divina*. Eerie silence penetrated the corridors. His toes edged toward the threshold to JC's former cell. His room had offered up no clues other than the missing Virgin Mary statuette. It was the other cells he wanted to turn upside down.

He peered into the one cell with the door left open. Brother Jerome sat at his desk, reading Scripture. He hadn't noticed Sebastian peering in. Or he no longer worried if he did. A chilled calm had descended over the abbey the past week. Rumors must have already circulated about the father's directive, bringing with it a tacit acceptance that the investigation into JC's slaying had run its course. Case closed.

But not for Sebastian. Apart from the father's demands or Brother Rodel's cryptic warning, he intended to see the case to the end. He refused to sit on a cold case for what might be the remainder of his life.

Frustrated, he found himself standing inside the administrative office. It lay empty, silent. Father Paolo and Brother Lucien were straightening up the chapter house for the dignitaries scheduled to visit the abbey soon after the final snowmelt. A wash of nostalgia for his old twenty-fifth district sucked breath out of him. He could almost hear the ding of computers, the relentless phone ringing, the incessant chatter, followed by the cry for political favors and cover-ups and the inability to accomplish anything due to the barrage of external and internal pressures.

Years ago, police work had turned into a kaleidoscope of appearances. He'd sensed its dismal evolution as a rookie. The dictates that flowed from a power base that exuded tentacles wider than a man-of-war's. From the mayor, trickled down to the district captains, underlined by a media obsessed with self-styled vendettas and a gullible public hungry for suffering. And now even Washington inserted its will in local policing. Politics saturated them.

The last decree had ended Sebastian's career. Once the local media had unleashed the headlines and sound bites, there was no turning back. In a world of instant information, culpability superseded innocence. A sacrificial lamb offered for the communal guilt trip, too tasty to pass up.

He'd fought for his reputation, but he knew from the first round he was a goner.

Sebastian still could see the whites of the man's eyes, rain saturating them while he stood over him, staring in disbelief. He hadn't meant to do it. But the entrenched power structure cared little about truth.

No one could beat the forces behind a power that literally razed cities, stirred riots, lost or won wars, caused suicides, and even led people to murder.

It took on a reality of its own. A cult-like presence that people had given up questioning generations ago. A powerless submission to image, manipulation, and a perplexing world encapsulated into bite-sized morsels. The hunger for a vague social justice that left men's brains battered. And the public opened its mouth like chicks waiting for their mothers to regurgitate into their throats.

Sebastian had been one of the meals.

Served up for ratings, sales, emotionalism, and radical ideology that had transformed into a new religion, complete with sensational dragons to slay and glorious iconoclasts to worship.

The Pilgrims, fleeing from the Catholic Church's clutch on Europe, had traveled five thousand miles on rickety ships to reach a world they'd never stepped foot on, full of fears, sickness, and uncertainty. Five hundred years later, Sebastian had escaped the Church's modern equivalent. Leviticus in the hands of secular tyrants greedy for contemporary witch hunts. He had hoped to find his refuge high in the Rocky Mountains behind the walls of Mt. Ouray.

In a way, he'd succeeded. Casey brought him a newfound joy he'd assumed he'd never find again. And despite JC's murder, even that, from an investigative end, thrilled Sebastian. He could not deny his instincts to uncover and sniff and dig. The detective lurked inside him, possessed his spirit. No priest could exorcise that demon. But the abbey's bureaucratic power structure proved almost as elaborate as the one he'd left behind.

Inside the abbey, Sebastian's desire to find JC's killer stemmed from love as much as hatred. Indeed, Sebastian had grown to love his fellow monks—even Father Paolo, in a way. They lived closer than any family. They prayed together, worked together, took their dinners together. They recognized each other's scents. Finding out who had murdered JC was as much for them as it was for him. Underneath it all, Sebastian held the potential to save a man's soul.

The light on the abbey phone's answering machine blinked red. Spring had already fallen over most of the country. People were stirring. Interested postulants and guests were filling the machine with inquiries into reservations and vocations.

Sebastian's heart thumped with a dizzying urgency. He needed to solve the crime. One way or the other. He refused to let the powers— whether they lingered inside or outside the abbey—control him. He sensed the investigation slipping from his hands. He must hold onto it, grapple with it until each speck and crumb lined up in a semblance of order.

He considered for a moment telephoning the police. Not to report the crime—he couldn't have that. This was *his* case. But to fish around for general information on missing persons or psychotics known to pose as clergy. Perhaps contact his old cronies in Philadelphia. Someone who might understand his predicament. But who?

He'd left Philadelphia like a shamed hound, his tail between his legs. Even his best friends from the force had refused eye contact with him his last day, siding instead with caution. The old saying, "Where there's smoke, there's fire," never resonated louder than inside police departments.

One colleague had found the courage to speak to him in the parking lot while Sebastian carried the last of his belongings to his van. Bart had gestured for him to step behind a pickup truck. "We can't fight it," he'd stated after ensuring no one saw them. "It's at the point we can't even speak our minds in private anymore. The other night at the dinner table I found myself whispering to my wife about everything that's been going on. That's how terrified they have us." Bart's words, barely audible above the chilly breeze coming off Lighthouse Field across the street, had left goose pimples on Sebastian's arms.

With a long sigh, he left the administrative office determined to solve JC's murder. During the Eucharist and Terce, Sebastian watched his brothers more intently. They had fallen back into their old postures. JC's death was fading from their perceptions. Soon, he feared, the events would connote nothing more real than the absurd Dalakis Curse.

He rested his eyes on Casey. He sat two brothers away, not next to him as usual. He was avoiding him again. Averting his eyes, which seemed moist and red most of the time, as if Casey spent his alone time crying. The one time Sebastian had tried to reach out to him and ask what ailed him, he'd wrenched from his hand and rushed off without a glance back.

Had Sebastian done or said something to disturb him?

Casey's red eyes fixed on his psalmody, and his voice rose stronger, with an angry energy. Even Brother Jerome beside him must have taken notice. He'd flashed him a quizzical glare, turned up his nose, and tweaked his shoulders.

Throughout the day Sebastian tried to find him alone, but whenever they had the chance, Casey chose to wrap himself in frivolous work or stand among the brothers so that they couldn't speak freely.

Resolved to reach the bottom of something, at least, Sebastian cornered Casey in his cell after Vespers. He entered without knocking.

Casey, lounging on top of his bed, raised his eyes from the pages of a book. "Sebastian...."

"How are you, Casey?"

"I... I was just reading Alban Butler."

"*Lives of the Saints*. Good book."

Casey closed the cover and sat upright. "How is the investigating going? Are you getting any closer to solving it?"

A heavy sigh escaped Sebastian's mouth. "I'm more concerned with another matter at the moment."

"What's that?"

"I'm curious why you've been so evasive and despondent."

Casey looked contemplatively at the floor. "It's nothing, really."

His downcast eyes suggested something more. Sebastian pressed him. Finally, Casey returned his gaze.

"What would you do if I left the abbey?" Casey said.

Sebastian remained silent. Difficult to imagine life at Mt. Ouray without Casey. But then, it was difficult to imagine life at the abbey with him. They were supposed to be celibate. How might he imagine taking a vow of celibacy with Casey always so near? Both of them, young and vital, harbored an earthy practicality that oftentimes demanded a sexual release.

"I don't know," he said. "Life has changed here a lot the past few months. I'm unsure what I want or what I'd do. Why do you ask such a thing?"

"Sebastian," he whispered, "Father Paolo is sending me away."

"What?"

"As soon as the forest service opens the road, at the end of April."

"That's only a month away. Where to? What were his reasons?"

"There's a monastery in Vermont. Father Paolo said the Church requested a shuffling of younger novices there. The average age of the monks there is over sixty. They need healthier novices to care for the elders and run the facility. It's dying."

"And what did you say?"

"Nothing. I was stunned. I sat and listened. He said that it was out of his hands."

Sebastian grew indignant. "That's not fair. Why not take Brother Rodel?" He hated saying those last words the second he caught the shock in Casey's brown eyes. Then it faded into a gentle glint from the overhead light, and a shadow of a smile appeared. He'd stated what he'd meant, and Casey did not judge him. Perhaps he admired Sebastian all the more.

"He thinks I did it, doesn't he?" Casey said to Sebastian. "He thinks I killed JC."

"That couldn't be the reason. Why would you say such a thing? Don't worry over something so silly."

"What if I'm right? That's why he wants you to stop the investigation at the same time he's sending me off."

"How does the abbot know any of us didn't do it? Me even?"

"He asked you to investigate. Besides, you liked JC. You wanted to help him. We all noticed. Everyone could tell I didn't like him."

"All the brothers found fault with JC."

"Brother Micah might have hated him more than me," Casey said almost to himself, "but he was the only one."

"The abbot doesn't suspect you of murder." Sebastian nudged closer to him. "It's not uncommon to move younger monks to struggling monasteries."

"And ours isn't?"

Sebastian stood planted before Casey. He wanted to squat and take Casey's head in his hands and utter reassurances. Not only was the case slipping from his hands, but so was Casey Galvan.

Casey lifted his head and inhaled. "Then maybe the father is seeking revenge," he said. "I rejected his advances once, and he's finally enjoying his retaliation after all these months. That's it, you think?"

Sebastian caught his breath. He'd guessed the father had tried to seduce Casey, the way he had with JC and most likely Brother Rodel. For a moment, relief pushed aside the dread of Casey's leaving. Casey hadn't succumbed to the abbot's advances after all.

"Don't allow this to turn you bitter," he said in a soothing voice, his arms stiff by his sides. "Everything will be okay. You can't take his sending you away to mean some kind of reprimand or indictment."

"Maybe he's the one who did it. He killed JC and wants to conceal the truth. He's worried I learned something when I went snooping on the computer. He's punishing me for... for being your secondary. He's guilty and jealous and all those horrible things." Casey's gaze dropped to the floor.

"Let's not worry about his motives right now. We'll think of a way to keep you here."

Sitting firmer, Casey eyed Sebastian. "Do you think we can?"

"Spring is a while off. There's enough time to figure out a plan."

Casey cocked his head and looked directly into Sebastian's eyes. "I don't want to leave here."

"I don't want you to leave here either, Casey."

– XIX –

STANDING before Father Paolo's mahogany desk, Sebastian waited for the abbot to finish writing in a notepad and offer him one of the Bergère chairs, as he normally would. Palm smudges on his eyeglasses suggested he'd been thinking hard on matters and would be in no mood for another confrontation. But Sebastian refused to sit back on the issue any longer.

Impatient for the abbot to acknowledge him, he uttered, "Why must you send him away?"

For the first time since he'd stepped inside the office, Father Paolo peered over the wire frames of his eyeglasses at Sebastian. He sighed heavily. "Sit, Brother Sebastian."

Sebastian flashed back to when he'd stood in his captain's office, leaning into his desk as he'd confronted Reems. Many times they'd butted heads. With JC's murder investigation in full force, there was scant difference between Captain Terry Reems and Father Paolo Cabral.

Seated, Sebastian repeated his question and punctuated it before the abbot had a chance to respond with, "He hasn't even professed his vows; he's not a full monk."

"It's what the bishop wants." The abbot pushed the notepad aside with another lengthy sigh. "He e-mailed me last week asking for young monks. What was I to tell him? I'm sure Casey will preserve just as well in Vermont as he would have here."

"Couldn't you have suggested he look at another monastery?"

"And why would I have done that?"

"We barely have enough young men here now," Sebastian said. "E-mail him back, or better yet, call. Tell him the brothers here are getting older and older, like at the abbey in Vermont. Brother Augustine needs full-time attention. He can't even feed himself. It's only a matter of time before Brother Jerome's arthritis forces him into a wheelchair full time like Brother Giles's gout has. We'll need younger monks to attend to their needs. Brother George can't be expected to do it all."

"I agree with you more than you realize, Brother Sebastian, but the bishop asked who among my younger charges would make the smoothest transition, and I simply told him. Why do you care where Brother Casey goes?"

"He's only just gotten here," Sebastian said. "Give him a chance."

Father Paolo peered at Sebastian over the bridge of his nose. "You've become mighty bold, Brother Sebastian. I feel that I'm partly responsible. I've unleashed the sergeant inside you. Shall I refresh your memory of where you reside and who's in charge? Mt. Ouray is not your old precinct in Philadelphia."

The heavy scent of extinguished juniper incense lingered over Sebastian's head, a reminder of whose authority controlled the workings of the abbey. Sebastian agreed with a few of Casey's suspicions. Revenge lurked behind the abbot's decision. Vengeance for his snooping and for Sebastian's snatching Casey from his clutches.

"I just don't understand," Sebastian mumbled.

The abbot's eyes dropped to the top of his polished desk. "I planned on calling you to my office before Retire today, in fact, Brother Sebastian, to elaborate on something we've already discussed. You might find it relates to your present torment."

Lifting his eyes, Sebastian said, "And what is that?"

Father Paolo cupped his hands under his chin and eyed Sebastian with tightened lips. "I'm going to assemble the brothers tomorrow and instruct that we forever conceal Brother JC's death. It's what the Lord would want."

Sebastian's head snapped up, and he peered at the abbot. "How could the Lord wish to cover up the death of an innocent man?"

"How do you know he's innocent? Have you learned why he came here?"

"No, but…."

"I've seen his type. He asked for trouble here."

"You once insisted he came to us because he was a devout Catholic. You even compared him with the old women of Vila de Seda who hiked to church on their knees."

"Are you defying me again?"

Sebastian's shoulders slumped, and he gazed toward his fidgety hands. "I just don't see how any of us can pretend that a man wasn't murdered, inside an abbey of all places."

"That's my point precisely." The father stood and began pacing. "There are larger issues at stake beyond that boy's death. We've gone over this, haven't we?"

Sebastian followed him with his eyes. "But you're asking us to participate in a cover-up, to lie."

"We'll go on here as if he'd never come," the abbot said as if to himself, pivoting on his heels faster and faster. "No one will be the wiser. We'll toss his body into the forest. We must act within the next few days. Already the snows are coming farther and farther apart."

"What about when they find him? What about the contusion on his temple?"

"They'll think he hit his head on a tree or a rock buried in the snow."

"They'll do an autopsy. They'll learn he died from asphyxiation."

Father Paolo's accent became garbled. "He suffocated in the snow," he said. "Many victims do in Colorado. Ever heard of avalanches? Rescuers find people who've died from suffocation in isolated mountain passes all the time. His being frozen all this time will only fortify their assumptions. The authorities will never draw a link between the abbey and him, between any of us and him."

"I... I can't do it."

Father Paolo stopped before Sebastian and looked down on him with flaming cheeks. "You must. You have no choice in the matter." He seemed to study Sebastian, pondering. Then he sat back at his desk and said in a calmer tone, "There is something I might do for you in return for your strict obedience."

Sebastian flashed him a look. "Does it have anything to do with you wanting to speak with me?"

Gazing toward the cold fireplace, Father Paolo said, "I can perhaps—perhaps, mind you—see that Casey stays put here with us at Mt. Ouray."

Acid inched up Sebastian's throat. "Are you... are you bribing me... with Casey?"

Father Paolo smirked and shook his head at Sebastian. "I'm merely stating a reasonable condition. Now's your chance to act the same. Isn't Brother Casey worth it to you? For you to forget any of this ugliness with JC ever happened and to keep your mouth shut?"

"So all along you set it up for Casey to be sent away in order to trick me?"

"I'm hardly that devious, Brother Sebastian. The bishop did, in fact, solicit me for a younger monk. It was one of those opportunistic nuggets to fall into my lap. I cleverly used it to my advantage. Can you blame me?"

Dazed, Sebastian stared at the abbot, but hardly saw him.

"I can always suggest that the bishop look for a monk elsewhere. As you've stated, we hardly have any brothers to spare here at Mt. Ouray, which is what I'd like to tell him. But that is up to you."

The father spread his arms, his flowing tunic sleeves long and impressive. Beneath the picture of Pope Benedict, he almost appeared like a pageant angel, which made his scheme all the more unreal.

"This is Mt. Ouray," he said. "My abbey. A place I intend to salvage in any way possible. Have I made myself clear, Brother Sebastian?"

Sebastian worked up the spit in his mouth. "Yes, Father Paolo, you've made yourself clear."

SEBASTIAN retired to his cell and refused to come out for his afternoon work assignment. He and Brother Eusebius had met the winter's rosary quota days before, and the abbot had relegated him to odd jobs around the abbey. The latest: to fix the display cases in the gift shop. In a sense, Sebastian hadn't fibbed to Brother Eusebius when he'd mumbled through his cell door that he'd fallen ill. He was sick. Sick of the ultimatum Father Paolo had forced him to face.

He rejected dinner and came out only for Vespers. The brothers' ogling bothered him not a bit. He made scarce effort to conceal his shaken gaze and his inaudible, listless chanting. Father Paolo avoided his eyes whenever he emerged from his cell. A smugness cut into the abbot's face.

Casey knocked on his cell during their evening free period. Sebastian asked only that he allow him time alone. "Whatever you need," Casey said into the door with a soft voice, and Sebastian heard the gentle slap of his sandals fade along the corridor until the sound disappeared from earshot.

Later that night, after Compline, Casey's sober flute playing drifted into his cell with the softness of spring's fragrant promises. Warmer weather did indeed lie around the corner, and Sebastian had only a few days to choose which oath to declare. Father Paolo's or his own.

Keep Casey and discard the truth or lose him forever in exchange for justice.

None of it seemed fair.

But when had life ever played fair for him?

Blue wedges of moonlight rubbed against the wall. One highlighted his statuette of the Virgin Mary. He begged her for compassion and mercy. Did she care? Had she ever even existed?

Casey's tender tunes, the same familiar melody that Sebastian had failed to place, pained his heart. Images of tragic lovers whirled in his mind. He reached under the bedcovers, touched himself through his tunic. He imagined Casey in the shower stall, lathering the soap over his sleek body, devoid of almost any body fat or hair. He rubbed himself while the music interlaced with his thoughts. A voice from somewhere flowed with the melody. Sebastian had whispered Casey's name, dripped from his lips like nectar from honeysuckle.

"Casey…."

Growing exasperated, he tossed the covers aside and sat on the edge of the bed, his bare feet flat on the cold floor. His heart raced. He dropped his head into his hands and bit his palms. He pulled them away, a string of saliva connecting his lower lip and the cleft of his joined palms.

He stared at his large hands, sparkling with saliva under the moonbeams.

God, prevent me from doing what I want to do.

He stood, gazed hard at the floor, and uncinched his belt.

– XX –

A SOLITARY tear left a cold trail along Casey's cheek while he played the flute. The moonlight that streamed through his bedroom window bathed him in a bluish-yellow light. Like a friend boarding a plane to fly far away, so, too, his music drifted absent of his touch, despite it coming from his own lips and fingers.

Whenever Casey had crossed paths with Sebastian during the day, he'd studied him. His demeanor had changed. He understood that Sebastian had been unsuccessful in convincing the abbot to allow him to remain at Mt. Ouray. That's why Sebastian had evaded him during the day. Defeat and guilt fueled Sebastian's torment. There was no keeping Father Paolo from his intentions. Dual emotions conflicted Casey. On one level, his leaving loomed as imminent. Yet on the other, Sebastian loved him enough to suffer over it.

Casey wondered what St. Simeon Stylites would do. Climb a pole and forget the world? Sometimes that's exactly what Casey wanted. Without Sebastian, no reason existed why he shouldn't torture himself as his favorites saints had done. He'd scale the tallest tree in the San Juan Range and refuse to budge. His stubbornness, like that of St. Simeon, would be taken for piety—or maybe insanity. Either way, Casey no longer cared.

Dispirited, he laid his flute aside, forcing himself back to a time when his loneliness was something for him alone. Upstairs in his bedroom in Hutchinson, surrounded by an indifferent family, he'd find solace in isolation while reading Milne or playing his flute or writing stories (as a boy he'd sometimes write plays on the lives of make-believe saints). The pleasure of self-imprisonment in a house full of strangers. But here? In Mt. Ouray? With Sebastian so near?

You will find love and beauty inside a monastery. Had the whispering voice inside his head meant to persuade him or to stress a warning?

He fell supine into bed. The dark ceiling gaped at him. He wrapped his arms around himself, massaging his elbows underneath his tunic sleeves. He felt cold, yet it was warm inside, with the dry heater boards pumping harder than usual.

What else was there? The pain stood more tangible than the San Juan Mountains puncturing the unrestrained Colorado sky.

Moonlight continued to cut between the window blinds, leaving slashes across the floor. The Earth had shifted. Warmer days lurked restlessly. Normally, spring would fill him with hope and excitement, inject his limbs with vim. But now, he realized, with the thaw he'd be shipped like a package to a Trappist monastery he'd only given the slightest inkling of joining when he'd first considered his discernment, two thousand miles from Mt. Ouray.

Irritating tears dribbled down the sides of Casey's face and tickled the back of his ears and neck. He wiped his face, sniffled. What remained for him to do?

In one continuous, bold move, he leaped from bed, tore the belt from his waist, and pulled off his tunic and boxer briefs. He stood exposed, almost shocked at his own bare rebelliousness. He trembled with a quivering smile that flexed his tear-stiffened cheeks.

Naked, a sense of liberty overcame him.

Temptation trembled through his limbs. Sheathed with nothing but his own skin, he crawled under the bedcovers and clutched the edges. How nice to feel the sleekness of sheets against his tender flesh.

He lay motionless for several minutes. Barely a breath swept past his dry lips. For the moment, his defiance proved his sole comfort.

He jerked upward. Someone—or something—lurked outside his cell. Second night he'd heard the sound. He clutched the covers tighter.

This time he sensed heavy breathing directly opposite the door. The doorknob jiggled. He tensed. Why couldn't he scream?

The cell door opened. Meager light parted the darkness, silhouetting a tall figure. No one spoke. Casey brought the covers closer to his nose. He wanted to shout out, but his tongue stuck to the roof of his dry mouth.

The form moved inside his cell. He sensed heat pulsating from it.

Was it the murderer? The same shadow that had chased him into the sacristy? A demon summoned by the Dalakises?

JC's ghost come back for revenge?

But ghosts did not exist.

A gasp escaped Casey's mouth, about the same time the figure moved closer, and Casey was certain it had spotted him. He shook with fear. Nevertheless, an odd sense of anticipation tingled along his bare limbs.

The slim mattress sank, as if the form had sat on the edge of the bed, forcing Casey to flinch. He felt hot breath on his knuckles that was not his own.

"I sometimes wish we'd met under different circumstances, in a different place."

The voice. The one he'd heard telling him to seek the monastic life years ago. God's voice? Then he recognized the shadow's earthy scent.

Casey shook his head to reorient himself, and he sat upright, holding the covers to his neck to conceal his nakedness. "Sebastian?"

"Did I startle you?"

"Only for a moment. Why didn't you say anything?"

"I'm sorry. I'm so weary."

"I've noticed. You're not feeling better?"

"A little. And how are you?"

"I'm okay." Casey scanned Sebastian more closely and discerned in the moonlight that he went without sandals. "What brings you here at this hour?"

Sebastian's silent gaze appeared brooding in the murkiness. "I spoke with the abbot," he whispered.

"The news isn't good. I've already guessed."

Another pause. Sebastian inhaled. "He's given me a horrible choice, one I'm certain he'll present to you too. To all of us. Tomorrow he's going to call an assembly and announce his mandate."

"JC?"

Casey sensed Sebastian nodding, and he buried his head in his pillow. The bland smell of nothingness from the cotton pillowcase burned his nostrils. "No," he said, roving his forehead over the pillow to wipe out the awful thoughts.

"Try not to let it upset you," Sebastian said.

Casey felt the mattress rise, and he heard the door shut, and for a moment he worried Sebastian had left him, providing him with nothing more than words for consolation. He expected to hear the slap of his bare feet die away behind the closed door. Instead he felt the mattress compress again and a hand rest on his shoulder. Heat traveled through the bedcovers and constricted his throat in relief.

"Casey, after all we've suffered through together in a few short months, we can face this tribulation."

Indignation stiffened his limbs, and he rolled to face Sebastian, careful to ensure the bedcovers did not slip from his grip. Sebastian's shadowy figure, a blur through his moistened eyelashes, fluctuated with a throbbing force of the moon. "I'll be carted away from here," he said in a raspy whisper. "Less than a month from now we'll never see each other again. It's because I won't let you lie on the abbot's behalf. I won't let you."

"Don't worry yourself, Casey," Sebastian said soothingly. "Let's face this like brave soldiers. Take courage."

"I can't take courage." Casey wanted to tear away from Sebastian's hold and again cover his teary face with the pillow, suffocating the pain until it expired, but Sebastian held him in place.

"We have no choice," he said. "This is what God has dropped into our laps. We must deal with it. You and I. I know we can."

Sebastian's lulling voice softened his anger into prickly warmth. There was quiet. Sebastian's hands held firm to his arms beneath the bedcovers. The chill had left him. Casey wanted to smile. But the mere idea of the abbot's pronouncement seared into his soul anew.

"I can't believe Father Paolo, of all people, would consider such a horrible thing."

"It's how things are done sometimes. I used to see it often in the police department. Cover-ups, political pandering, bribery. All of it. It's the way the world wags."

"But you're not going to do it."

"I've made up my mind."

"I'm flattered, really, but you can't. Let me leave here. Let it all be over with." He swallowed a sob, wanting to appear braver for Sebastian's sake.

"What would life be like here without you, Casey? Without my secondary?"

They looked at each other in the subtle light of the moon. Sebastian lowered his eyes to the bluish slash marks on the floor. Casey, following his somber gaze, nearly gasped aloud and choked back his instinct to bury his head. The moonlight revealed Casey's garments and underwear, which he'd stripped from his body and tossed to the floor.

With heavy, almost hostile breathing, Sebastian's eyes fixed on the heap of bodiless clothes. Casey's heart thumped in his ears, and his neck and cheeks burned.

Gulping, Sebastian uttered, "You're... you're not wearing your tunic."

"It was only this first time," Casey said. "I was warm. I meant to put it back on before I fell asleep."

The mattress lifted. Sebastian moved for the door, stopped, turned back for the bed. It was the first time that Casey noticed Sebastian did not wear a belt with his tunic. Casey held the covers higher to his chin. In an instant, Sebastian reached for them, and, dreamlike, Casey relinquished his hold. Using the most precise movements, Sebastian lowered the covers.

Sebastian stood straight and stared at Casey's exposed body, highlighted by the moonlight. Letting his eyes fall away, Sebastian sat beside him again and buried his head in his hands.

Against his better judgment, Casey flung his arms around him, unconcerned for his exposed flesh, which burned against the itchy fabric of Sebastian's tunic. Tears flowed. Sebastian grabbed him in return, squeezed him tighter.

Casey's heart drummed against his chest. He pursed his lips, tried to will away the sense of light-headedness that left him trembling.

Sebastian nudged him back and stood before him, speechless, solidified with a piercing resolve. With a slow, thoughtful turn of his hands, Sebastian flipped his tunic over his head and let it drop by his feet beside Casey's.

Sebastian Harkin, his flesh a sheet of smoldering strength, stood naked before Casey's eyes. Within a mere arm's reach. Sebastian stepped closer, never once removing his eyes from Casey.

The afternoon they'd exposed themselves to each other in the showers, Casey had seen Sebastian only semiaroused. Now, something like spit or lubricant glistened on his shockingly long and thick full erection.

Casey reached out, and Sebastian grasped his hand. No words. More staring. Slowly, Sebastian's grip tightened. Casey winced, but he didn't want him to let go. Sebastian softened his hold and crawled on top of him, his hardness like a sword pressing into Casey's abdomen.

Their tongues pressed into each other's mouths with measured strides. Sebastian reached along Casey's slick chest and abdomen and grasped him. His large hands massaged Casey's shaft, inched along the planes of his belly, fingering his ribcage, halting behind his nape, where he pulled him in tighter to meet his watering mouth.

They kissed deeper, Sebastian covering his face and neck. Casey roved his head, taking in more of Sebastian's kisses. Steamed with dizziness, he traced his fingers down Sebastian's bare back. His hands stiffened in a moment of incredulity when they found the astonishing mound of flesh.

Casey squeezed hard, rolled his head back and forth, allowed Sebastian's lips and tongue to move across his mouth, neck, chest. Pulling Sebastian onto him, he brought his knees to Sebastian's sides.

Already lubricated (had he come prepared to make love to Casey?), Sebastian lifted Casey's pelvis and rubbed against him. Eyes focused on Casey's expression, Sebastian slowly inserted himself.

Unused to anyone entering him—especially of Sebastian's size—Casey flinched. Sebastian held back, waited. Casey sucked in his breath, smiled, and indicated with a blink of his eyes and a soft release of breath for him to continue.

Sebastian pushed in farther, gauging Casey's face for pain or pleasure. Both let out a mutual dull moan. Casey breathed in Sebastian's musky scent. Sebastian held onto his long shaft, letting go only when Casey exhaled. Then, in that phenomenal split second when unbridled pain transposed into pure bliss, Casey surrendered himself, and he drew in Sebastian completely.

Sebastian responded to Casey's unremitting tremors and dared to push harder and more deliberately. Casey dug his fingers into the flesh on Sebastian's back and buttocks, spreading his legs wider to communicate his consent. Sebastian wrapped his arms around him and, with their mouths fixed on each other, gave him the totality of his arousal, moving on top of him in a rhythmic rush.

Sebastian lifted Casey's torso and leaned into him with his complete power. Casey spread wider, needing Sebastian to take him. Time leaped into a blur of passion. Some kind of medal, a religious icon, the same he'd noticed in the shower stall, hung from Sebastian's neck and brushed Casey's chest, setting his flesh aflame.

The medal swept over Casey's face. He let the cold chain brush his lips, bit the icon as it fell into his mouth. It was all Sebastian, all of him. And Casey wanted him fully.

Sebastian pushed Casey's knees to his chest and sat on his haunches, never missing the potency of his driving force. Casey flung his arms above his head, gripped the headboard, melded with the motion of Sebastian's pushing into him.

He sensed Sebastian getting closer. His thrusts grew faster and harder. Casey squeezed his eyes shut, waiting for the final, burning release. Sebastian leaned into him, and his weight shifted to his hands by Casey's head. Casey bit into Sebastian's forearms and nipples, his head dizzy with wanting and disbelief.

Then Sebastian stopped. Casey opened his eyes, puzzled.

He pulled out of Casey, causing Casey to stiffen, and forced Casey's legs closed and straight. He spit into his palm and lubricated Casey, massaging the entirety of Casey's erection. Next he straddled him, allowing Casey to enter him without pause. Casey twisted and squirmed, mesmerized by the unanticipated turn. Casey, smaller than Sebastian, had no trouble penetrating him completely.

Casey grasped Sebastian's sinewy hips, feeling the muscles flex and the veins throb with each upward drive. He could still feel Sebastian inside him, a shadow of pain and pleasure. The combined sensation compelled Casey to move up to meet Sebastian's downward motions with even more potent thrusts.

Sebastian rode and rode until the medal slid to his side and he tossed his head back and squeezed his eyes heavenward. Uttering a guttural sigh, he spilled on Casey's belly, some striking Casey's face. Casey licked his lips. The saltiness made him dizzy. He filled Sebastian almost simultaneously, while looking into Sebastian's blue irises, which reflected the shifting moonlight.

Sebastian collapsed on top of him. He held Casey like he was rescuing him, like he had with JC when he'd carried him into the abbey from the snowstorm, and afterward when he'd laid him naked on the infirmary's bed.

Casey suspected Sebastian had fallen asleep. His breathing came heavy and steady. Suddenly he raised his head, leaped from the bed, and dressed in a rush. Without a glance back, he scurried from the cell.

Casey lay staring at the door, wondering.

Had it all been a dream?

– XXI –

AN HOUR before Brother George's signature rap on the doors for Rise, Sebastian awoke alone in the early morning darkness of his cell, like so many times past, hardly believing what had transpired overnight. Had he dreamt it? No, it had happened. The stickiness left on his body, along with the familiar dull ache inside him, proved it was so. He brought his hand out from beneath his tunic and wiggled his fingertips under his nose. Still smelled of Casey. The lingering taste of Casey's kisses sweetened his lips too.

His cheeks pushed upward into a grin.

For the moment, Father Paolo's onerous and devious plan to conceal JC's murder dissipated. Sebastian relished his exhausted body.

He and Casey Galvan had made love. Deep, penetrating love. He'd finally given in to his desires. The mounting craving had built up inside him until he had needed but one release. A discharge he'd fantasized about since Casey's arrival at Mt. Ouray.

The past week, he'd foreseen it coming. Growing beyond his control. He'd stood outside Casey's cell door late at night on a few occasions already, listening and waiting in his bare feet so no one would hear him stomp about. Trying to muster enough nerve to knock. Then that time Casey had unexpectedly opened his door, he'd run off like a truant schoolboy spotted by cops.

He'd tried to return to his cell, but Casey had trailed after him, and he'd had no choice but to scurry toward the kitchen. Casey was a rambunctious man. Probably had wanted to impress Sebastian with catching the murderer. Bolstered by longing, Sebastian had decided to follow after Casey. But he'd shut himself in the sacristy. He'd hated frightening Casey and wanted to console him. Delores had spoiled everything. Or maybe it had been best that he'd returned to his cell and left Casey unaware.

None of that mattered now.

Last night he'd gone to Casey's cell, lured by the melody of his flute (and lubricated with globs of his spit), and waited outside his door. Then the flute playing had ceased. Almost without forethought, he'd reached for the doorknob.

The moment he'd shut the door to Casey's cell, Sebastian had understood the true motives for his coming to him. The crumpled garments and belt hadn't spurred him on. Before knowing Casey lay naked under his bedcovers, he had already decided what he was to do, even if it had meant tearing Casey's tunic off his body.

A fiery lust had ignited inside his breast. He had grown dizzy, faint with longing. Strange buzzing in his ears had shut out any surrounding noise—and semblance of reason. Burning need had swept aside caution.

And then, depleted, he'd cried.

With the exception of that one unwanted encounter with Brother Micah, he'd gone without for nearly six years. The feeling of abandoning self-control for passion had left him a mere mass of quivering flesh. Casey might've supposed Sebastian had rushed from him in shame after their lovemaking. No, his humiliation came with his wetted cheeks. He'd wanted to hide his tears in the privacy of his cell, where he had sobbed himself to sleep.

Now, his own cell stood cold and empty. In the darkness, the statue of the Virgin sat on the wall shelf, gazing out with white eyes. He eyed it a good while, catching the glint from the moon setting beyond the western peaks that cut between the blinds. Was it normal for anyone to experience such simultaneous joy and misery?

Brother George's rap came. Sebastian rose from bed and dressed for the day as if it were any other. But it wasn't. A major change had taken place. Nothing at Mt. Ouray would be the same again. In more ways than one.

He could still smell Casey's scent rising from under his cowl on the way to Vigils. Would the others detect it too? They might wonder, "Why does he smell like Brother Casey today and not himself?" Sebastian wouldn't mind if they did.

Inside the chapel, Casey sat next to him the way he had hundreds of times before. Sebastian refrained from making direct eye contact. He watched him from his peripheral vision. Casey kept his head downturned, his eyes concealed by his hood. Sebastian gripped his psalmody all the tighter to resist clutching Casey's hand while they chanted their ancient prayers.

Sebastian spent his meditation period alone in his cell, staring out the window, where snow blew from barreling gusts off the San Juan Mountains. The sky, however, was a brutal blue. He craved another retreat outdoors, if only for a half hour. If the wind ever settled, he'd slip on the old snowshoes or cross-country skis and go for another hike. Yes, that was the medicine. Fresh air and sunshine. To clear his head. But spring brought two pending threats: either Casey's leaving or the probable cover-up of JC's murder. He'd rather live forever imprisoned by winter than face either.

He carried his toiletry bag to the bathroom, eyeballing Casey's cell along the way. He could not see him there, and his shoulders slumped when he wasn't in the showers either. He brushed his teeth using slow strokes, waiting, hoping. Even during his shower, Casey failed to show. He was half-glad. Now that they had crossed that physical barrier, how would he keep from grabbing him, right then and there, naked and wet in the shower stalls?

He ate his breakfast at his usual spot by the cloister garden, but Casey did not follow him. He hesitated to finish, knowing what was to come. After a while, he carried his empty tray to the kitchen and rinsed his dishes. He could almost see Casey lying nude beneath him while spending the remainder of the morning replacing burned-out bulbs, giving Brother Giles's wheelchair a tune-up, and tinkering with the faulty commode.

Before lunch, the father called for the short meeting in the chapter house that Sebastian had dreaded. They assembled around the ornate table gifted to the abbey many years before. Standing before the seated brothers, Father Paolo, absent the tiniest flinch, gave his directive as calculated. The brothers listened. Through the sheen of their eyes Sebastian detected a trace of relief. They, too, wanted to put the ordeal behind them. Who cared if they never learned the truth behind JC's death? It stood behind them. Already relegated to a story of myths from long ago.

Only two or three brothers visibly cringed when Father Paolo stated that they would toss JC's body into the forest to appear as if he'd died there, "for the good of the abbey and the Church." If anyone ever discovered him, there would be no way to trace him to the abbey. "In truth, he had no connection to us here at all," he said.

Sebastian imagined living with the guilt, the sinister secret for the remainder of his life. The idea reared itself unbearable. He'd at least have Casey to ease the darker days of his torment.

An hour later, the abbey grapevine disclosed that Brother Lucien and Brother Micah had made good the abbot's orders. During siesta, they'd trekked to the barn, dressed JC in winter gear so it would look like he'd been hiking if anyone were to find him, and pitched his body from the side of a cliff into a tree-loaded gully. Sebastian could smell the incinerator burning the trash bags they had used to mummify JC up until Compline, along with anything else Father Paolo worried might incriminate them.

By Retire, he still had yet to reconcile the abbot's wishes with his own moral convictions. He sat at his desk with his Bible opened to Job 11, but his attention had drifted, and he wondered how he might leave JC's murder unsolved—and never set eyes on Casey again if he failed to submit to the abbot's orders.

Father Paolo held a sword over his head, but Sebastian also poised one over the abbot's. Father Paolo had assumed Sebastian and Casey would remain at Mt. Ouray for their entire lives. What if either of them chose to leave? What power would the abbot wield over them then?

Sebastian, or any of the other brothers who failed to preserve, could report the events that had transpired inside the abbey to the authorities, and then… and then…. And then what? Face another media maelstrom? Once reporters learned Sebastian's backstory, wouldn't they zero in on him and crucify him a second time?

The finality of JC's death stood as Sebastian's Via Dolorosa, his Trail of Tears. The Avenue of Suffering.

He laid his face in his cupped hands. Something tickled his chest. He pulled it out from under his tunic. The St. Michael medallion. He held it up to the light, feeling the chain pull on the hairs on the nape of his neck. He inhaled, reading the universal inscription: "Saint Michael, pray for us." Us? The police, the victims, earthly overlords? Didn't criminals and tyrants seek God's prayers too? Seek sanctuary inside God's house around the globe? He almost chuckled at the theatrical depiction of the angel slaying a dragon.

Sebastian had imagined himself as a fighting force seeking to destroy evil. But the world no longer wanted that. He'd come to Mt. Ouray believing prayer cut mightier than a sword. Now that idea seemed to have fizzled.

On the back of the medal he read: "For Sebastian, Congratulations." His mother had given it to him as a present upon graduation from the police academy. Almost eleven years to the day. Only after deciding to travel to Mt. Ouray had he taken it off for the first time.

Unprepared to remove it again, he let the medallion fall back under his tunic, the cold chain teasing against his chest, and he flipped ahead to his favorite proverb. A few minutes later, he dragged his finger to the first verse and reread: "The wicked flee though no one pursues, but the righteous are as bold as lions."

Perhaps Father Paolo had a point. He should abandon the already botched investigation. But never in all his years investigating homicides had he given up a hunt, regardless of its complexity. Even cold case files fused to his mind.

He pictured him and Casey again, tangled in each other's arms, submitting to one another. The way they had kissed. So full of longing and need. Yet a haunting question remained fixed in Sebastian's mind: Could he—or should he—continue a physical relationship with him?

Sebastian had intended to take his vows within the coming year, which would include a pledge of celibacy. With Brother Micah, he had been a postulant, but that had not made his infraction any less severe. Though he had not coveted Brother Micah, he had permitted him to follow through with the act until Sebastian had stood in shock, assuming innocence. Sebastian wanted Casey beyond physical pleasure. He imagined them in a special partnership. Like the one Brother Lucien and Father Paolo enjoyed.

Had he and Casey done anything more wrong than they?

With a deep sigh, he closed his Bible, switched off the desk lamp, and crawled into bed for another fidgety night of sleep.

– XXII –

BROTHER AUGUSTINE sat propped up in bed like an oversized silver Raggedy Andy doll. A string of drool connected his chin to his lap and glistened in the sun rising above the mountains, framed by his window. Brother George must have moved him off the wheelchair after he'd asked Sebastian to fix the squeak. Didn't take much strength to lift Brother Augustine. Probably weighted less than one hundred pounds, by the look of him.

"Good morning, Brother Augustine," Sebastian said with a cheerful voice, stepping fully inside the cell with his toolbox weighted at his side. "Brother George says you got a squeaky wheel that's driving him crazy. I'll try not to be too long."

A sudden sense of failure and hopelessness struck him with the glaring sunlight oozing through the grimy window, which needed a good scrubbing. Spring cleaning perched upon them. He forced a smile, tried to garner strength from helping a fellow brother and the warmer days ahead.

Life hadn't changed much, he realized, as he set his hefty toolbox on the floor and fumbled among the contents. Yes, he and Casey had taken their relationship to a new intensity, but other than that, the days inside the abbey moved ahead, one like the other.

He appreciated the jarring clank of the stainless steel tools while he looked for what he needed. Clutching a Phillips screwdriver, he squat-walked to the nearby chair. Seemed to be a lot of wheelchair trouble lately. He'd only fixed the squeak on Brother Giles's chair two days ago. Soon, he figured with a self-effacing shake of his head as he turned the chair to its side, he'd need to maintain wheelchairs for several of the brothers, including Casey one day, perhaps.

He pulled off the rag he'd wedged under his belt and wiped the part of the chair he wanted to fix. Brother George had said the squeak came from the left wheel, near the axle. He rotated it several times and agreed. Must be a bearing problem.

Grateful for the opportunity to focus on something other than his own worries, Sebastian set to tinkering with the chair. He tightened the nuts and the axle plate and guaranteed it could withstand a few strong tugs of his hand. Brother Augustine seemed to ogle Sebastian while he toiled. His silver eyes stared in his direction, empty and eerie. Almost as if he were a full-scale monk puppet, complete with white cowl and long gray beard.

Sebastian spent fifteen minutes on the chair, and gave one final spin of the wheel to ensure he'd solved the squeaking problem. He checked the rest of the chair, including the front caster wheels and rubber tubes, and gave it a good wipe down. Standing, he brushed his hands on his scapular and smiled at Brother Augustine, who remained fixed in bed.

"All done," he said.

Brother Augustine made a strange, guttural sound. Had he messed himself again? Sebastian neared him, expecting to wince. The brother, shaking from his Parkinson's, tried to raise a hand from his lap. Sebastian wiped the drool from his mouth with a tissue from his bed table and sat beside him. "What is it, Brother Augustine?"

One finger, trembling like an electricity meter, rose to knuckle level. Sebastian followed where he pointed. The closet? Could he even see well enough across the room?

Sebastian humored the old-timer and opened the one small closet each of the brothers had in his cell. He peered in. Smelled moldy, like Brother Augustine. He had a suitcase on the top shelf and only one stark white cowl hanging on the rack. Most of them had two. Sebastian figured Brother Augustine barely had need for one, since they rarely wheeled him into the chapel, save for special occasions. He shut the closet door and sniggered under his breath.

What did he expect to find? A pile of bones?

Brother Augustine continued to grunt and quiver his index finger. Sebastian studied him. He was about to turn for the door and find Brother George, when he realized the brother pointed to the wall shelf behind him.

Several trinkets rested on the shelf: books Brother George often read to him, old votive candles that had gone unlit for years, and a few other iconic figurines, including the statuette of the Virgin Mary. Sebastian turned and held up some of the knickknacks for Brother Augustine, but he continued to grunt. The instant he lifted the Virgin, the brother quieted and his finger lowered in line with the others.

Solid in his large hands, he hoisted the statuette closer. Part of the Virgin's face was chipped, and paint had peeled off from the nick, which made it look as if her right eye were winking. He tested its heft and imagined using it as a weapon. With enough force and a wide enough swing, someone might successfully knock out a man JC's size. He held it for a while, thinking.

"Is this what you want?" he said, stepping closer so that Brother Augustine might see the statuette clearer. "Did you wish to have this near you?" Sebastian placed the figurine on the bed table beside him. For a while he analyzed Brother Augustine's silvery eyes. Such a tiny gesture to make him happy.

The ascending sun bathed the Virgin in a shimmering spray of white light. The brother sat stiffer, but his gaze remained fixed toward his toes. Perhaps the closeness of the statuette comforted him, despite his inability to see beyond shapes and shadows.

He was becoming difficult to care for, Sebastian realized. Brother George, who had taken on the task nearly single-handedly, seldom complained. He'd sacrificed much for a man who could not even converse. Brother Augustine probably made the perfect pal for him. Sensitive to criticism, Brother George wouldn't have to worry over hurtful words coming from his mouth. But how much longer before they'd have to consider moving him to a hospice facility?

Again he wondered what Brother Augustine might know. He'd love to hear him speak, if only one tiny word. What might he say? Utter an "Amen"? Cry out in agony? Mumble a simple greeting?

Bother George, carrying a small wash basin, strolled into the cell with a happy-go-lucky expression on his chubby face. He must have wished to sponge bathe Brother Augustine before Sext. Brother George set aside the wash basin and noticed the statuette by his bedside. He beamed at Sebastian and tilted his head to the side. Certainly the uncomplicated Brother George was pleased to get back to business inside Mt. Ouray, where cherished icons and daily tasks filled his world.

He began to remove the old brother's garments, and Sebastian, toolbox clenched in hand, backed out of the cell with a mutual smile and nod.

THE first of April arrived with more snowfall, but winds off the San Juan Range came mild. Streams of sunlight pierced between gaps in the nimbus clouds and sparkled against the falling snow like shards of glass. With the unusual, brilliant snow shower came a strange and shadowy presence that unsettled Sebastian. Someone had been pursuing him around the abbey. Watching him from behind corners and doors, apart from Casey's characteristic trailing of him. The moment he'd sense eyes upon him, he'd turn and see nothing but a blur of white and black racing away.

Later, upon Retire, he heard the slightest sigh in the corridor. He flung open his cell door, but whoever it was had vanished, leaving behind a lingering whiff of stewed tomatoes. The next morning, plating breakfast, he noticed a set of eyes upon him, wide and filled with an uncanny gleam. The same shiver from the past few days traced along his spine. Sebastian had guessed it might be him. The night before in the corridor, he'd recognized his scent.

Brother Micah stared at him with more concentration than typical. A simper accompanied his beaming blue eyes. He'd even nudged Casey aside to pour Sebastian's coffee, his smile and ogling unchanged.

During *lectio divina*, he spied Brother Micah nearby again, but he maintained a stealthy distance. Sebastian led him on a slow-paced pursuit, ending in his cell where he sat on his bed, the door purposefully left open.

As Sebastian had orchestrated, Brother Micah followed him in a few minutes later. He shut the door and stood quietly, without announcing himself. He had a strange leer on his face. A child seeking credit. Sebastian knew the brother had wanted to tell him something. He'd been following him for days with giddy anticipation.

Sebastian gazed toward his hands nesting in the hollow of his tunic skirt. After three or four solid breaths, he said, "What can I do for you, Brother Micah?"

"I've got something to share with you."

"Does this have anything to do with your extra attention?"

Brother Micah's sandals appeared in Sebastian's vision. He'd taken a step closer. "It does," he said. "I wasn't sure if I should or not, but I think it's a good idea now. My telling you is a kind of gift."

Sebastian hesitated, wondering how far he should allow Brother Micah to carry out his performance. He gazed up at him, perhaps matching Brother Micah's odd smile. "Is there something you need to tell me about?"

Snickering, Brother Micah said, "I feel safe knowing you're here with us. But even you must realize that brave men like yourself need *backup* now and then."

Sebastian allowed his ambiguous words to settle in his mind, and he found himself reaching for the bedcovers beside him and squeezing.

Brother Micah went on, his voice eager, self-assured. "Now that the JC issue is all over and the abbot has ordered us to never tell outsiders, I figure you should know. You spent so much effort searching for his killer. Well," he said, opening his arms wide in showmanship style, "you can rest easy now. I did it."

Sebastian jerked up the moment Brother Micah had released those last words. *I did it.* His mind spun. Had he understood him? "Are you making an actual confession to JC's murder, Brother Micah?"

Brother Micah looked away, then peered back at Sebastian with a light smile. "I killed JC," he repeated softly, yet with conviction. "I clubbed him over the head." He gestured with his left hand how he might have struck JC, a wide, sweeping motion from left to right. "I had no choice, you see. I did it to save your life. He'd stolen my fillet knife to come after you."

The shifting sun cut amid a band of clouds and heated Sebastian's cheek. He turned his face to avoid the blinding light in his eyes, wanting to both shake Brother Micah until he fell flaccid by his feet and encourage him to continue. "What do you mean?"

"He wanted to kill you. That's why he'd come to Mt. Ouray. He'd traveled from Philadelphia to find you. You were old enemies, or something like that. I followed him, close behind, to his cell and tried to stop him. He raised the knife to me, and I walloped him. I carried him to the kitchen, covered him in plastic bags, put him in the freezer so he wouldn't rot, and returned to his cell to clean the remnants. All along I did it for you. To save your life."

His confession sunk into Sebastian's mind. The sensation tasted bitter on his tongue. There was no relishing the revelation. Like eating a Philly cheese steak without the cheese or onions. Something lacked oomph. "Didn't JC suffer from amnesia?"

"No, it was all an act until he could find the right time. That night I found him in the kitchen clutching the fillet knife, he decided to waste no further time carrying out his plan to kill you."

"Why didn't you mention all this weeks before, when the father asked for a confession?"

"I covered up everything for you." He waited, as if expecting Sebastian to ask him a slew of questions. When Sebastian remained silent, staring, he said, "If the others learned JC had come because of you, they might have become hostile toward you. Father Paolo might have even confined you to your cell indefinitely, or even worse, banish you from the abbey. I had no other choice. I acted in an instant, and all for you. The only thing I cared about was saving you. He was going to kill you, Sebastian. You should've seen the rage in his eyes. I couldn't have stopped him any other way."

"If he was in so much hurry to kill me, why had he rushed to his cell rather than mine? Didn't you say you followed him to his cell?"

Brother Micah moved closer, out of the direct rays of the flickering sun and into the shadow of Sebastian. "When I caught him in the kitchen, we began to argue. Everyone else had turned in for Retire. I had much to clean up in the kitchen. JC, as usual, was leaving a mess. That's when I no longer could hold back. I told him I knew he was scamming us. He confessed everything, grabbed for the knife, and hurried off toward the cells. I followed after him. I suppose he wanted to get rid of me, so he ducked inside his cell first. I cornered him. Let me tell you, Sebastian, I was trembling with fear, but something provoked me. I had to save you. I couldn't let any harm come to you."

"Why didn't you pull the alarm to warn us?"

He edged closer again. "He acted too quickly. All that concerned me was stopping him. I know I wasn't thinking clearly. Nothing else mattered but to keep him from harming you."

Sebastian looked away at the tiled floor. "And then in a heated moment, you struck him. What did you use?"

"My bare hands. I must confess, when I get angry, I can make a tight fist. I used to box in my younger days."

Sebastian gazed at the Virgin Mary on his wall shelf and exhaled. He held his breath for what seemed many minutes. With a spasm of his shoulders, he wanted to fall back and demand that Brother Micah leave him. Composing himself, he looked directly at Brother Micah, who now stood solidly before him. "So you saved my life?"

A flush brightened Brother Micah's blue eyes. "Aren't you worth it, Sebastian?" He gazed at Sebastian with a smile. "I'd do it again too. I'd do anything for you. You know I would." He dropped to his knees before Sebastian, praying to him almost, like an icon to worship.

Sebastian maintained an easy smile, wanting to provide Brother Micah the assurance he always sought from him. Clutching tighter onto the bedcovers, he said, "Thank you, Brother Micah. That was very considerate of you."

"Then you don't think of me as horrible? You're happy about what I've done for you?"

Sebastian nodded. "You saved my life, after all."

"You can tell the others now if you want. Since we've been ordered to keep our mouths shut, it won't matter, I guess, unless you don't want them to know about JC coming after you. I don't mind that they know that I acted in your defense. Do you think any of them would have risked their lives to save you, Sebastian?" He gazed up at him. Deep shadows cast over his narrowing eyes. "Even Brother Casey?"

Sebastian kept his eyes on him, but he barely saw him. A mound of white and black fabric camouflaging pale flesh streaked with lines and indents and rivulets of slacking tissue. With a peculiar indifference, he noticed the brother's receding hairline and the age spots that had appeared on his scalp. "I doubt any of them would have risked their lives for me," he mumbled.

Reassured, Brother Micah placed both hands on Sebastian's knees. "Do you remember that time when you first came here? About three years ago? In this very same spot? How I helped you then too?"

Images flashed in his mind. He'd been a frightened and confused postulant then. Only a few years had passed, but it might have been a lifetime. The sameness of abbey life, day in and day out, an endless routine of work and prayer, had in many ways forced time ahead.

Sebastian had run hard from his life in Philadelphia. With no place to go, he'd come to Mt. Ouray, a trembling man just turned thirty-two. Brother Micah had taken away that indecisiveness and fear, but only for a few minutes. And afterward, he'd added to his worries.

He was a different man now. Of course he wanted none other than Casey.

Sebastian brushed away Brother Micah's hand when he reached under Sebastian's tunic skirt. "Maybe later, if you don't mind, Brother Micah."

Reddening, Brother Micah stood and straightened his scapular. "If that's what you want," he whispered. "I'm glad I was able to put to rest the investigation. Now you no longer have to worry over it. We'll see each other later, won't we?"

"Yes, of course."

With a demure nod, Brother Micah left Sebastian alone in his cell.

– XXIII –

THAT night Sebastian bent Casey over the bed, his body molded over his. They were like two amorous falcons, fused together, soaring higher with each thrust. Casey kept steady with Sebastian's moving back and forth over him. Slow, purposeful, enjoying each and every sensation. Their sweat adhered them to each other.

Overwhelmed with his body's power, Sebastian stopped and breathed. Casey's light moans forced Sebastian to continue. He slipped back inside him and allowed the electricity to shudder through his limbs. His arms stretched wide over Casey's figure, relishing the heat and firmness of his flesh and the cadenced beating of his heart against Casey's back. He pecked his nape, back, arms. Casey reached for Sebastian and held him firm, encouraging him to completion.

Sebastian lifted him backward to press against him while he massaged Casey's shaft. Finally, Sebastian erupted inside him. Casey flinched, and Sebastian felt Casey's oozing discharge heat his hands. He fell on top of him, pushing him back against the bed. Breathing heavy, neither moved for what seemed several minutes.

Sebastian, still gasping for air, eventually slid out of him and stood. They cleaned up with tissues and collapsed back into Sebastian's bed. Casey lay in his arms, fingering the St. Michael pendant that entwined with Sebastian's moist chest hairs.

"Is everything okay, Sebastian? You're being rather quiet." Casey's voice flowed like the tunes from his flute.

"Tired, I guess," Sebastian said, unwilling to mention Brother Micah's confession for the moment.

"Does it have to do with us?"

"I told you, I'm happy about that." He squeezed his shoulder to reassure him.

"Is what we're doing wrong, you think?"

"Depends on in whose eyes."

"It's yours that matter to me."

He stared at the dark ceiling, imagining Father Paolo and Brother Lucien (and perhaps one or two of the other monks, including Brother Micah), disregarding their vows. The brothers did many things wrong in the eyes of God—and the law. He knew his relationship with Casey was different. He did not abuse Casey for a sense of power, nor did he view him as a shameful temptation.

He pictured the two of them years down the road, older, wiser. Less infatuated with each other, but still emanating love and respect. Casey wouldn't remain youthful forever. Like a rose bloom that faded with time, so would their beauty. But he'd always yearned to grow old with someone. Inside the abbey, they'd chant their prayers side by side, knowing that, no matter what, they could count on each other for solace along with the psalms. Steal tender moments together. Like now.

"I don't think it's wrong," he said at last.

"Then why did you run away the first time we made love?"

"It had nothing to do with you." He paused. "I was overwhelmed with everything. Afraid someone might catch us, I suppose. You've been somewhat evasive yourself the past few days."

"I wasn't sure how you felt about everything. I didn't want to come across as too pushy."

"I don't mind pushy."

Casey hunkered down, and Sebastian could feel his cheek muscles on his chest move into a grin. "I don't think what we're doing is wrong, not between the two of us, anyway. It's hard to believe all that's happened. I've dreamed of you since my first days here. Did I ever tell you about the voice that whispered in my ear once, not long ago? It told me that inside a monastery I'd find love and beauty. I think I have."

Chuckling, Sebastian said, "I'm glad you listen to the voices inside your head."

Casey looked up from Sebastian's unexpected and sudden quiver. "What's wrong?"

"Just a chill." Sebastian laughed it off. "You know how drafty it gets at night this time of year. Brother Eusebius always turns down the heaters once April hits."

They remained silent, Casey's head resting again on his chest, the heat of his soft breath warm on the tight flesh across Sebastian's ribcage. A moment later, Sebastian whispered, "Casey, I'm going to be busy the next few days. Will you allow me some time?"

"What do you mean?"

"I know I mentioned how I don't mind pushy, but there's a lot I need to take care of inside the abbey. Spring cleaning, you know."

"Can I help with anything?"

Sebastian shook his head. "You'll help me by giving me some space. Besides, you have your own responsibilities here. Will you give me a few days?"

"Whatever you need, Sebastian."

"Good." Sebastian moved to sit up. "You better get to your cell now, before Brother George knocks on our doors for Rise."

Casey rose and pulled on his tunic, and stood beside the bed as if waiting for further instructions.

"Remember now," Sebastian said, holding his hand. "I'll be preoccupied the next few days."

"I won't disturb you. You can count on me." And Casey gave him a light kiss on the forehead before tiptoeing away.

Next morning, Casey provided Sebastian the space he'd promised. He'd even refrained from taking his breakfast tray by the cloister garden where Sebastian brooded and stared at the blackness outside. Sleepiness from his long night with Casey sapped his body and scratched at his eyes, but his wide-awake mind churned with many considerations, leaving an almost burning taste in his mouth. Having Casey around would have only distracted him.

Brother Micah, on the other hand, continued to posture for Sebastian's attention. Every chance, he'd break into a figurative dance around him. Sebastian's body language pressed for Brother Micah to back off. He even gave him one of his stealthy winks, indicating they shared a secret and must keep cool. Brother Micah, flushing and nodding, understood the implication.

Throughout the day, Sebastian kept his ears and eyes wide open. A day in the life of a Trappist monk. That's how Sebastian carried out his routine. He shared smiles with his fellow brothers, saving the extra robust ones for Brother Micah whenever they crossed each other's paths.

During the prayer stations, they chanted as they had hundreds of times before. Sebastian joined their rising and falling voices, unleashing the best of his lungs. He went along as if the only curious impression hanging over their heads was the sunlight that filtered through the stained glass windows.

At dinnertime he watched them seated at the long oak table in the dining hall. He kept his eyes glued to his cheese casserole and lentil soup, his peripheral vision never keener. They ate in silence. The clink of silverware rang in Sebastian's ears. The fireplace ran cold. Their winter wood supply had run out weeks ago.

He examined everyone. Casey buttered a roll he held with his left hand. A minute later he used his right to cut into his casserole. Sebastian had noticed his ambidexterity a few weeks after he'd first arrived last October. Just like Sebastian's youngest brother and sister. Must be something about the newer generation, he mused. Casey flashed his wide eyes at him from time to time while they ate. Obeying Sebastian, he kept still, his curiosity wrapped tight inside him.

Brother Giles's grizzled beard, a virtual sift for everything that went into his mouth, looked more like a fuzzy a la carte of the Trappist meal. Brother Eusebius's heft belied the easy movements of his hands, which went from tray to mouth in graceful fashion. Even from four men away, Sebastian noted the veins pumping in his strong hands. He'd seen them so often while they'd sat shoulder to shoulder and day in and day out, fashioning rosaries in the sacristy.

Brother Rodel, the youngest of their brotherhood, ate like a bird. He used his spoon for both his soup and his casserole, which had always amused Sebastian. Despite their fleshless diet, Brother George seemed to get rounder and rounder. Soon, Sebastian speculated, he'd be as big as a cart, and they'd have to put him in a wheelchair if he didn't exercise more or eat less. He shoveled food into his mouth as if he had but minutes to spare before the call for Vespers.

Brother Jerome burped. He dabbed at his mouth with the napkin, unembarrassed by his natural sound. Aging faster and faster each day, he seemed to flick aside decorum. He'd even stopped combing what was left of his hair, which stuck out in a wild frenzy. Brother Micah, although he always managed to clean his plate, needed the entire forty-five minutes allotted for dinner to finish. Taking slow, methodical bites, he glanced at Sebastian with a tight smile, but heeded Sebastian's eyes, which sustained the gentle warning, "Don't let the others know about our little secret."

Seated side by side, Brother Lucien and Father Paolo seemed to fret over their meals. Their shoulders hunched up, and their backs appeared to have humps. Steam from their soups washed over their faces and fogged Father Paolo's eyeglasses. Spring's onset worried the abbot. JC's ghost might haunt him worse than any of them.

Sebastian slurped his soup, eyeballing the brothers above his bowl. Curious what they were thinking, but at the same time no longer really caring. Save for one. His gaze settled at the far end of the table, where Brother Hubert sat with a steady tempo to his eating. For an instant, they met each other's eyes. Brother Hubert's right hand froze midway to his mouth, his cheeks puffed with food. Sebastian prolonged his stare until Brother Hubert flushed and, swallowing, looked back toward his food.

After dinner, Sebastian kept close to Brother Hubert in the kitchen, where they emptied their trays into the sink and washed out their dishes. When Brother Hubert knitted his eyebrows in his direction, Sebastian nodded a grin. Brother Hubert screwed up his forehead further, darting Sebastian a bewildered glimpse over his shoulder before disappearing out the kitchen door.

During their evening free period, he followed Brother Hubert into the library, where they sat at opposing tables. Together they stared into the wintery scene, the cobalt sky shellacking the dwindling snow with subtle blue.

Sebastian stretched his long legs while seated sideways at the table. Brother Hubert glanced at him over his dark-framed glasses, cleared his throat. He turned back to the window, his hands cupped under his chin and his elbows on the armrests. Sebastian mirrored his sounds and gestures, fully aware Brother Hubert could see him reflected in the windowpane, framed by hoarfrost. At that point the brother stood and took his leave. Sebastian followed.

In the bathroom, Sebastian sat on the bench by the shower stalls, waiting. Brother Hubert, dressed in a bathrobe and carrying his toiletry bag, stopped in his tracks when he spotted him. He shook his head and sighed, and went about prepping to shower. Sebastian left him privacy.

While chanting the Salve Regina at Compline, Sebastian continued to study him. Brother Hubert maintained concentration on the psalmody, yet his rising shoulders pointed to his growing unease.

The following morning, Sebastian burned his eyes into him at every chance. He carried his breakfast tray to where Brother Hubert liked to eat, by the large window in the back foyer. When Brother Hubert made to leave, Sebastian got up and bumped straight into him, feigning clumsy ignorance. Brother Hubert scurried for the kitchen.

They exchanged more awkward stares and unusual encounters deeper into the day. Acting as the abbey's barber, Brother Hubert visibly tensed when Sebastian entered the laundry room for his monthly trim. He sat in the chair, and Brother Hubert swathed him with the smock. The sweep of Brother Hubert's sandals as he shuffled across the hair-covered floor gave Sebastian that tingly feeling he enjoyed.

Brother Hubert's breath, sour and warm, fell over Sebastian's neck while he squirted water over his hair and combed out the tangles. Flexing the razor-sharp shears, he commenced first by trimming Sebastian's hair above the neck, the way Sebastian always liked it, and next along the sides. Sebastian closed his eyes, placed his trust in Brother Hubert's capable hands, refusing to allow the sudden discomfort to subdue him.

When he finished, Brother Hubert removed the smock and shook it free of the russet hair, after which he brushed Sebastian's neck with cooling talcum powder. Brother George, waiting patiently, took Sebastian's place in the barber's chair. Brother Hubert returned Sebastian's appreciative nod and clicked on the clippers, filling the laundry room with gentle buzzing.

The second morning, he again followed Brother Hubert into the bathroom. He scrutinized him in the mirror while they both shaved, shoulder to shoulder. Brother Hubert had taken off his black-framed glasses, and his irises appeared like raisins. His upper lip and shaving hand twitched. He left without bothering to rinse his face.

His chanting lagged during Vigils and Lauds. Sebastian, standing next to him in the chapel for the first time, noted he'd become less focused than the previous days. His hands trembled, and once he'd even dropped the psalmody, the sound resonating in the chapel like a blow.

In the kitchen, where Sebastian washed his lunch dishes, Brother Hubert showed the first signs of resentment. He dumped his dishes in the sudsy water and stomped off. Sebastian, unhurried, cleaned his dishes, strolled to the cells, and leaned against the wall across from Brother Hubert's cell with arms and legs crossed. A minute later Brother Hubert stepped into the corridor, grimacing as he passed Sebastian.

He followed Brother Hubert past the cloister garden, where he allowed a moment of pleasure listening to the chatter of the finches nibbling on the bread crumbs someone had left atop the melting snow, and into the chapel for None. Again Sebastian sat beside him, chanting louder than ever before.

Brother Hubert forewent his free period and scurried for the administrative office, glancing over his shoulder to check Sebastian's trailing him. Sebastian, smile muscles stretching his face into what he was certain was the same smirk from the past few days, watched from the doorway as the brother sat at the "off limits" computer. Brother Hubert tried to ignore Sebastian's presence and affected a professional stance while jabbing the keypad and jotting in a notebook. After another minute or two, Sebastian turned to leave for *lectio divina*.

As the afternoon progressed into evening, Sebastian maintained a steady gaze on him. Never once did they speak. Yet Brother Hubert's irksome expression had begun to fade into one full of lethargy and fatigue. By Compline, red eyes behind his thick lenses appeared ready to burst.

Nearing midnight—a time when the abbot would have surely reprimanded the brothers if he'd caught them lingering outside their cells—Sebastian knelt at the transept. Votive candles flickered and danced with an expectant energy. He mumbled Psalm 84, his folded fingertips rested under his nose. He kept his eyes closed tight. The scent of burning candles and dry wood filled his nostrils.

He prayed for many minutes. But prayer had not been the main force ushering him to the chapel. He squeezed his eyes tighter, inhaled. The sensation of completeness, what he lived for back at the PPD, overpowered him.

The pit in his stomach goaded him. He was waiting. Like back in Philadelphia. He and his colleagues would stew for hours—days, even—waiting for a suspect to show himself. To make the final move.

He heard the steps of someone enter the chapel, but he did not budge from his prayer spot at the transept, nor did he open his eyes. He continued to mouth his prayers, his hot breath brushing his fingertips. The footsteps grew louder, then ceased a mere few feet to his left. He sensed someone entering the pew ahead of him and then sitting. He knew who even before opening his eyes.

Sebastian ended his prayer by whispering aloud, "Give me a sign of your goodness, that my enemies may see it and be put to shame, for you, Lord, have helped me and comforted me." Following a reflective pause, he opened his eyes, crossed himself, and sat back in his chair, his hands loose on his knees.

"Have you known all along?" Brother Hubert said after a moment of silence between them.

Sebastian stared at the back of the brother's head, none too surprised to find he wore his cowl with the hood raised. He kept his own head unmoved, pointed toward the fluttering candles. "I wasn't certain until a few days ago."

"What can I tell you, Brother Sebastian?"

"How about the full story?"

– XXIV –

BROTHER HUBERT crossed himself, keeping his eyes directed on the candles. Sebastian watched from his side vision. The hood concealed Brother Hubert's face. But Sebastian did not need to see him to imagine the grim expression that must have elongated his features. Sebastian savored the moment. He also swallowed a sickness that welled up in his throat. The same affect from when he stood on the cusp of solving a case with the PPD.

"How much do you know?" Brother Hubert said, his voice hollow but stable.

"I pieced together most of it. The rest I suspect you'll fill in for me."

Mottled color from the moonlight filtering through the stained glass windows washed over the crucifix above the altar. Sebastian gazed at Jesus, waiting for Brother Hubert to find the courage to continue. The eyes hypnotized him a moment. They were blue, as are many depictions of Christ. In reality, Jesus most likely resembled Casey—and JC.

Brother Hubert peered at his hands, and with a shudder, he concealed them in the folds of his cowl. "There was a strange snowstorm that night," he began, his voice distant, as if he were transported back in time. "The winds and the thunder had kept me awake. My mother used to say that thunder during a snowstorm was an omen for bad things to come. How I wished I hadn't laughed at her for saying that when I was a boy.

"But it was more than the snowstorm that agitated me. I'd been wracking my brain for days, wondering what I should do, or if it even warranted action. You understand, I discovered who JC was and why he'd come to Mt. Ouray about a week before that horrible night. Or at least I thought I had. I had no way of knowing for sure. How could I prove anything? Finally, I had to confront him.

"I slinked to his cell. I knocked, and he answered. I stepped inside and found him sitting at his desk, dressed in his street clothes that I had laundered for him and drumming his fingertips on the desktop. He looked up at me. A strange gleam shone in his eyes. Stranger than usual. Sinister and dark. The look of someone wanting to do harm. I no longer doubted my assumptions.

"'I know why you've come here,' I whispered, my heart pounding in my chest. 'I know all about it.'

"Unblinking, he stared. 'And?'

"'I think you should call for a helicopter as soon as possible and leave us.'

"'What if I don't want to?'

"My insides turned to ice cubes. I realized that I was already in over my head. Who was I dealing with? I should've presented everything I suspected about JC to Father Paolo days ago. He had researched missing persons as well, but I think he had yet to build a connection why he'd come. But I worried about the ramifications if I were wrong. I knew how much the father had cherished JC.

"Without warning, JC stood and nudged past me for the corridor. I turned to follow him to see what he was up to. I found him standing in the kitchen, a fierce expression cut into his face. Wanting to keep him calm, I asked what his true intentions were for coming, although I already knew. He merely stared straight through me and stated, almost trancelike, that his memories had been trickling back to him, and right before I'd come into his cell, everything had fallen into place. He said that he was going to do what he'd intended all along, to take care of the business that had brought him so far. To finally make good the promise to himself that had forced him to suffer in the blizzard. A chill darted up my spine. It was all the things I had grown to suspect and worse. He hadn't faked his amnesia. Now I had to deal with a man who'd awakened without realizing much time had elapsed. A man without time is a man looking for trouble.

"He said he'd planned to come during winter, knowing that Mt. Ouray would be empty of visitors. I suppose he had underestimated the mountain snowstorms. From the information provide in our website, information that I partly wrote, he knew only the monks would be here. Funny how nowadays we use the Internet to spy on each other. He'd mentioned taking a bus from Philadelphia so that he could conceal a gun without detection. He kept whispering between clenched teeth how he wished he still had it. I informed him we never found a gun on him. He insisted we'd stolen it, along with his wallet and cell phone. That's when I noticed the knife clutched in his right hand, by his side. I'd been so focused on his menacing eyes I hadn't noticed he'd grabbed one of Brother Micah's kitchen knives from the wall magnet. I shuddered, realizing he was crazed, worse than anything I had imagined. Although my suspicions for why he'd come proved true, I had yet to comprehend what he was capable of. With the instinct of an alley cat, I blocked the door from his leaving and demanded he put down the knife.

"'Step aside, or I'll let you have it too,' he said with a horrible, gravelly tone.

"'Why must you do this?' I pleaded with him.

"'Don't you know?' he said, and he elbowed me aside, forcing me against the doorframe. Of course I scurried after him, my mind in a whirl. I don't recall seeing anything other than the heels of his sneakers growing smaller and smaller and the terrible glint of the knife clutched in his hand.

"I turned the corner and saw a shadow disappear into Brother Augustine's cell. My mind whirled. Why on earth would he go in there? But I suppressed my puzzlement and honed in on one realization: I had to stop him. I raced inside the cell and found him standing over Brother Augustine's bed, the knife gripped in both hands, ready to plunge it into his chest. In the light coming from the corridor, I could see poor Brother Augustine gaping up at him, unable to move or scream. He must've been terrified and confused. A strange focus overcame me. My mouth went dry, my hearing dulled, and I saw him as if I were staring down a tunnel. I pulled JC's arm back, and he shot me a fierce, monstrous glare.

"'Keep back,' he spat. 'This is what he deserves. He's el Diablo.'

"I remember a blast of thunder just before I reached behind me for the statuette of the Virgin Mary on the wall shelf. Filled with anger and desperation, I clutched it. I wasn't thinking. I was acting like an animal, on pure instinct. I remember the odd sound of Brother Casey's flute emerging above the wind and thunder at the precise moment I struck JC on the side of his head. He dropped the knife with a horrible clank and fell instantly, right by my feet.

"The Virgin had broken in two, and her precious torso had tumbled onto Brother Augustine's bed faceup, right into the hollow of his lap. Her white eyes seemed to gape at me, as if she were in shock at my deadly act. There wasn't much blood, but JC didn't respond to my nudging him and pleading that he wake up. I panicked. When I saw Brother Augustine's wheelchair in the corner, an idea struck me. How quickly we resort to thinking like common criminals.

"I grabbed for one of Brother Augustine's cowls from his closet and pulled it over JC, making sure to cover his face with the hood. My scheme was to wheel him to the walk-in freezer to preserve him until I could carry out my plan to toss him into the woods once the storms passed, just like how Father Paolo had eventually wanted, ironically. If anyone caught me wheeling him away, I could say I was taking Brother Augustine to the bathroom. I was panicked. My instinct was to cover my tracks, nothing more or less.

"What else was I to do? I had defiled the commandments, the abbey, the Church, Father Paolo, myself. There would be no explaining to anyone how everything had unraveled. I still failed to understand it myself. I started to believe in the Dalakis Curse. That JC had become possessed by demonic spirits—or perhaps I had been myself—like Brother Micah had once said.

"I was unsurprised when Brother Rodel said he'd seen me pushing who he assumed was Brother Augustine the night of JC's murder. I thought I had noticed his dark eyes peering at me right as I passed his cell. But my plan had worked. Why I didn't scream for him and everyone else to awake or pull the alarm, I don't know. I suppose I was worried what the monks might say. Primitive instincts surpass even faith and reason during desperate, horrifying times like that.

"I wheeled him to the kitchen and instantly began to cover him in the plastic trash bags. After I had hidden him as best I could behind boxes of frozen vegetables and fruit, I wheeled Brother Augustine's chair back to his cell, where he still lay, unmoved and his eyes wide open. Yet somehow, while I was gone, he'd managed to reach for the upper half of the broken Virgin Mary. When I got there he was clutching it to his heart. I tried to ignore the anguish in his eyes. Oh, don't misunderstand. He can see all right. There's no doubting the horror painted on his face. He'd seen everything unfold before his very eyes, glaucoma or not.

"I removed the statue from his trembling fingers and cleaned up the blood with some towels I'd carried with me from the kitchen. How I ever considered such details, I still don't know. Desperate, I grabbed up the knife and wiped it clean of blood, then hid it along with the broken statue inside Brother Augustine's suitcase in his closet. You'll find them there still if you care to look. Afterward, I began to feel giddy. Yes, giddy. I remembered that JC had informed us of his intention to leave only the night before. I was home free, as they say. No one would miss him. My original plan appeared more cunning than ever.

"But that meant I still had to get rid of his belongings. I went to his cell and grabbed his knapsack and coat. At the last minute, a pang in my side reminded me how I had destroyed Brother Augustine's statuette. I grabbed the one Father Paolo had given JC (I was sick that he'd given it to him) and replaced the one I'd ruined in Brother Augustine's cell. I then traipsed to the incinerator and torched JC's belongings, along with the towels I used to clean up. Since I work in the laundry, I was able to stash my soiled tunic, which had some blood smears on it, and wait until wash day to clean it. After that, I crept to the showers, washed up, and stole away to my cell in nothing but a towel. Dressed in a fresh tunic, I lay in bed as if nothing had happened. But the demons that haunted my restless sleep told me otherwise.

"Upon Rise, I considered recounting my horrifying ordeal to Father Paolo, but I bit my tongue. There was no point, and as long as everyone believed JC would be leaving, what harm could there be? I stood there, trying my best to conceal my tremors while Brother George voiced surprise JC had left so soon. Thank goodness Father Paolo ended any speculation.

"That night, after I'd assured myself everyone was asleep, I sneaked to the freezer to follow through with my plan to carry his body into the woods. I didn't care if I had to face the blinding snow. Only you had discovered his remains minutes before I had come to retrieve the body. Frantic, I feigned shock. I suppose in a way I still was in a daze. Later, when I learned he hadn't died from the blow I'd given him, but from hypothermia and suffocation, I nearly got sick. I could've saved him if I had been thinking like a normal person."

Brother Hubert paused, and his head fell farther toward his lap. The side of his white hood reflected the flames of the votive candles. He didn't sob or shudder. Sebastian supposed he'd shed enough tears over his crime that his ducts were tapped dry.

"If I ever hear the tune Brother Casey was playing on his flute that night," he said, "I will not be able to think of anything but striking JC across his head with the Virgin Mary. Funny how 'A Time for Us', a melody about misfortunate lovers, will forever remain emblazoned on my brain to connote a much more ghastly tragedy."

"Is that what that tune was?" Strange those words should be the first to fall from Sebastian's parched lips. He had wondered about the haunting melody that often flowed from Casey's cell right before Retire. He supposed Brother Hubert's revelation left his mind anesthetized. Yet he still needed to know more. "But JC wasn't after Brother Augustine, was he?"

Brother Hubert sighed and shook his head. "I knew immediately he'd gone into the wrong cell. I suppose in the dark we brothers do look an awful lot alike in our Trappist garments. I remember he kept getting turned around in the corridors, and how even Brother Jerome had found

JC in Brother Augustine's cell, thinking it was yours. I suppose you've pieced together why JC had come here too, and why he'd meant to target you."

Sebastian nodded despite Brother Hubert's being unable to see him. "An idea of his identity came to me about two weeks ago, but it wasn't until a few days ago that I knew for certain."

"I learned about your past shortly after you'd arrived at Mt. Ouray, of course." Brother Hubert snickered. "You know me, always prying into the details of the lives of the people who come here, like with JC. I kept it to myself, not wanting to embarrass you. That was part of my uncertainty in coming forward about JC. Imagine how difficult it was for a gossip like me. I didn't blame you, anyway. We're both in the same boat, so to speak."

Thunder clapped in Sebastian's mind, followed by a flash of blinding lightning. He was standing in the rain in an alley on Philadelphia's north side along with two of his fellow detectives, searching and waiting. The hot, muggy June night pressed on them. He could smell the wet, hot pavement and feel the sogginess in his socks. The patter of rain and thunder so loud they could barely hear each other shout.

They'd been hunting for a known drug kingpin, one who'd orchestrated a slew of hits on rival drug gangs, targeting mostly adolescent carriers. The latest victim of the ceaseless turf war was a teenager shot thirteen times—ironically, one for each of his short years on Earth. Six prior kids, all but two from Puerto Rican gangs, had been shot dead during the past twenty-four hours. One of the bloodiest weekends in Philadelphia. Few of the overlords ever pulled the triggers themselves. They had kids shooting kids.

Everyone—including the mayor, the captain, the citizens, the media—demanded action. Yet Sebastian and his colleagues knew that those very same people limited their options. Most of the "tiptoeing" they did came not from pursuing criminals on the lam, but from avoiding the scrutiny of a society that insisted on protection without the ugliness of bloodshed, and in many cases, incarceration.

The PPD had had its sights on the reigning drug leader for months, but they had to make a quick move or risk the loss of more youth—along with the expected augmentation of political swaggering if they failed. A tip-off led them to a party in Fairhill, a part of town Sebastian knew well. It was only five blocks from the twenty-fifth district station.

When they drove by the party on Westmoreland to assess the scene, they estimated about five hundred people crammed inside the row house. Music vibrated the rain-shellacked windows to their van, which they parked a block away, across from McIntosh Playground.

They scattered along the adjacent streets, communicating with each other on their two-ways. Although they'd protected their radios with weatherproof holsters, the downpour made hearing and speaking cumbersome. Despite the relentless thunder and rain, the heavy bass beat as they neared the party made Sebastian's guts roil. For several minutes he worried he might mess his pants from the deep vibrations. He crept alongside two other plainclothes detectives. Four uniformed officers covered their backs out of sight, and two more flanked the parallel street.

They slinked to the side of the row house with their guns still tucked in their holsters. The majority of party attendees were not involved in the illicit drug trade, and the police had to use caution. They guessed that someone might have tipped off their suspect (probably the same informant who'd squealed about the party), and soon a man dressed in a thousand-dollar Italian suit marched out front, his entourage shielding him from the rain. The posse entered a waiting fully decked dark Escalade. From his spotty, diagonal observation, Sebastian recognized it as the suspect's car they'd tailed in the past.

Squinting into the rain, Sebastian shouted into his two-way for the uniforms to surround the SUV and detain the suspects, but he received no recognizable response. Right then, three shadowy figures dashed out of the side door into the alley. The three detectives requested they halt. Two of the figures obeyed. One hesitated, and with his hands thrust deep inside his jacket pockets, darted straight for the undercover detectives.

Sebastian reached for his gun and stood his ground, demanding again that he stop. The man turned to his side. A flash of something metallic pierced Sebastian's vision below the streak of lightning. Gunfire split the night. The man dropped onto the rain-slick pavement. The other detectives rushed the two companions and forced them against the wall. Sebastian stood over the downed man while blood mixed with rainwater puddled around his feet.

Later they would learn that the two bullets that had struck the man had come from Sebastian's Glock. One bullet tore off a small section of his shoulder. The fatal shot pierced the heart. The metallic object Sebastian had noticed was his cell phone. He had been speed dialing his wife.

When the media learned that a white cop had shot to death a weaponless forty-five-year-old Latino father of five with a full-time job and a wife of twenty-three years, Sebastian's world forever changed. A few of Sebastian's supporters (mostly independent bloggers) uncovered that, five years before, the deceased had a suspended sentence for possession of twenty-one grams of marijuana, a misdemeanor under Pennsylvania law. Unfortunately, the well-intentioned supporters set the media off like a hound on a fox.

Local columnists labeled Sebastian everything from a white supremacist (ironically, using his Irish roots to prove his racist inclination) to a steroid-crazed cop. The sensationalized reports took on a life of their own, like a mold spore. The other two detectives were labeled as racists too, regardless that both were Puerto Rican. None of that mattered. Half a dozen local politicians marched alongside one hundred irate Fairhill residents, calling for justice. Included in the protest was the man the PPD had targeted as the mastermind behind the weekend bloodbath.

Five months after battling for his job and reputation, he caved to pressure. Captain Reems and the D.A. demanded he resign or face prosecution. They presented their ultimatum as if staging a play for the benefit of the media. Not a private one on one, but a public spectacle. So that everyone could save their collective butts.

On the bright side, the story bypassed the national media's radar—it was otherwise too consumed with the presidential campaign, the mortgage crises, and the end to the Harry Potter series, Sebastian supposed. Fresh out of a job, he opted out of his lease on Leiper Street, distributed his possessions among his five siblings, and hopped a plane for his sanctuary nestled high in the Rocky Mountains—Mt. Ouray.

He didn't bother to tell Brother Hubert the entirety of what had unfolded after that dark night in the alley back in Philadelphia nearly five years ago, mostly because Brother Hubert had probably read the reports on the Internet anyway. He cared little to clear his name, especially in relation to Brother Hubert's own confession. Both had experienced similar fight or flight responses, and suffered the consequences. But he believed Brother Hubert was owed something more.

Inhaling, he said, "JC's family and I kept our distance during the ordeal, but I did receive more than my share of threats. At least one hundred. Some fairly violent. One of them was signed Juan Carlos Valesco. It was JC. I remember because he'd said he would track me to the ends of the earth to avenge his father's murder, 'no matter what.' He'd referred to me as 'el Diablo.' JC would've been about sixteen then. His father, Manuel, had the nickname Manny. I remember when JC uttered the name while I interviewed him, I'd instantly pictured the man I'd wrongly shot. My first and only case of mistaken identity. I saw his face so clearly, dripping with rainwater. But I had failed to make a connection at the time, at least consciously. After nearly five years, JC had come to make good on his promise."

"I read in one of the Internet articles that someone had played the flute during Mr. Valesco's funeral," Brother Hubert said reflectively. "Do you think, in addition to the thunderstorm, Casey's flute playing might have helped trigger JC's memories?"

Sebastian allowed the quiet to settle over them, along with the faint scent of the candles. Neither man moved. Sebastian watched the dancing flames and the orange orbs oscillating against the pine wood of the transept. He recalled the achy feeling in his gut the night JC had died, while Sebastian had listened to Casey's music. Deep inside, he had always known why JC had battled the snows to reach Mt. Ouray.

"How did you come to suspect me and not the others?" Brother Hubert uttered toward the candles when Sebastian remained mute.

"Basic reasoning," Sebastian said, a tingle shooting along his spine as he recalled how he had fit the pieces together with the power of deduction. "I knew Brother Micah fabricated his confession almost from the start. I eliminated him along with Brother Eusebius because they are both left-handers, making them unlikely suspects. JC had blunt force trauma on his left temple, indicating the killer had used a wide right to left medial sweeping motion. Besides, I'd seen enough false confessions in my day to know one. Brother Giles is confined to a wheelchair, and the blow had come from at or near eye level. I figured the killer and JC were probably about the same height. And Brother Augustine…? Well, apart from blaming demonic possession, I couldn't imagine him as a suspect. Once I figured the culprit had burned evidence, I eliminated Brother George as well. I'd smelled the incinerator going the night of JC's death. Of course, I didn't think anything of it at the time. But later I assumed the killer, wanting to dispose of evidence, had burned JC's coat and knapsack. I have the leftover buckle and zipper in my trunk to prove it. Our beloved Brother George has a fear of even the smallest flames under the bins that warm our food. If he fears that, certainly he wouldn't have wanted to face the incinerator's raging fire. Brother Jerome and Brother Rodel also face physical limitations that led me to eliminate them. Due to his osteoarthritis, Brother Jerome can't lift his arms above his head. He would have had a tough go reaching for the statue and striking JC and then covering his tracks. Besides, Brother Jerome most likely would have checked his pulse. Brother Rodel, at a mere five two, couldn't have hit JC unless he'd been standing on something when he'd struck him, an improbable scenario. That left Father Paolo, Brother Lucien, Brother Casey… and you."

"And why didn't you suspect any of them?"

"I did at one point."

"Including Brother Casey?"

Sebastian flushed. Had he and Casey flaunted their attraction for one another? "I'm afraid I had at one time even suspected Casey," he said. "But what most made me consider you as the primary suspect was what Brother Rodel had said the night we found JC in the freezer. He'd said he'd seen you pushing Brother Augustine to the bathroom. Brother

George usually takes care of Brother Augustine, especially late at night. And later I remembered you had come up behind me in the walk-in freezer right when I discovered the body. You had wanted to carry the body to the woods, as you stated. Again, I didn't think anything of those things at the time."

"And the figurine? How did you know I had used the Blessed Mother as a weapon?"

"When you replaced Brother Augustine's statuette with JC's, you'd forgotten that JC's had a chip on the face from when he'd dropped it in Father Paolo's office after he'd given it to him. I realized they had been swapped, but still had no idea for what reason. I began to suspect the missing statuette was what had struck JC, and that Brother Augustine's cell had been the actual scene of the struggle and not JC's cell or the kitchen. One thing I don't understand: how did Brother Micah know that JC had come here to seek revenge against me?"

"I'd confided in him after Father Paolo's directive to toss JC's body into the woods. I figured it could do no harm. I needed to unburden myself. He can be comforting at times, Brother Micah. I held back providing details, but he knew JC had come for you." Brother Hubert snickered. "So Brother Micah took credit for it, huh? Why do you suppose he did that? Oh, don't bother to answer. We all know how he's smitten with you. Almost more than Brother Casey."

Another rush of blood heated Sebastian's cheeks, but he cared little for how the monks judged his relationship with Casey. "If you needed to unburden yourself, why not confess to Father Paolo after he'd asked for the responsible party to come forward in private?"

"I did."

Sebastian gaped at the brother's stiff head. "What?"

"I confessed the very next night, right after Vespers, after the father had requested the guilty brother to step forward. I was shaking like a leaf, trembling worse than I'd ever experienced. The reality of everything descended upon me in a great sweep, and I needed help. I realized that I had done wrong to cover my tracks and should have confessed from the moment everything happened. The abbot listened to me silently, nodding with understanding throughout my entire confession, even while I sobbed at his feet. When I finished, he swore me to secrecy and said that he would find a way out of it. Promised no one would know, that he wouldn't even tell Brother Lucien. Said it was for the good of everyone, including the Church, if I kept my mouth closed. 'Never acknowledge what you've done except to God,' he'd said. Father Paolo reminded me that his word was the word of God. And so I obeyed." Brother Hubert lifted his eyes to the crucifix. "The father's directive wasn't my only reason for keeping quiet. My own fear persuaded me to agree to his decisions and keep my tongue from wagging. It's partly why I hadn't wanted to call anyone to my aid when I first struck JC."

"What do you mean?"

"My family came to the United States from Poland in 1939, you understand. My father had difficulty there. He was a proud meat cutter. While most of the Jewish families had changed their surnames to blend in with other Poles, my grandfather and father kept theirs. And of course I experienced little issue with my surname growing up in America. So when I converted to Catholicism in college, I thought my aging father might disown me. He always hated that the Vatican had shielded the Nazis and made that awful pact with Mussolini. But I could not deny the religious awakening I had experienced while watching the sun set over the Lower Bay near our home in Brooklyn. It might sound crazy to you, but out of the golden brilliance I saw Mary and the boy Jesus appear to me in a rowboat launched from Staten Island." He raised his head higher, and his hood slid back enough for Sebastian to see his left eye fill with tears. "All I can recall for a reaction was a smile that seemed to fill my soul. I feared I might explode from the good feeling welling up inside me." His voice lowered, and his eyes rested back on his lap. "Because I was raised Jewish and a convert, I feared the brothers here might hate me if they ever found out I was responsible for JC's death. Of course Father Paolo had conveniently reminded me of that to ensure I never disclosed the truth."

"What made you change your mind, Brother Hubert, and speak now?"

"I knew you had me cornered. But even if you hadn't used your detective skills to wear me out until I spilled the truth, I'm sure I would have eventually come forward. I was tired of the charade. If I could go against my dearly beloved father and even my own people, as he put it, surely I can defy the abbot, especially when I know now he was in the wrong."

Sebastian cast his eyes down to his lap. "And the father had me investigate JC's death to keep me occupied. He'd summoned me to his private office, setting me up for a scam."

Brother Hubert nodded. "We all know how inquisitive you are, Brother Sebastian. He wanted to keep you busy, knowing I could never tell you the truth. He later told me it was part of his plan, and not to worry if you snooped around or asked questions. If I kept my mouth shut, you'd never learn what had happened that night. I was so tortured. But when you started to, well, stalk me, I cracked, as they say. I was tired of the covering up. It was so unfair to Juan Carlos and his family. Hadn't the Valescos suffered enough?"

Lowering his hood, Brother Hubert turned his head and faced Sebastian for the first time since coming into the transept. "My duty is to pray, and I failed. I reacted instead of placing myself in God's hands." He faced the candles again. "I hope he has forgiven me."

"He's forgiven you, Brother Hubert. Like I'm certain he's forgiven me and JC."

Enough experience notched Sebastian's belt that he could tell the difference between a man who'd reacted from sheer instinct and a cold-blooded killer. Unless they met in a dark alley, and.... Sebastian cringed. He didn't want to think of that anymore. He willed his past to recede into the distance, where it belonged. Set free to the mountains.

Besides, Brother Hubert had rescued Sebastian, the way Brother Micah wished he had. In actuality, Brother Hubert had saved Brother Augustine too. The law would understand. Brother Hubert—and Father Paolo—would most likely face criminal negligence charges and never see a day in jail, unless a testy district attorney with a grudge against the Catholic Church sought heavy penalties for obstruction of justice and tampering with evidence.

"Did you know that *repent* in Hebrew means *return*?" Brother Hubert said with a merry lilt to his tone, as if speaking to either himself or Christ on the crucifix, or a ghost from his Brooklyn childhood. "Shuwb. To return to God."

"Lovely," Sebastian whispered.

The quiet of the transept massaged Sebastian. His head grew heavy.

Standing with the crack of his bones reverberating off the acoustical walls, he said, "Come, Brother Hubert. Let's retire to our cells. In the morning, we'll both have our dragons to slay."

– XXV –

SEBASTIAN said his good night to Brother Hubert outside his cell, after which he strolled five cells away and listened by the door before opening it. He found Casey asleep. A wheeze brushed the side of his pillow, where a dime-sized spot of drool pooled by his tender lips. Sebastian squatted beside him and stroked his hair.

Casey stirred. His eyelids opened, the unfolding of an angel's wings. "Sebastian," he whispered, "I was just dreaming about you. We were holding hands while soaring in the sky like birds."

"Sounds like a wonderful dream." Sebastian slipped off his scapular, tunic, and boxer shorts and nudged Casey closer to the wall. After sliding under the bedcovers, he helped Casey squirm out of his tunic and tossed it alongside his on the floor. Although he grew aroused, he lacked the focus to push Casey onto his back, to show him he wanted to make love. Feeling his warm flesh against him proved enough.

Sebastian slept beside Casey peacefully, and before Brother George's rap on the doors he slinked to his cell, where he sat at his desk and plotted his next plan of action. After Vigils, he confronted Father Paolo in his private office. The abbot gazed at him over his wire-framed eyeglasses, his veiny fingers knotted together atop the polished desk.

"So now that you know everything," he said once Sebastian had recounted what had transpired between him and Brother Hubert in the transept, "what do you plan on doing? Brother Hubert has already confessed. He's asked for God's mercy, which I'm sure he'll receive. He did nothing more than defend himself and our brothers here. What else is there?"

"Juan Carlos and his family."

"And how do you plan on addressing that?"

"Oddly, by upholding your original command." Sebastian understood the abbot's wide eyes to say, *Whatever do you mean?* He licked his lips and answered the abbot's implicit inquiry. "You are right about Brother Hubert. In the eyes of the law, his—and your—biggest crime would be obstruction of justice, tampering with evidence. All that, in reality, contributed to JC's death. Brother Hubert will have to live with that for the rest of his life, much like I will for having mistakenly killed Manuel Valesco. People panic, and horrible consequences can result. I've seen worse. I don't condone his actions or mine. But I don't see why we should carry this out any further. In this case, the truth would only harm more people. Perhaps there is a higher justice. Maybe God's mercy is enough."

"And...."

"And I want JC's family to believe he came to Mt. Ouray seeking to live among us as a brother. It would warm his mother's heart. My gift to JC's family. I don't want anyone to ever know JC came here for revenge. Not for my sake, but for his family's."

"Whether we speak the truth or not," the father said, his Portuguese accent thickening, "there's a hefty civil lawsuit in all this, yes? We've already been sued a while back because of an unforeseen death on our property."

Sebastian inhaled. "I never met with Manny Valesco's wife and children—other than JC here, obviously—but I heard a lot. They aren't that type of people. After the incident, they never filed a lawsuit against the city. Most of the outcry came from activist groups. Mrs. Valesco was a part-time receptionist and full-time mom. Manny worked at a meat packing plant. He was ten years younger than her and had probably done his share of partying, but basically he was a good, hardworking man. From all accounts, JC was much like his father. Decent and unafraid to earn a living. But rage had consumed him. The violence around him, like vapors, blinded him. He'd given up everything because of the frenzy stirred by people he'd never met, by forces he couldn't even see, and made it the venture of his lifetime to exact revenge. In a strange way, he's a victim of big-city swaggering as much as his father and me. Mrs. Valesco would prefer to believe her son suffered in a similar manner as Jesus during his long trek along Via Dolorosa. That would be more valuable to her than money, I'm sure of it."

"Don't you think there'll be questions?"

"There'd be questions regardless. But like you once said, we'll have answers. We'll stick by your story, Father Paolo." Sebastian, wanting to make his position clear, stood and leaned toward the father with his palms flat on the cold desktop. "Brother Lucien and I will fetch JC's body before the snowmelt. We can rappel into the gully and retrieve it. I have some experience."

Father Paolo's neck disappeared into his shoulders. "You think that's wise?"

"No less than your plan to cover up JC's death." Sebastian waited for Father Paolo to return his averted eyes to him before he stretched to his full six-foot-two stature, leaving two palm prints on the desk, and continued. "We'll lay him out in the chapel and call the authorities. We'll tell them we found him and brought him inside, hoping to revive him. We'll say a young man from Philadelphia had written us last summer wanting to come here, to prove himself before God. He insisted on journeying at the height of winter to experience pure suffering, like Jesus had during his walk to Golgotha. We'll insist that, despite our advisement against it, we suspect the young man in our chapel might be him. Officials will learn that he was. And they'll convey our story about his noble intentions to his family, perhaps the world. Everyone will look glowing and wonderful, including you, Father Paolo."

Lies, the tongue of the devil. Those in power lied, but not everyone for the same reasons. Some lied to make people or situations appear worse. Others lied to exaggerate greatness. For the sake of everyone in the abbey, including JC, Sebastian would speak the language of power. Lies.

"You'll praise JC for his piousness," he went on, his eyes fixed on the diminutive abbot slumped in his Victorian chair. "You had originally compared him to the old ladies of Vila de Seda. You'll maintain that venerable opinion whenever speaking with the authorities or his family. Everyone will think of him as a Christian martyr."

"And what about you? What will you do once everything has settled, Brother Sebastian?"

"I'M LEAVING as soon as the road opens."

"Where will you go?" Casey asked Sebastian while they spent their afternoon siestas in the library, discussing the future.

"I have a friend who's a PI in Las Vegas. Perhaps I'll do something like that. Might take a while to build up a reputation. I like the idea of working on my own, out from under all the politics. Start over again. I'll get a cell phone, a new bank account. Father Paolo and I settled the finances in a magnanimous manner, rest assured. I'm taking with me about an eighth of the two hundred seventy thousand I brought along." He snickered. "If all else fails, I can always get a job making necklaces."

"I'm afraid of it out there."

"It's not much different than in here, so I learned," Sebastian said toward his twiddling thumbs on the tabletop.

"But in a way it's easier for us to be ourselves here, as weird as it might sound. You're the real reason why I chose to come back to Mt. Ouray," Casey whispered.

Breathless warmth pinched Sebastian's heart. He nearly clasped his chest to steady himself. "I'm glad you came back."

"But now you're leaving."

"I can't imagine staying after everything that's happened."

"You mean what's happened with JC or between us?"

Sebastian peered toward the San Juan Range, the snowcapped peaks glowing orange in the setting sun. How Sebastian loved the twilight hours. Bending of day to night, and then back again from night to day. A perfect egalitarian sharing of supremacy.

Spring inched closer over Mt. Ouray Abbey each day. April's arrival had awakened the landscape. The branches of the spruce and aspens had shaken off their snowy armor, and the expanse of green against the snow-covered floor and surrounding mountains added a sense of renewal and hope.

He no longer blamed himself for what had happened in Philadelphia. Coming to Mt. Ouray had exacerbated the guilt, in a way, emphasizing the sense that he had run from something. But now he felt cleansed, refreshed of culpability. He'd taken a man's life, but had given his son immortality.

"Neither you nor JC have anything to do with my decision to leave here," he said to the trees outside. "It's me. If I remain here, I'll feel like a hypocrite."

"I don't feel like a hypocrite."

"You're not one."

"My mother and stepdad thought I was crazy for joining the Trappists," Casey said with a gentle snicker. "Maybe they were right."

"We all have different reasons for wanting to come to places like Mt. Ouray," Sebastian said. "Most are genuine, I suspect. For the rest of us"—he returned his eyes to Casey—"it's part of life's journey."

It was Casey's turn to look toward the mountains for inspiration. Brown eyes far away, beyond the abbey grounds, high upon twelve-thousand-foot Mt. Ouray. "It's scary out there," he murmured.

"I know it is, but I've seen worse than you have."

"I can't imagine life here without you. But the idea of leaving… I'm afraid."

"Are you saying you'd rather stay safe here without me than face the uncertainty of the world with me?"

Sebastian watched Casey, waiting for him to answer. Casey remained focused outside. He did not speak, nor did he show any sign of being conscious of their present space. Inhaling, Sebastian allowed his gaze to drift along with Casey's, and they continued to stare out the window without words.

BROTHERS EUSEBIUS and Lucien gripped the rope while Sebastian rappelled into the gully. Howling wind screamed in Sebastian's ears as he lowered himself inchmeal, careful to avoid letting any more snow fall on top of JC's body. A snowdrift had already covered most of him. Sebastian could see part of his head and left leg sticking above the snow.

Eerie peacefulness enshrouded Sebastian once he made his way down. He stood beside the body, inhaling the cool air, listening to the wrens and warblers in the imposing pine trees. Animal droppings and tracks indicated the woodland creatures had become curious about the strange object semiburied in the snow. When Sebastian reached to uncover JC, he realized his body was still too frozen for any creatures to devour.

He untied the rope and secured it onto JC so Brothers Eusebius and Lucien could haul him up. Sebastian's determination allowed him to focus on the gruesome task. Ten minutes and a few close calls later, JC's body was brought up from the gully and resting by Brother Lucien's feet. Brother Eusebius untied the rope and tossed the frayed end back to Sebastian. He knotted the rope around his torso and groin and signaled for the brothers to tow him up in the same fashion they had JC. Next, they carried JC's corpse into the chapel, where a coffin they'd fabricated out of three wine crates (thanks to the ladies' auxiliary) waited for him.

The brothers filed in one by one, observing his body laid out like a venerated saint. Smoke from dozens of incense cones wrapped JC in a haze and masked the odor of his thawing body. In lieu of lunch, they recited the traditional Catholic funeral rite. They held candles throughout the service, chanting in low voices the Office of the Dead with a solemn recitation of "Requiescat in pace." Sun streaking through the stained glass windows highlighted smoke from the incense cones. Father Paolo played Dvorak on his cello for an underscoring of respect—and repentance.

Abbey rumor had exposed Brother Hubert's role in JC's death and why JC had traveled to Mt. Ouray. The compassion shown to Brother Hubert confirmed they held no harsh judgments. After the funeral, the brothers laid gentle hands on Brother Hubert's shoulders, as if they were consoling a mourning relative.

With Sebastian beside him, Father Paolo telephoned the San Miguel County Police. A callback ten minutes later informed them a forest service helicopter would arrive around three, for speedier recovery of the body.

Meanwhile, Sebastian sat in his cell and examined the contents of Brother Augustine's suitcase. Brother Hubert had handed it to him the day after his confession. "I suppose this will help tie up any loose ends," he'd said before walking away.

Sebastian handled the halved Virgin Mary figurine and Brother Micah's fillet knife—a weapon intended to pierce his heart. Then an idea came to him. He hid away the "souvenirs" and dashed outside, where he peered around under the library's arched windows.

"Do you remember the exact location where you spotted JC from the library?" he asked Casey, who he had grabbed from his cell along the way.

"Over there." Casey, squinting into the sun, pointed twenty yards to his right.

They stomped about like they had when they'd first searched for the figure Casey had spotted lying in the snow, circling in a denser and denser area. About a foot of snow still remained on the ground in some places, but in many spots, the grass and rocks showed through where the ground lay exposed to the sun. The echoing silence of the past several months seemed absorbed by the open sky. Mt. Ouray's peak rose above the canopy of trees, a chiseled masterpiece holding up Heaven.

All of a sudden Sebastian stopped short. There. The sun captured it. A spray of metal. He trudged over and lifted it.

"My goodness," Casey said, eyeing the object alongside Sebastian.

"What I suspected we might find."

The weapon JC had intended to use to seek revenge for his father's death. Sebastian held in his very hands the means of his own execution. The second such instrument of death in a mere capful of minutes. He recognized the gun as a common Austrian-made Glock, easily bought on the black market from gun thieves and favored by gangs. Even the PPD used them. But the pistol represented more than death. It signified a simultaneous beginning and end—orchestrated by a blind, autocratic brokering machine that possessed a godlike muscle. Deep inside, he imagined how different events might have unfolded.

They built a healthy sweat under their snow gear, searching for an accompanying wallet and cell phone, until the grinding of a helicopter brought them into a tight cluster by the abbey door. Sebastian concealed the Glock in his parka and stood beside the other brothers with cool expectancy. The whirlybird grew larger against the brilliant blue sky. Snow swept up in a wide gust when the Bell Cobra landed in the parking area. Two uniformed forest rangers and an officer with the San Miguel County Police Department debarked.

Father Paolo greeted them with a compulsory smile and invited them inside. The solemn expressions of the officials gazing upon JC's body laid out in the pine box after the father relayed their tale corresponded with Sebastian's intentions. They already thought of JC as a venerated martyr. A saint.

The photograph the county police officer brought with him of Juan Carlos Valesco verified his identity. His family had issued a missing persons report a month before, the county officer mentioned.

And so as the Bell Cobra whisked away JC's body, a new distaste for Father Paolo soured Sebastian's tongue. He'd known JC's family was searching for him, but concealed the facts. He had devised a sneaky plan, and stretched it with all his power. Yet Sebastian's last words reestablished his Irishman's stubbornness. He was the primary to the end, regardless of fifteen hundred years of tradition.

A few days later, forest rangers snowmobiling along the road from Monfrere tracked JC's path and discovered his cell phone, wallet, and some of his clothes lying in a channel. They'd pieced together JC's moves: he'd taken a bus from Philadelphia to Telluride, left the ski resort in a van-for-hire destined for Monfrere, set out on his trek up the mountain, rested along the way—possibly even slept or passed out—and after awakening set off again on his journey, leaving behind some of his belongings. By then delirium had possibly set in and he'd no longer realized where he was or what he was doing. One ranger had even suggested Juan Carlos had "wanted to experience true austerity" like Jesus would have.

Already Sebastian's sham had taken root, massaging those who wanted to believe in the best of human nature (rather than the worst). Sebastian and Father Paolo had nodded in acceptance while listening to the rangers recount their findings, biting their tongues to keep from revealing the truth.

The remainder of the week passed, and not a word from anyone except Mrs. Valesco. She'd e-mailed the abbey to thank the brothers for recovering her son's body. She would rest, knowing he'd come to Mt. Ouray seeking salvation and the consecrated life. So profound was his commitment, "He never once mentioned his intentions to his friends or family," she'd written.

The Thursday before Easter, Sebastian dressed in his civilian clothes—sneakers, khakis, light blue oxford (the St. Michael medallion visible around his neck)—and stepped outside the abbey with his tote bag clenched in hand. A quiet fell over the abbey grounds. Cocking his head toward Mt. Ouray's peak, he listened. Did he hear the mountain wishing him farewell?

About a dozen Rocky Mountain sheep had wandered off the higher elevations and grazed near the cottage, where tall grass poked through the remaining snow. Soon they would come in larger numbers and munch on the wild alfalfa that grew along the forest edge, and their droppings would spur the growth of yellow daffodils.

Sebastian still heard the brothers' chanting in his head from when he'd gathered for the last time with the men he'd called family for nearly four years. Their voices had expressed potent finality.

The seven stations of prayer had provided him solace. A quiet solitude of splendor, where pain and euphoria coalesced to form a sturdy pillar. The monks sought such tangible acceptance of mystery and life. Sebastian needed more. Or was it less?

Brother Eusebius, who had just finished plowing the parking lot for the second time in two days (for it took that many attempts to remove the top layers), approached him on the footpath.

"You are ready to leave, by the look of your suitcase," the brother said, facing him soberly.

Sebastian nodded. "What about you? After everything that's happened here, do you still wish to stay?"

"I will die here," he said unequivocally. "My faith will keep me at the abbey. I feel more dedicated than ever."

"I'm glad for you."

"You learned an important lesson," Brother Eusebius said. "You need to be a detective. That's your true vocational calling. Mine is a monk. A life of endless prayer and contemplation and to work my fingers to the bone."

Eye to eye, they shared a gentle smile, and Brother Eusebius wrapped his exquisite and powerful hands around Sebastian's. "Goodbye, my brother," he said, after which he stomped the snow from his boots and disappeared inside the abbey. Sebastian envisioned someday the brothers electing Brother Eusebius as their next abbot. He'd follow in the footsteps of his pioneering ancestor, and carry on tradition to make his father proud as the first black abbot.

Sebastian looked toward the cells and saw Brother Hubert sitting by his window, looking at him. A tender smile curled his lips. The middle-aged brother would maintain the monastic life for the remainder of his days too. He'd atone for his actions, and for that brief moment in time when a lapse in judgment had ignited their bittersweet tragedy.

And Brother Augustine, the man who had on some level solved the mystery for them (or had it been the Virgin Mary?), would die at Mt. Ouray with the diligent Brother George looking after him until he'd require caring for himself. Brother Rodel also had stated his intentions to stay put. Brother Micah (who'd avoided Sebastian after realizing he'd found out his scam) would likely remain. As would the aged Brothers Giles and Jerome. Brother Lucien and Father Paolo's joint reign over the abbey would continue unfazed, as if nothing had upset the status quo. Perhaps the abbot might move about his abbey more quietly during the upcoming summer tourist season.

No supernatural power had descended upon them. Although, in a way, good versus evil had taken place inside their abbey. But it had been of the manmade kind. Ignorant "evil" waged by those with power. People with dirty thoughts and dirty minds who see only dirtiness in their eyes. He'd been the victim of it in Philadelphia. That had been the Satan he'd battled inside Mt. Ouray. It had followed him two thousand miles, tracked him into the Rockies. In the end, he'd slain his dragon.

The crunch of hard-packed snow yanked his attention away from the abbey and the men inside. The van-for-hire was pulling into the parking lot to take Sebastian to the Telluride airport. He waved a final good-bye to Brother Hubert in the window and grinned when Casey, wearing dark jeans, a red oxford shirt, and a brown down jacket (the same clothes he'd worn when he'd first arrived at Mt. Ouray six months ago) strolled down the front steps, his single bag and flute case by his sides. Sebastian's grin widened, which seemed to stretch wider than Mt. Ouray's peak.

"All ready for Vegas?"

"I think so," Casey said.

"Let's go, then." Sebastian carried his and Casey's bags to the waiting van.

Barking forced the two of them around. Delores trotted from the barn and stuck her wet, cold nose against Sebastian's hand. She wanted to say her good-bye too. "See you, old girl," Sebastian said, patting her head. "Keep those mice in check." Delores licked his and Casey's faces and dashed for the front steps where she barked and reared up on her hind legs. She would remain at Mt. Ouray the rest of her life also, Sebastian mused, where she belonged. Chasing mice and nibbling crumbs off Brother Micah's kitchen floor and Brother Giles's meal tray.

"I'm going to miss her," Casey said.

"She'll do fine here. The summer crowd will keep her happy and well fed."

They greeted the driver, who took their suitcases and stored them in the back. No one else was in the van, and Sebastian took the opportunity to hunker down closer to Casey.

"It's a crazy world out there," Casey said, interlocking his fingers with Sebastian's, "but with the two of us, it'll come easier."

Sebastian squeezed his hand back, almost instinctively, as if their fingers had meant to be fused. Joined in communal prayer.

"Yes," Sebastian said, nudging closer to Casey as the van driver conveyed them out of the parking lot and along the recently cleared forest service road into the valley, where the world with all its ambiguity opened to them. "It'll come easier."

SHELTER SOMERSET enjoys writing about the lives of people who live off the land, whether they be the Amish, nineteenth-century pioneers, or modern-day idealists seeking to live apart from the crowd. Shelter's fascination with the rustic, aesthetic lifestyle began as a child with family camping trips into the Blue Ridge Mountains. When not back home in Illinois writing, Shelter continues to explore America's expansive backcountry and rural communities. Shelter's philosophy is best summed up by the actor John Wayne: "Courage is being scared to death but saddling up anyway."

Also from S<small>HELTER</small> S<small>OMERSET</small>

SHELTER SOMERSET

On the Trail to
MOONLIGHT GULCH

http://www.dreamspinnerpress.com

Romance from SHELTER SOMERSET

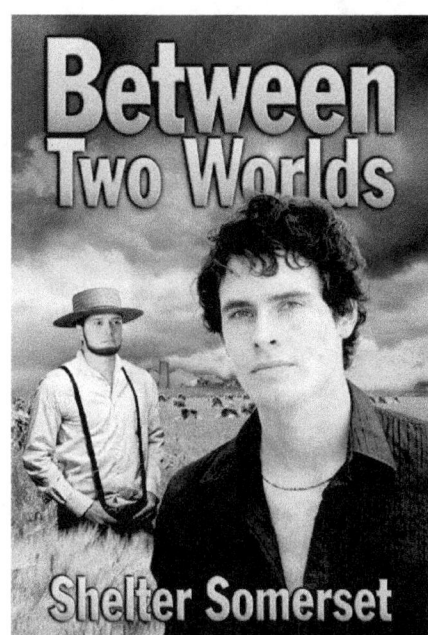

http://www.dreamspinnerpress.com